Child of My Winter

Books by Andrew Lanh

The Rick Van Lam Mysteries
Caught Dead
Return to Dust
No Good to Cry
Child of My Winter

Child of My Winter

A Rick Van Lam Mystery

Andrew Lanh

Poisoned Pen Press

First Edition 2017

10 9 8 7 6 5 4 3 2 1

Library of Congress Catalog Card Number: 2016961974

ISBN: 9781464208461   Hardcover
      9781464208485   Trade Paperback

Poisoned Pen Press
6962 E. First Ave., Ste. 103
Scottsdale, AZ 85251
www.poisonedpenpress.com
info@poisonedpenpress.com

Printed in the United States of America

Child of my winter, born
When the new fallen soldiers froze
In Asia's steep ravines and fouled the snows.

—W. D. Snodgrass, *Heart's Needle*

Prologue

Late Saturday night a light sleet pings the old windows of my apartment. Drowsy, I switch on the TV. Midnight: Turner Classic Movies is showing *The Deerhunter*. Vietnam all over again. It's a movie I've resisted because the fierce gunfire and brutality and napalm-burnt landscapes drag me back to my boyhood at the orphanage in Saigon—Most Blessed Mother Catholic Orphanage.

But I'm a grownup, I tell myself as I wrap myself up in my warm quilt comforter, a birthday gift from Gracie, my landlady and good friend who lives one floor below me. Hot cocoa in a mug, untouched and now filmy and cold.

My eyes keep closing, then opening, tired but strangely alert. Then, horribly, that chilling scene arrives when maniacal Cong guards and the terrorized American GIs play Russian roulette. One bullet in the chamber. Your turn. Fire. Hesitate. Stark horror on the American faces. The demonic faces of the Cong—eyes hard as flint, twitching fingers.

Do it. Do it. *Mau di di.*

I freeze.

A pistol to the head.

Hurry. Now. Quick. Now. Do it. Move. Move.

Frantically I switch off the TV.

Those horrible words. *Mau di di.*

Maybe I'm ten or eleven, living in the orphanage since around age five, dropped off by a weeping mother who disappeared into the ruins of Saigon. Not Saigon…Ho Chi Minh City now. *Doc lap va Tu do.* Independence and Freedom. The words drilled into our schoolboy souls, our morning mantra. No matter because I'm the hated child, *bui doi*, a child of the dust, awful breed of that frightened mother and some breezy American GI.

Occupying the far back corner of the barracks, my narrow cot under the dripping walls where the mice chatter at night and water bugs crawl onto my eyelids when I sleep, I spend my days dreading the shoving, the sneers. Satan's child. Mongrel American. Sister Do Thi Bich uses me as a moral exemplum of failure and some sort of original sin. Me, bastard boy.

On a hot August day, so humid my baggy blue shorts and white shirt melt into my skinny body, I line up with a dozen other boys. A fat man with a piercing laugh points us into two old Russian Malotova trucks. Drivers waiting, cigarettes bobbing in their lips. The nun warns us to behave, to follow orders. To listen and obey. She glances at the fat man and smiles nervously. She's afraid of the Communists, I know. We all are. The North Vietnamese swagger and spit and curse. Men in hard-pressed uniforms stomp into the chapel during services and watch us. The nuns clutch their rosary beads and look into their laps.

We ride for an hour, bouncing in the truck with bad springs. A boy shoves me when my body falls into his, and the others jeer. "The American can't sit still."

I push back and we tussle. Someone punches my neck, another pulls my hair. Disorder. The driver hears the commotion behind him and leans on his horn. "If I have to come back there…" He taps the small window behind him with a pistol. We get quiet.

We're dropped off twenty or so kilometers outside Saigon, near Long Thanh, near old supply buildings, ramshackle structures with rusted corrugated-tin roofs and shot-out windows. A man shambles toward us, lines us up, and announces our work for the day. We will clean the fields around what he calls the depot, gather the scraps of wood and metal and glass scattered

around, half-buried or leaning up against the sprawling buildings, haul off debris, and toss it into a truckbed.

"Americans died here," he tells us. "Cowards."

He spots me as I lean on one foot, and scowls. "Americans."

He's from the north, I know from his rough, unlovely accent,
an old crusty veteran from the National Liberation Front. Uncle
Ho's followers. Missing his right arm, he swings his left wildly.
A skinny, leather-faced man, shabbily dressed, he stumbles over
his words, looks away, then back, each movement of his face
a lesson in what's wrong with war. His shorn head reveals scar
tissue and part of an ear missing. One of his eyes isn't there.
"Captain Le. You will call me that." Then he repeats it. One of
the boys snickers and the man jumps so quickly that we all start,
nervous. He's crazy.

While we work, he disappears into a shed, but soon sum-
mons two of the boys. They drag an old metal chest outside,
snap it open, and Captain Le holds up a military uniform—or
the remnants of one. A moth-eaten shirt with stripes on the
shoulders. Boots without laces. A helmet.

"An American deserter," he announces. "A coward."

At midday, exhausted under the blazing summer heat, we are
given water and a bowl of rice. Captain Le disappears for two
hours, but when he returns, he's blind drunk, staggering. His
one lazy eye focuses. "American boy, come here."

As I stand in front of him, he nearly topples, rights himself,
but points at me. Broken fingernails, black, chipped. "You tried
to kill me."

I keep my mouth shut, my heart racing.

He turns to the other boys. "When we capture American
infidels, we do not kill them. Yes, maybe some torture. A bamboo
cage." A sickly grin. "But we make them into animals." He reaches
back into memory. Then he shouts at me in garbled English:

Xo ren doo dai
Not mu
Xai lon
Go quich

A memorized list of brutalized English commands for the captured American soldiers: *Surrender. Don't move. Silence. Go quick.*

He spots the American uniform on the ground. "American," he yells at me, "wear it."

I don't move.

"*Mau di di.*" Hurry. Now. Move.

The other boys, nervous at first, begin to laugh. Tottering, Captain Le yells for them to put the helmet on my head. One of the bullies, thrilled, grabs my arm and twists it. Another grabs my sleeve.

I squirm, fight them, but it's useless. They lock my arms behind my back. The helmet drops on my head, so large it covers my face. My shirt is torn off, replaced by the wormy shirt. Finally they strap me to a bamboo post jutting out of the ground.

Mau di di. Hurry. Now.

They circle and jab, kick, but then get bored, as the captain demands they get back to work. "You are all lazy. There's a reason none of you has a mother." They leave me hanging for an hour, my head dipped from the heavy helmet, my arms hanging by my side. The musty old cloth smells of rat droppings, ancient sweat, decay…

The sun beats on my exposed neck. I pass out.

When a superior drives up, he's furious, demanding Captain Le release me. I topple to the ground.

Back at the orphanage, delirious, I'm carried to the room where the sick boys convalesce. Alone, writhing, crying, the back of my neck so burned I can't find a comfortable spot on the cot, I have wild dreams: the American soldier in his uniform looking at me, a maniacal smile on his lips. *Mau di di.* I can't lift the helmet off—it weighs a ton. My neck snaps. I hear my mother's voice as she says goodbye.

When I wake up, sweaty, parched, I look into the face of Sister Mary Chi Hanh. She's a new nun, the quiet one who always looks nervous. Sitting on the edge of my cot, she dabs my forehead with a damp cold cloth. Seeing me awake, she rushes to give me a sip of water. It dribbles out of the corners of my mouth. When she speaks, she has a slight accent. Maybe French, I think. A whisper.

She anoints my burning neck with lotion, maybe tiger balm, and though I wince and cry, she shushes me.

"The cruel boys..." She is speaking to herself.

I sputter out my name for some reason. "Lam Viet Van."

"Sssh."

"My name is..."

She reaches behind her, glances over her shoulder, and suddenly she is placing something in my mouth. "What?" I ask, my tongue rolling over the sweet wonderful taste.

"Chocolate," she says with a smile on her face.

I swallow it but the smooth taste lingers, welcome, delightful. I grin. "Wow."

She laughs quietly.

A voice from outside calls her. Alarmed, she jumps up. "I can't be here."

"Stay."

"I can't, American boy."

"Stay."

She sits back for a moment, touches my cheek. "You'll always be a lonely boy, Viet."

"What?"

She whispers, "You will always wear the loneliness of the people you meet."

"I don't understand."

"But what you don't understand is that it's your gift from a loving God."

Confused, I stare into her face. "That is not a gift."

"Our Lord does not make mistakes."

Chapter One

Anh Ky Trang lived in his own world.

Sometime during the fall semester I spotted the young man sitting alone in a corner of the Student Union, his body angled away from the crowded room, his face buried in a textbook or staring blankly out the window at the campus, his hands folded into his lap. A young man, though I thought of him as a young boy because he was so small and skinny. Once or twice, coming from behind him, I'd see his head follow the movements of passing, laughing students, and when he turned his head I thought I detected eagerness there, a hunger to say something. Maybe simply to have someone talk to him. Loneliness covered him, or maybe I projected that emotion onto him. One time, startled by a group of students who'd bumped into his table, his eyes got hooded, wary.

Lonely. But how was I to know that? Because I also spotted him as Vietnamese—and I suppose I saw myself when I saw him. A boy afraid of others, a boy who felt he didn't belong in a world where others could point at him and shout, cruelly, Look! There! The outcast.

Stone him.

One day in late September, I thought I'd approach him. I'd been born in Vietnam, I said as I leaned into his table, but he started, his eyes frozen with fear or maybe dread. His lips tightened into a disapproving line, then, surprisingly, into a thin smile, though not a friendly one. I backed off. As I headed to the coffee bar, I watched him gather his books, sling his backpack over his shoulders, and scurry out of the room.

Another time I spotted him heading to class. He hugged the wall, his shoulders dragging against it. His left arm was cradled into his chest, tucked inside his jacket, and his head dipped to the right. Blue jeans, shiny new, but a foot too long, rolled up so that the underside nearly reached his knees. A plaid hunter's jacket, one side of the tattered collar turned up against his neck. Huge goggle eyeglasses with clunky black frames. A helter-skelter haircut, uneven in places, spiked in the back.

A week later a football lummox, all testosterone and heat, sprinted by, reaching for the waist of a young girl. He bumped into the boy, who jerked back. For a split second his tiny face darkened, his eyes flashed, and that cradled hand formed a fist. A whistling sound escaped his throat. The jock didn't notice, thank God, maneuvering the willing girl into his sloppy embrace.

What the moment did was make me curious about the lost boy at Farmington College.

Everything shifted at mid-semester when my buddy Hank Nguyen, now a Connecticut state cop, appeared on campus for a six-week, two-hour-a-week semester as part of the State Crimes Investigation course. Teamed with an older lieutenant, the two fielded questions in a practicum for prospective state cops enrolled in the college's Criminal Justice program. Hank welcomed a return to the campus where he'd been a student a few years back. In fact, the hostile, withdrawn young man who harbored kneejerk bias against me had been *my* student in Criminal Procedures. Pureblood Vietnamese, though born in America, Hank had inherited his father's myopic distrust of Vietnamese *bui doi* like me. Yet, working through his jaundiced view of me, he'd emerged as my buddy for many years now. He was part of my social world—and I was welcomed into his family's home.

So his stay on campus one night a week was opportune. I'd be finishing my two-nights-a-week course on Forensic Investigations when he'd emerge in his crisp uniform from his classroom, giving us a chance to have coffee or a bite to eat together. My day job was as an insurance fraud investigator out of Hartford, working with Vietnam vet Jimmy Gadowicz in Gaddy Associates, another pal of mine, but my adjunct status at the college provided me a few extra bucks for weekends in New York City or, occasionally, a stolen holiday in Barcelona or London.

Headed into the College Union for coffee one evening after class, I stood at the counter and realized Hank was not behind me. When I strolled back from the counter with two cups of coffee on a tray, Hank had settled into a chair opposite a boy who stared unhappily at the uniformed state cop who was leaning into him and smiling.

Hank motioned me toward an empty seat. "Sit, Rick." Amazingly, in the minute or so he'd sat there, he'd learned the student's name. "This is Anh Ky Trang. But he prefers Dustin. The name he gave himself. Dustin Trang."

He smiled at the boy, who did not smile back. Instead Dustin wore a scared look, his shoulders hunched.

Hank laughed. "He thinks I'm gonna arrest him."

The boy sputtered, "You are?"

Hank pointed a finger at him. "Why? You commit a crime?"

Dustin actually trembled, but shook his head vigorously back and forth.

"Don't mind him," I reassured Dustin, nodding toward a beaming Hank. "He's a jokester. You'd think a man in a state cop uniform would be better behaved, no?"

Dustin didn't say anything.

"Dustin, do you know Rick? Professor Lam? He was my prof a hundred years ago."

Dustin still said nothing.

"See where you end up when you take my class, Dustin?" I said warmly, but nervously.

Dustin's head swung from me to Hank, almost mechanically, but miserably.

"A life of crime or a life arresting criminals." Hank grinned at me.

I downplayed it. "Don't mind him."

But Dustin suddenly found a voice. "He's scaring me."

That bothered Hank, who lost his smile. "Hey, sorry. Not my intent, Dustin. I saw you, figured you were one of us"—his finger pointed to me and then to himself—"and…" His voice trailed off.

"It's all right," Dustin mumbled.

"You a freshman?" I asked.

He nodded. "Yes." A clipped response, very polite. "Two courses a week." But he was already standing up, closing his book and tucking it into his backpack. He stepped back. "I gotta go."

"Hey," Hank began quickly, "it was good…"

Dustin was already moving away, banging into a chair, hurrying out of the College Union.

"Nice work, Hank. He's practically running away. You really charmed him."

Hank, bewildered. "I needed more time."

"I think your uniform scared him. A cop approaches a solitary boy in a college cafeteria, you know how the story ends—handcuffs, leg irons. Do words like *freeze scumbag* come to anyone's mind?"

Hank sat back and folded his arms over his chest. "As I said, I needed more time." His eyes followed the departed Dustin. "A strange boy, no?"

"I've thought so all semester. Lonely."

"By Christmas we'll be friends."

"Maybe you should leave him alone, Hank."

Hank tilted his head to the side, a mischievous grin on his face. "State cops save the world." Eyes twinkling. "It's a bumper sticker I proposed to my captain."

"No wonder you're assigned to freshman KP at the college. You know, sometimes the world doesn't want to be saved, Hank."

"Neither one of us believes that."

• ● ● ● •

A week before Thanksgiving the solitary life of young Dustin Trang shifted, a metamorphosis I'd not expected. Yes, Hank had persisted in greeting the young man in passing, even dipping into a seat to annoy him, but Dustin had remained stoic, withdrawn, resisting Hank's charm crusade.

That changed.

One night, sitting by myself with a hamburger and coffee in the College Union, I watched a teacher sidle up to Dustin and loudly praise a term paper he'd just graded. He was walking past Dustin's table, followed by a swarm of buzzing acolytes, and suddenly he stopped and announced in a loud, enthusiastic voice, "Dustin, I gotta tell you—your paper on local evangelical churches and the New England Great Awakening—you nailed it."

Dustin sputtered feeble thanks, then dropped his eyes down at his textbook. But the professor wasn't through. Stepping near, he tapped him on the shoulder and said, "I mean it, Dustin. You *nailed* it." Dustin refused to look up.

Ben Winslow—Dr. Bennett Winslow, Professor of Sociology—was the campus firebrand activist and all-around good-natured prof. "Call me Ben," he told his students, and they did, though some with derision and mockery. A man in his sixties, a roly-poly Falstaffian man with round cheeks, white beard stubble, skimpy salt-and-pepper hair, an infectious laugh, he had the noisome habit of lecturing so loudly other teachers closed their doors in his corridor. An unreconstructed sixties radical—his own Facebook definition and Twitter handle @ socialdemocrat—he was immensely popular, not only because of his dynamic, off-color, pun-sputtered lectures, but because his real concern was his students. A rarity. With his rolled-up work shirt sleeves and Beatles neckties, his corduroy sports jacket with ripped elbows, he was the campus oddity. A claque of worshipful students trailed after him. Twice a week, after his Social Problems course ended at seven, he'd linger in the Union, surrounded by a coterie of students, and the gabfest would go on.

Suddenly, surprisingly, Dustin Trang became a part of his circle. Certainly not one of the boisterous kids who celebrated everything Winslow said as though they were part of the studio audience of, say, Jimmy Fallon on late-night TV. No, Dustin sat on the edge of the group, inordinately happy that someone included him in a party. I doubt whether he ever spoke—the few times I spotted him among Winslow's followers he sat at attention, ready to bolt if too much notice came his way. The fact that he had found his way there pleased me.

"See," I nudged Hank one night when we strolled past the chatting students. "Ben Winslow hath charms to soothe the lonely boy."

"I needed more time," Hank quipped.

He was pleased, I knew. Passing, Dustin glanced at us, and Hank flicked his finger toward him and smiled. Dustin actually smiled back.

"Professor Winslow wants everyone to love him," Hank told me.

"So do you."

He made an exaggerated monkey face at me, which startled a young girl walking toward us. The tall state trooper in dress uniform made a grotesque face. Her eyes got wide.

He leaned in. "I'm gonna have to arrest you, Rick. Otherwise she'll think the state police are crazy."

"Perhaps you should assume a more stoic look when you walk through these hallways."

"I don't like going out of character." He raised his eyebrows. "Look."

Professor Winslow's group had dispersed, but Dustin was walking alongside the teacher as they headed out the door. His body language was troubling—walking too close to Ben, bumping into his side, talking, his face animated. The teacher was attentive, two short men eye-to-eye, but he kept pulling back, trying to put some distance between them. It resembled a skit from a high-school performance, but there was nothing humorous about it—something serious was being said.

"What in God's name?" Hank muttered.

"But something is wrong, Hank."

We watched the two disappear out the doorway.

Bothered for that moment, I put it out of my mind until two weeks before the finals and the Christmas break. I'd been sitting in the adjunct faculty office, reading student term papers and then quietly reviewing a fraud case for Aetna Insurance, my mind numb with the banality of white-collar crime, when I decided to head home. Seven p.m., the late-afternoon classes ended, students swarming into the dark wintry night—headed back to dorms or to cold cars in the lot. I waited until the hallways were clear, then wrapped a scarf around my neck, grabbed my gloves, and walked out of Charlton Hall.

Raised voices stopped me. At the end of a wing of faculty offices a door swung open, slammed back. Ben Winslow's office, I knew. At first I saw no one, but immediately I recognized the voice: Dustin Trang.

His words shrill, panicked. "You promised."

Winslow's answer. "I can't keep a promise like that."

The sound of a book slammed to the floor. A hand banging a wall.

Dustin's voice broke. "You said you were my friend. You acted…"

Winslow spoke over Dustin's words, hurried. "C'mon, Dustin. Listen. I told you…"

Suddenly Dustin stepped out of the office but faced in. From where I stood I could see his purplish face, his spiky hair sticking up, his fists raised in the air. "You promised…"

"You gotta believe me, Dustin. This is…wrong."

Dustin cuffed his ears. "It isn't. It isn't." Then, his voice lowering, "I'm sorry I told you."

"But you did."

Silence as Dustin breathed deeply. "I lied, Professor. I made it all up."

Winslow appeared in the doorway. The small, round man with the fuzzy hair appeared tense, his reddish skin now blanched. He pointed a finger into Dustin's chest. "I have no choice."

"But you promised."

"Stop saying that."

Dustin backed up, then stamped his foot. "You could get in trouble, Professor."

"No, *you* could get in real trouble. The cops."

A long, drawn-out, "Noooo."

Dustin spun around, his fist in the air, and suddenly he slammed his book bag against the wall. "Damn it all."

Ben approached him, but Dustin held up his hand, traffic-cop style, and Ben froze. Ben slammed his office door behind him, leaned against the hallway wall. His voice roared: "Damn, damn, damn."

A few students, walking out of other faculty offices, had bunched in a corner, watching and whispering. One, grinning, held up his cellphone and was recording the quick encounter.

Dustin stormed away, giving the finger to the kid with the cellphone, and came face to face with me. For a second he paused, deliberated what to do, then caught his breath. A weird smile covered his face as he rushed by me.

An office door swung open, and Professor Laramie stood in the doorway, his arms crossed over his chest. He frowned at Ben, who ignored him. He was a small, wiry guy I'd never liked—and an avowed enemy of Ben Winslow's out-there politics. I'd sat at faculty meetings and listened to Laramie and Winslow go at it, their dialogue mean-spirited. Laramie was notorious for standing outside Winslow's classroom, jotting down suspect remarks and forwarding them to Academia Fact Check, a right-wing alarmist group convinced professors were poisoning the minds of American youth. Winslow was his main topic—which Winslow relished. Indeed, when the shadow of Laramie lingered in the hallway, he upped his sensational remarks.

Now as I passed Laramie, I stared into his face.

"You find this funny?" I asked bluntly.

Surprised by my words, he shot back, "Nothing is funny that comes out of that madman's office."

"You have a grin on your face."

"It's not a grin, Mr. Lam."

"What would you call it then?"

He watched me closely. "Did you ever read Hawthorne? *The Scarlet Letter*? Chillingworth. It's the look Satan has when he knows he's checked another soul into hell."

"And you're Satan?"

"God, no. I work for the opposing team."

Chapter Two

At six o'clock on a Thursday night Zeke's Olde Tavern, down the street from my apartment off Main Street in Farmington, had a used-up feel to it. The barmaid dragged a grimy cloth over old oak tables, and the bartender polished glasses so scratched I was certain bacteria smiled back, taunting him. Nearly empty—my favorite time of the day there—Zeke's was established in 1907, according to the sign outside, which no one believed. Some recall another sign, blown away by Hurricane Carol back in the fifties, that said, simply: c.1900. No one believed that either.

Sometimes beautiful young girls in finishing school dresses from nearby Miss Porter's School peered into the window as they strolled into town, but the place was too Dante's *Inferno* for delicate minds.

Sitting at a back table, I was talking about the encounter—Dustin Trang and Ben Winslow, a scene that still shocked me. I shivered in the drafty room. Munching on a burnt hamburger and sipping a tepid Sam Adams, I brought Hank Nguyen, now in street clothes, and Liz Sanburn, my ex-wife from my Manhattan days, now a psychologist with the Farmington Police, up to speed.

"Rick, you gotta be kidding." Hank narrowed his eyes. "Dustin is…shy. I can't imagine him fighting with anyone."

Liz sipped her glass of wine. "Rick, why are we talking about this student?"

"I can't get him out of my mind. He was so belligerent." I took a sip of beer. "It wasn't pretty."

Hank leaned on the table, "I know what you mean about him—it bothers me. He looks so…lost at the college."

"I wonder how he ended up there."

Hank grinned at me. "I got *some* answers. In one of my feeble interrogations—friendly, I might add—I learned a little about him. He lives in a housing project with his family. He's from the next town over—Bristol."

I raised my eyebrows. "But Farmington College?"

Hank nodded. "A scholarship from the Bristol Lions Club or the Rotarians. Some civic group. He's a half-time student, works days at a dairy bar restaurant on Terryville Avenue near his home, drives over for two or three classes. A freshman."

"A smart kid?"

"Yeah, that's the thing. Not talkative, but comes off as real bright. A few offhand remarks—clever. But afraid of his own shadow and with that oddball behavior."

Liz had been quietly listening. "If I can add my two cents' worth—though as a psychologist I should charge you for the advice—maybe he's insecure there. Farmington College is another world from hardscrabble Bristol."

"Maybe," I answered. "Still, we've got lots of scholarship kids." I shook my head. "I've watched him in the hallways. There's anger in him. And that's what I saw when he confronted Ben Winslow."

"But it sounds to me that Ben was also angry," Liz said. "You said *he* was fighting back." Her eyes got cloudy. "And that doesn't sound like the Ben we know."

I tapped my fingers on the table. "Something nasty is going on. True, I didn't expect it from Dustin, though I don't know him. But students don't talk like that to professors. They…"

Hank interrupted, his eyes flashing. "I was always tempted to."

"Yeah, I remember." I pointed a finger at him. "But this smacked of some deep-seated disagreement—something personal."

Liz sat back, tilted her head. "Are you sure you're not reading too much into this, Rick?" She was wearing dangling emerald earrings that caught the overhead fluorescent light. Ex-wife or not, I often found myself staring at her beautiful face, that alabaster skin setting off her dark eyes. A woman in her forties now, our failed marriage years in the past from student days at Columbia, she often caught me looking. Stop that, Rick. A look that said: Sometimes I think *you* think we're still in love.

We were.

"But I was also surprised by Ben," I went on. "The friendly professor that everyone loves."

Suddenly Liz sat up. "That reminds me of something Sophia said about Ben being rattled. Just the last few days or so."

"Sophia? What? Tell me."

"My, my." Liz's eyes twinkled. "The once and future investigator."

Sophia Grecko, Liz's friend, was an instructor in Art History at the college, a fiftyish widow who'd been dating the divorced older Ben Winslow for a few years. Ben lived on the first floor of a triple-decker apartment house in Unionville, while Sophia occupied the second floor. We'd socialized with them a few times. A melodramatic woman who often got on my nerves—"Call me Natasha," she'd warble after too much wine one night—she wore thick makeup to cover up a pocked face and skintight knit dresses that made male students trail after her through the hallways. Liz always told me I was narrow-minded. She defended her. "She's warm and funny and—my friend."

Ben Winslow, the ragtag hippie professor who resembled an unmade bed, was smitten with her. The unlikely couple lingered over cocktails on a Friday night at the local Applebee's while a piano player sang an anemic version of "The Way We Were." I know this because, unfortunately, Liz and I were sitting at the same table.

"Tell me."

"I really didn't pay it much attention. We were talking about our little get-together this coming weekend to celebrate Ben's new book, and she said Ben didn't seem interested."

"Maybe the end of the semester. Christmas almost here. Term papers…"

She shook her head. "No, not that. Overnight Ben has become secretive. He hides away in his home office—mumbled conversations on the phone when she comes near. When she asked him why he was so distracted, he wouldn't answer."

Hank was anxious to talk. "Do you think it has to do with Dustin?"

"A little far-fetched." But I hesitated. "Who knows? Ben does get involved with his students' lives. They run to him with their problems. Sort of a campus legend."

Liz smirked. "Campus legend, indeed. Getting involved with students got him a divorce a century back, no?"

"What's that?" Hank was curious.

She leaned in. "A stupid half-second romance with a teaching intern from the UConn School of Social Work, some blushing co-ed who charmed the craggy professor."

"Illegal," Hank said in his state-cop voice.

I made a shocked face. "Not back then, Hank. No one cared who slept with who back then, especially in hushed, ivied halls. We've added a few more academic felonies to the ledger since then."

"I don't think peace activist Ben is wooing little goofy Dustin," Hank said.

"Agreed, but something *is* going on."

"Since I've been on campus," Hank was saying, "I've been talking to a kid named Vinh Thanh Luong, aka Brandon Vinh, who's in my seminar. He's a part of this Asian-American Alliance at the college, a social club, I guess."

"Yeah," I broke in, "I've seen him around campus. Back-slapping, in-your-face politician."

"Not a favorite of mine. All buddy buddy—but arrogant. He's seen me—even you that one time—talking to Dustin in the College Union."

"And that's a problem?"

Hank rushed his words. "He has it in for Dustin. Brandon is a sort of jock, a muscle-bound loudmouth student who talks too much in class."

"BMOC," I said. "He swaggers."

"That's his only gait," Hank laughed.

"Where are you going with this, Hank?" Liz asked.

"Well, Brandon wants to be a cop, which will never happen. Too gun happy in a mindless hey-anybody-see-my-Colt-45?-I-left-it-somewhere-duh way. If you know what I mean. Anyway, when he spotted Dustin on campus back in September he approached him. Vietnamese to Vietnamese. Heartwarming, right? Strangers in a strange land. Dustin rebuffed him, and pretty rudely."

"So?" I took a swig of my beer. "He rebuffs everyone."

Hank waved a hand in the air. "Brandon didn't like it. So Dustin has an enemy. But what I'm trying to say is that Brandon said something strange to me. I was telling him that he should encourage Dustin to come to Asian-American club meetings—Brandon's pet project—and he said 'No way.'"

"A real democratic soul." From Liz.

"No, he told me. No. Capital N-O." Hank stressed the word. "Me, the state trooper, yes. Honored guest." Hank bowed. "Then, Brandon said, 'You know, Officer Nguyen, that kid is gonna murder somebody someday.'"

"Christ, what did you say?"

"I told him he talks too much."

Ben Winslow was standing at a vending machine at the end of the hallway, staring blankly at the glass. His hand clutched a dollar bill, but he seemed frozen. When I approached him from behind and called out his name, he jumped, spun around, dropped the bill onto the floor and then, shuffling, stepped on it.

"Sorry, Ben. I didn't mean to startle you." I smiled at him. "Such concentration on the choice of a candy bar."

A blank stare. "What?" Then he snapped out of it. "I don't even eat candy."

He stepped back, ignoring the crumpled dollar bill, but I stooped to retrieve it. "Here." He stared at my palm.

A weak smile. "Thanks."

"Everything all right?"

"Yeah. Of course." An edge to his voice. "Why wouldn't it be?"

"Saturday night still on at your place? Liz mentioned…"

He broke into my words. "I guess. Sophia wants to celebrate my book."

"It's an event."

"I guess." He gazed over my shoulder.

I stepped closer. "What's the matter, Ben?"

He shook his head absently. "A lot on my mind."

"Wanna talk about it?"

He didn't answer but offered a sheepish smile. "Sophia keeps saying the same thing to me."

I walked away but turned back, stared into his face. "You know, Ben, I overheard you the other night. That nasty send-up with Dustin Trang outside your office. A little heated. It bothered me…"

I stopped because his hand flew up into my face. He blinked quickly, color rising in his cheeks. Jittery, his fingers crumpled the dollar bill I'd returned to him. "No," he spat out. "It's none of your business."

That surprised me. Ben was a man who cultivated likability, the clown who told too many stale jokes in class, a man who liked to laugh. Yes, he could be biting with those who opposed him on academic and even worldly politics, but those exchanges were largely cerebral. He avoided *ad hominem* attacks, even as others hurled them at him at faculty meetings. David Laramie once called him a "butterball turkey with a clucking harem of adoring henhouse coeds." Not nice, and reprimanded by the college.

Ben found the line hilarious and repeated it everywhere.

Now, realizing what he'd just said to me, he tucked his head into his chest. "Christ, Rick, I can't believe those words came out of my mouth."

"Forget it. But, Ben, maybe you *do* want to talk about it?"

He smiled thinly. "I wouldn't know where to begin." He waited a heartbeat. "No, I'm lying to you, Rick, but it's something I gotta deal with."

"Are you in trouble?"

His eyes were tired. "Sort of."

"Legal?"

He didn't answer.

"Illegal?"

"Just...trouble."

"Serious?"

A bittersweet smile. "More than I ever expected."

Frustrated, I leaned in. "Does this have to do with Dustin Trang?"

He pulled his lips into a razor-thin line and gazed over my shoulder. When he looked back at me, his eyes were shrouded, dark. "You're Vietnamese, right, Rick?"

"Yes, but..."

His lips trembled. "I'll never understand what that war was about, you know."

"Ben, what are you talking about?"

He laughed an unfunny laugh. "When I was young, like fifteen or sixteen, I marched in protests against the war. My father was a firebrand protester. I held up signs. 'Hell no, I won't go. Get out of Vietnam.'"

I shrugged my shoulders. "Well, America eventually did."

His voice got sharp, hard. "But that war never ended, did it?"

"Not for a lot of folks, I admit."

"You?" He locked eyes with mine.

"I have my own battles. Yes."

A low rumble to his words. "After 1975 I never thought about it."

"Until now?"

He glanced over my shoulder and shook his head. "No, it's just meeting you."

I plunged in. "Meeting Dustin Trang?"

A trace of anger. "He's not what I'm talking about."

"Then what are you talking about?"

He inserted the dollar into the vending machine but nothing happened. He banged on the glass, harder and harder, until a candy bar dropped into the slot. But he walked away without it. At the end of the hallway he turned and yelled, "You know what Plato said, right?"

"He said a lot of things."

"He said: 'Only the dead know the end of war.'"

● ● ● ● ●

Late that night my phone rang. I'd been sitting at my desk in my apartment, dreamily organizing files on the fraud case I was working on for Aetna Insurance, a routine bit of embezzling by some district manager whose felonious footprint was so obvious I considered it corporate suicide. I'd finished up, pressed SEND to the HR rep, and stared at the screen.

"Rick, you awake?" Hank's voice sounded wary.

"Yes. What's up? I thought you had a shift."

"At midnight." He put his mouth close to the receiver. "Rick, I wanted to tell you that I met Dustin when I left my seminar this evening. I walked to my car and saw him leaning against the old bucket of bolts he calls a vehicle."

I waited. "And?"

"I surprised him, walking from the side. He didn't see me until I was next to him. When he saw me, he let out this yelp and jumped into his car. He tore out of the parking lot like a bat outta hell, almost sideswiping a kid walking across the lot."

"He didn't say anything?"

"That's my point, Rick. In the second before he slipped into the car, I noticed that he was shaking."

"It's cold out, Hank. It's December. It's—"

He interrupted me. "Rick, he was crying."

Chapter Three

I was late getting to Ben Winslow's apartment. I'd dawdled at home, contemplating where to hang a Joan Miro print I'd picked up at the local Salvation Army. I tried it over the fireplace mantel, then over a cabinet in the kitchen, its vibrant pop-out colors warring with the black-and-white linoleum of the old-fashioned kitchen. Finally, disgusted, I laid it on the coffee table, a project for another day—a piece of reproduced art that was nothing more than a feeble excuse to put off leaving my apartment. Ever since that brief, unhappy encounter with Ben in the hallway, despite his knee jerk apology, I'd avoided him. Echoes of his unhappiness might surface at the dinner Sophia Grecko made him agree to.

Ben's apartment was on a side street in Unionville, the working-class corner of affluent Farmington, a street of modest homes that once housed mill workers. I stumbled up the steps to the front porch, the overhead light unlit, nearly dropping the bottle of chardonnay—"He likes Pioneer Valley brand," Sophia has whispered when I asked her—and colliding with a bank of plastic Walmart webbed chairs covered with slick ice. A shabby wreath hung on the front door.

Ben answered the doorbell with a smile on his face, and gave me a hearty handshake. "You're not late," he said, though I'd said nothing but hello.

"What?"

"Sophia lives upstairs and she's late."

I trailed after him to the back of the apartment, an old-fashioned spread of rooms, high-ceilinged, warped floors covered with scatter rugs, thick dark walnut molding with ornamental scrolling. I'd been in his apartment a few times, and had marveled at the helter-skelter furnishings—a lumpy sofa, side chairs with broken springs, paintings hanging crookedly on the walls. What Ben cared about was school—the lives of his students, yes, but also books and his research. Stacks of printed sheets slipped off tables and chairs, a pegboard dangled over an unused upright piano from the Scott Joplin era, tacks holding in place jotted-down websites and phone numbers and reminders to: "LOOK UP BILLY GRAHAM Kansas 1956!!" That kind of memo jumped out at you.

At the back of the apartment was a space where folks gathered. I spotted Liz tucked into an overstuffed side chair, her body nearly lost in the folds of sagging cushions, one hand gripping a glass of wine. She smiled mockingly, and pointed to a chair next to her. "You'll sink into oblivion."

"I've done that before."

"Yes, but we're no longer talking metaphors, Rick dear."

I slipped into a chair next to her and nodded to the other two guests in the room. Marcie and Vinnie were watching me with childlike grins on their faces. My closest friends on the faculty, dating back to my first years as a part-time instructor, Marcie was tenured English with a fascination for the 1930s proletarian fiction of the James T. Farrell sort—she'd done her thesis on *Studs Lonigan*—while her husband, Vinnie, was in the history department. They were childless, in their early forties, travelers, troublemakers; they fascinated everyone because Marcie was a fierce liberal and Vinnie the unapologetic Republican in a crowd of academics who viewed him with suspicion. They loved each other to death, though they squabbled and harangued each other, the James Carville and Mary Matalin stand-ins at the college. They cared for me as though I were a refugee washed upon their charitable shores, a benevolence I found a little grating at times, but I mostly basked in the glow of their friendship.

Marcie was pointing to a newspaper on a table, and I'd obviously walked in during her discussion of an article she'd read. A small, chubby woman with a round pink face, she wore a simple diamond cross around her neck, a gift from Vinnie dating from their collegiate days. She constantly fingered it, playing with the gold chain, especially when making a point. "As I was saying…"

Vinnie grunted, "Marcie, we all *read* the article."

A stocky man of medium height with a thin moustache over a large mouth that displayed a slight overbite, Vinnie now placed his palm down on the news article.

"Hiding it," Marcie joked, "will not prevent me from giving my opinion."

Liz interrupted. "Rick, the *Bristol Press* has an article on Ben's new book."

Ben's voice was low, scratchy. "So it begins again."

"Where's Sophia?" I asked.

At that moment, with theatrical timing, the front door opened and shut, the clack of high heels scurried from the front room, and Sophia appeared, out of breath. She was carrying a lopsided cake that tilted dangerously, dark chocolate frosting seeping to the edge of the platter like molten lava. She grumbled, "Baking is not an artform."

"It's lovely." Marcie squinted at it. "Very Tower of Pisa."

Sophia placed the cake on a side table, frowned at it, and poured herself a glass of wine, settled into a straight-backed chair by Ben's desk with the groans of an exhausted long-distance runner.

An unlikely couple, Sophia and Ben. Her real name was Sophie, we'd learned, but she'd appropriated Sophia because, she told us more than once, "it possessed a better rhythmic flow." She always added, unnecessarily, "Keep in mind Diane Ross became Diana Ross."

"So that's where you got that beehive hairdo," some junior faculty member once quipped. "An old late-night Supremes video from *Ed Sullivan*." Unfortunately the remark, reported back to her, had some currency. At the next faculty meeting the hairdo was higher, ink black.

"What are we talking about?" she asked now.

Marcie pointed to the article. "The old story resurfacing."

Sophia grumbled, "I know, I know. Lord, another religious war—like years back. The One Hundred Years War capsulated into a few protesters outside the college. 'Burn in Hell.' That was my favorite."

Ben's sociological interest was American evangelical religion. As a graduate student at NYU, he'd written his dissertation on the music employed by Kentucky snake worshippers—those fervent believers who take up serpents because of that curious bit in the Bible—and he'd spent time in the field. Most folks never realized that such religious frenzy had a soundtrack: strains of chanting, howling, tinkling banjos, and strumming fiddles. His study was revolutionary, though one night a maddened worshipper ran at him with a disgruntled, hissing rattlesnake, and Ben narrowly escaped an awful price to pay for doctoral scholarship. That study morphed into a study of American evangelical Protestantism, which included a popular essay in *Hartford Magazine* five years back on a mega church in nearby Bristol: The Gospel of Wealth Ministry, led by a charismatic, overfed minister in a white satin suit and a pompadour hairdo. Ben's article, though based in history, was almost a tongue-in-cheek—some said an unforgiving satirical—look at the popular church and the bags of money that the Reverend Simms packed into the trunk of his Cadillac on the way to Bank of America. What followed—death threats, pickets, the faithful horrified by a cynical glimpse at a church they adored. The *cause célèbre* died down, of course, but now, five years later, the *Bristol Press* had revived the story. The Reverend Simms, it seemed, was richer than ever—and madder than ever.

Ben's new tome, *Evangelical Fury: Essays on the Reinvention of Protestantism in New England*, just issued by the University of Massachusetts Press, would have been routinely reviewed in scholarly journals and then forgotten, but Ben had cherry-picked the Reverend Simms' mega church as an example of his unflattering thesis, though his arguments were wrapped in scholarly jargon. The local press, always ready to skewer the bombastic clergyman, highlighted Ben's new references in the book.

"Death threats," Sophia said.

Ben sighed. "All over again. But stupid. To be ignored."

Sophia wore an anxious look. "No one should ignore things like that, Ben. Nasty phone calls."

Ben reached for the article and tucked it between some books. "That's not why we're here tonight."

Sophia sighed. "To celebrate your book. Among friends."

"A pre-Christmas dinner," Ben corrected. "Okay?"

But it obviously was not okay, given the shadow that clouded his eyes.

"To Ben and Sophia." Marcie raised her glass.

We raised our glasses, too.

Five years ago he'd been bothered by the unexpected attention in the local press, paced the hallways of the school, dropped some pounds from his round figure, and missed classes and faculty meetings. Back then, Sophia had been a saving grace, a new faculty member in the Art History department who suddenly discovered Ben's charms. Ben, long resigned to a single life since his explosive divorce many years before, had moved into this apartment from the house on Avon Mountain that his ex-wife Charlotte kept. His meaningless fling with that graduate student ended messily, though Charlotte hammered at it in court and Ben bowed to her demands. Their two children, Martin and Melody, sided with their mother. A bad time for Ben, who then lost himself in his books and research and his students' lives—until the flamboyant Sophia—she was still Sophie then—squired him to parties and dinners and her bedroom. Upstairs.

Ben slopped wine on his sweater, didn't notice, his mind elsewhere. His hand trembled. Marcie asked him something about the book, but he didn't answer. She repeated the question.

"What?" Ben looked up.

Sophia answered for him, a hint of concern in her words. "Ben had a visit from Martin earlier."

Ben said slowly, "My son has never been happy."

Sophia addressed us, not Ben. "He's the prodigal son who returns to beg fellowship with his father, and then finds fault. Blames. Curses..."

"Stop." Ben's word filled the room.

"Well, I'm sorry," she said. "He's a thirty-year-old man. He acts like a pouting child."

Ben shrugged his shoulders. "He's never forgiven me for my sins."

"Sins?" From Sophia.

Ben frowned. "Sin. The original sin. Me, the atheist who devotes a life to religion, sinned."

Marcie spoke up. "Charlotte is an angry woman."

"A decade later?" Sophia sat back. "When the nonsense began with that faux minister in Bristol, five years ago, Charlotte was sympathetic, even calling Ben to give support. But when she found out that I was in his life—gossip provided by his roving-reporter daughter Melody who spotted us in town—all hell broke out."

Ben grunted. "Could we stop this now?" A weary smile. "We're supposed to be having a good time."

Marcie sat up. "I am. I love gossip."

Her husband touched her elbow. "The town crier."

"I'm the psychologist," Liz interrupted. "Does anyone want to hear my take on this?"

"No," I said.

"I have one thing to say," she went on, ignoring me. "Vinnie and Marcie, two people who don't belong together but actually do—perfect. Ben and Sophia, both from different corners of the universe but together—perfect. And then there's Rick and me. Two people who are the only ones in the world that everyone said belonged together but..." Her voice trailed off.

"Ended up apart," I concluded.

"And yet we still finish each other's sentences."

I reached over to squeeze her hand.

Marcie, flushed with too much wine, started to applaud.

When Ben left the room, banging around the kitchen, Sophia whispered, "Ben isn't himself. For two days now he walks the floor all night long."

Glancing toward Ben, Liz told her, "I noticed. Distracted."

Sophia's voice dropped. "It has to be Martin—or Melody. His grown children will be the death of him. I could hear Martin here today…yelling at him."

"Why?"

She clicked her tongue. "Martin doesn't need an excuse."

We all knew the tiresome tale of Ben's wayward children. Martin, at thirty, was in the middle of his second divorce and probably last year as a biology teacher at the high school in Southington. Long hours in therapy, explosive marriages that began in ecstasy and ended in court. Two years at the high school, on probation, he alienated the principal, which meant he'd be unemployed this spring. He blamed his father. A tired mantra—the adulterous affair years ago that detonated his mother's fury and her civil war. "Dad," he'd announced the one time we'd met, "never knew how to be a father."

His younger sister, Melody, drifted from community college to nursing and secretarial schools—even a beauty academy. Then to California to be an actress. Crestfallen, a little scarecrow of a woman, she'd dragged herself back to Connecticut and now slept the days away in the bedroom of her mother's house in Avon, the Dutch Colonial she'd grown up in when the family was intact. Charlotte blamed Ben for their daughter's spaciness and movie-magazine listlessness. Melody agreed with her mother. "Dad was never there for us." A snicker—I'm repeating Marcie's words, heard first-hand—"He preferred the adoration of simple-minded students, especially when they had no clothes on." So Ben salaamed his pain and hid away. He stayed long hours at the college exploring the animadversions of Cotton Mather as they resurfaced in the lower Connecticut hills. Until he met Sophia.

The doorbell rang. Ben rushed to meet a deliveryman. He'd ordered Indian food from Bombay Kitchen two streets away. We watched Ben shuffling around in his kitchen, emptying containers into bowls and onto plates. The tantalizing smell of *chicken tikka masala, lamb saag.* Curried goat. A huge pile of *naan.* The pungent aroma of curry, chutney, and saffron. On the counter were two six-packs of Kingfisher beer he'd taken out of the fridge. He never cooked, he'd told us—"I can scramble an egg"—and his refrigerator was covered with take-out menus from Chinese, Indian, Peruvian, and Japanese restaurants in the area. And pizza-delivery joints. A dozen of those. Maybe more.

The deliveryman had stumbled on the porch steps, and we'd heard his thick subcontinent accent, "Sir, pardon please, but a porch light would help." To which Ben answered, "The bulb is out and the landlord lives in Brooklyn."

Watching Ben's silhouette as he concentrated on arranging the food, I felt quickness in my chest—something else was going on. My gut brought me back to Dustin Trang and that explosive scene in the hallway. Ben's battles royal with his children were the stuff of routine and, according to Marcie, he'd reconciled himself to periodic skirmishes in the name of love. No, this was different. He looked marrow-deep sad.

The conversation over dinner meandered through academic politics, always petty and familiar old territory, to Ben's new book, stacks of which were precariously piled on a sideboard. "The solitary item in a goodie bag for each of you," Sophia joked.

Ben quietly watched her, warmth in his eyes. When Sophia lapsed into silence, he began rambling about the field research his grad students were working on, no doubt spurred by his own obsession with tent-revival religion. He talked of a young woman who spent some time in Middletown at a charismatic Catholic church, a squirrely sect that published diatribes each Saturday in the *Hartford Courant,* messages from the Virgin Mary that were unfortunately ungrammatical. "I'd recommend her to an ESL class," Marcie noted.

The only person who didn't laugh was Ben, sitting with his arms folded over his chest and observing our banter with slatted eyes, looking unhappy.

I plunged in. "Ben, I remember hearing you praise Dustin Trang's paper on the Great Awakening—"

I stopped, so fiery was his glare.

Liz probed, "What in the world? What are we talking about?"

Ben hissed, "Very good, Rick. I was waiting for you to bring him up." He paused, but faltered. "I mean, yes, that boy has a wonderful mind, his paper was amazing, a personal slant because his family is mired in some cockeyed mixture of evangelical Buddhist Protestantism, whatever that is."

I was confused. "But that scene in the hallway..."

"Nothing. Nothing at all."

But I'd ruined the evening, if I could judge by the censorious—if baffled—glances heaped upon me by Marcie and Liz. I'd broached a forbidden topic, taboo among the remnants of *tikka masala* on the stained tablecloth.

So the evening stumbled to an end as we moved back into the den where Sophia, rattled by the shift in tone, cut enormous slabs of her chocolate cake. We drank tea and ate cake and waited for the clock in the dining room to announce ten o'clock and our polite departures.

A sudden rapping on the front door made us jump. Sophia let out a throaty bark that made Marcie giggle. I checked my wristwatch. Nearly ten.

With a quick glance at Ben, Sophia rushed to the front door and quietly pulled back the curtain to peek out. Facing Ben, she mouthed a word: *Student.*

"At this hour?" Ben wondered out loud. He stood up.

Sophia was unhappy. "You have to stop letting your students know where you live. This isn't the College Union, Ben."

Walking to the window, Ben was muttering. "Nobody should be here. You know I don't invite students..." Stepping around Sophia, he pulled back the curtain, pressed his face against the glass, and gasped.

I moved behind him, strained to look out onto the dark porch.

A slight, shadowy figure rapped again, insistent, then stepped back to the edge of the porch and waited, rocking back and forth. Bundled up in a hooded parka, a thick scarf wrapped around his neck, he seemed a short jittery snowman.

His face reddening, Ben pulled open the door, although I reached around him to stop him. Too late. A flood of light flooded the porch, and Ben and I stared into the trembling, frozen face of Dustin Trang. Of course, he'd expected to see Ben, but his eyes popped as they flew to my face, and he stumbled backward.

"I told you, I told you…" Backing up, he collided with the balustrade, spun around like an out-of-control wind-up toy, and staggered down the steps, running lopsidedly until he disappeared from view.

"Ben," I pleaded, "what aren't you telling us?"

"None of your business."

Chapter Four

Brandon Vinh sat with Hank in the cafeteria late in the afternoon, that hollow time when few students hung around. Three other Asian students clustered around him as he spoke. One young woman, maybe Korean, leaned into Hank, the uniformed cop at leisure. She was ignoring Brandon whose words dominated, and Brandon wasn't happy at this impromptu meeting of the Asian-American Alliance, a small group lately energized by Hank's recent appearance on campus.

Hank waved me over.

A Criminal Justice major who'd never taken any of my night classes—I was convinced he purposely avoided me, although I had no proof—Brandon was the loudest member of the seminar Hank was mentoring. Hank had told me Brandon's goal was the FBI. Quantico or bust. Terrorist underground activity. Homegrown wacko jobs from Oklahoma. To carry a gun twenty-four/seven. Hank had recounted this one night in a wary voice. "Dead-end dreamer," he'd finished. "Imagine him with a gun."

I sat down facing Brandon. He unlocked his hands from behind his head, crossed his arms, and watched me with questioning eyes. When Hank began speaking, he broke in. "We're talking about our end-of-semester Christmas get-together at The Silo down the street. This Thursday after the seminar. At seven. You wanna come, Prof?" His smile was not inviting.

"Maybe."

Hank cut in. "Of course Rick's invited."

Brandon was all business. "We got twelve people committed. Check the invite on Facebook, gang. I arranged it."

The other students shuffled papers, mumbled about obligations, stretched out arms, one young man crumpling his Coke can as he narrowed his eyes at Brandon. Smiling at Hank and even at me, they left the table, but Brandon stayed, jotting some notes into an iPad he balanced in his lap. Leaning back, Hank watched him, though occasionally he glanced at me. I knew Hank well enough to read his irritation—his dislike—but I also understood that, curiously, he was enjoying this.

"You don't take Rick's classes?" he asked Brandon.

Brandon contemplated me as he rocked in his seat. "Rumor has it he's too hard a grader."

"You don't like a challenge?" I said.

"I like to pick my battles."

"Are we done here?" Hank reached for his jacket.

"A minute, okay?" I faced Brandon. "Could I talk to you about something that's bothering me?"

Brandon sat up, his face brightening. His long legs stretched out under the table, the tips of his expensive Timberland boots visible. A junior at the college. I'd read his bio in the campus newspaper. Campus leader—and the noisiest student in the quad. Lacrosse captain. Varsity tennis. In some ways he reminded me of Hank as a young student: tall, confident, self-assured. But Brandon lacked Hank's...not softness, but kindness. Maybe humanity is the word I'm searching for. The obligatory Criminal Justice buzz cut inherited from the Eisenhower years no student remembered gave him a look that exaggerated his larger-than life ears. A smallish head that perhaps wasn't that small but Brandon, a weightlifter, had broad shoulders and a thick upper chest on that frame. In the middle of December he wore a sleeveless muscle shirt.

I watched him closely. "Perhaps an unethical talk."

He grinned. "Even better."

Hank was bewildered. "Rick, what?"

"Dustin Trang," I said in a flat voice. "Anh Ky Trang."

Brandon's face closed up. He pulled his legs back from under the table and sat up straight. "Yeah? What?"

"A comment you made about him."

He glanced at Hank. "You squealing on me, Officer?"

Hank shrugged, glaring back. "Maybe you should be more careful when you talk to cops."

Brandon grinned widely, performed a half-bow.

I wasn't buying it. "I'd like you to tell me why you said what you said about Dustin."

"Little Anh?"

"Same person." I waited. "You said he'd kill somebody someday."

"I said that?"

"Yeah. That's sort of hard to forget, especially if you're talking to a cop."

"All right, all right. Who the hell cares?" His eyes accused Hank. "I was just talking, you know." A little nervous now, a bead of sweat on his brow that he brushed away with the back of his hand.

"Tell me."

Hank tapped his finger on the table. "Yes, Brandon, tell us." He started playing with his empty Styrofoam cup, rolling it around in his fingers.

"I don't like him. That's all."

"Why?"

"Have you seen him? Christ, the way he dresses. Those shiny cheap jeans from Walmart, rolled up to his knee, baggy at his ass, a spiky haircut you wouldn't give to a boy you hated."

Hank tapped the cup on the table. "He's poor."

"He's *odd*. When he first came here—God, I was surprised they let in a dumb scholarship kid like that—I walked up and said hello. I mean, I *knew* who he was—knew *about* his family. He shrugged me away." He spoke through clenched teeth. "A bastard." He caught his breath. "I mean..."

Bastard. *Bui doi.* A dangerous word in his community. In my community. My mother. My father.

"Brandon…" Hank cautioned.

"Hey, I'm sorry." But he laughed nervously. "What the fuck."

"Look," I said, "I'm worried about him. I witnessed a scary scene with Professor Winslow."

Brandon waved his hand in the air. "Yeah, like everyone talks about that. It started a couple days back—out of nowhere. Some asshole shot the fight and uploaded it onto YouTube. With funny comments. 'The Geek and the Prof, Round One.' Here's this pipsqueak kid, who never opens his mouth in class. Like he knows he doesn't belong here. But suddenly he's in the hallway yelling at the professor, threatening. It's like—like Dr. Jekyll and Mr. Hyde. You know, this inner demon coming out."

I broke in. "What started it?"

He shrugged. "Dunno. Somebody in the Alliance—I'm chairman, by the way, my idea a year back—anyway, this kid, a Chinese exchange student—he told me the professor asked him a question in class he didn't like. I mean, Professor Winslow's got a rep as a softie—everyone goes to him to solve problems. Easy A. You can cry on his shoulder, they say."

"That seems a little preposterous," Hank interjected. "You don't flip out over and over because of that."

"Yeah, true. Maybe you get mad at a prof, but you don't bang on his office door and bay at the moon. Jesus Christ! They tell me he did it again. Today. Real loud. He's weird. What can I say? If you're a goddamn nut, and certifiable—look at him—then the slightest thing can set you off."

I sat back, considered his words. "It has to be more than that."

Brandon eyed me curiously. "Why do you even care?"

I held his stare. "Why don't *you* care?"

"It's not my business."

Mind your own business. Echoes in the college hallway. Ben hissing at me.

Hank's voice got brittle. "Brandon, for God's sake. A little decency, no? What do you know about his background?"

"That's the trouble, Officer Nguyen. I know *too* much about his background. More than I want to know. Bristol, that stinking hellhole."

"So you know his family?"

"By reputation. Ba-a-a-a-d reputation."

"Tell us."

He surveyed the room and nodded at a young woman passing by. She debated walking toward us, but Brandon purposely swiveled his body away, leaning into me. "In a world of success, I mean, Asian success, you know the children of the starving boat people going to Harvard and buying vowels on *Wheel of Fortune*—hey, the Trang family slipped a notch on the old wheel of fortune. Worse, because they were *programmed* for American dreaming."

"I don't follow this," I said.

Hank's voice was sharp. "Dustin is a college student. That says something, doesn't it?"

Frustrated, Brandon assumed the manner of someone compelled to blab an unpleasant truth he'd rather not—but secretly relished it. "They're dirt poor because all they do is *dream*." He let that sink in. "The Vietnamese community in town, small though it is, twenty or thirty families, is close-knit, you know. Families that are…joyously middle-class. Maybe upper middle-class. Proud of it—we wear it when we cruise around in our BMWs. My father escaped by way of Thailand at the end of the eighties, met my mother at Fort Pendleton, had a cousin down here, ran a grocery. Now we own two gas stations, a dollar-value convenience shop, a laundromat." He sat back, beamed. "Money for nothing, chicks for free."

"What?" From Hank, irritated.

"Pop music gives me my lines."

Hank scowled at him. "Maybe you should read Shakespeare."

"Then most Americans won't talk to me. If I quote a golden oldie by Spyro Gyra, I can get laid."

I pushed him. "Could you get to the story?"

"All right, all right. Jesus Christ." He tented his fingers. "Here's the dope. When Americans fled Saigon in 1975, you've seen the footage, folks hanging off helicopters and scaling the walls of the embassy, the Trang family had no need for such whoop-it-up fireworks. Uncle Binh and his wife, Suong, worked for the Americans. He'd been an aide to General Westmoreland. A military man himself. Privileged and pampered, he was fed rice that smelled like lotus blossoms. Slept under mosquito netting. Used toilet paper flown in from California. So the U.S. had to get *them* out before the Commies put them in bamboo cages, sent them to reeducation camp, and smashed out their teeth. They got to an air force base a day or so before the craziness. Flown to Guam, put in huts, not makeshift tents like the rest."

"Who exactly?" Hank asked.

"Well, Anh's mother and father, who was Binh's brother, two young sons, babies, a year or so old, maybe. Uncle Binh and his wife. She was a translator at the embassy. Suong, her name. A package deal."

I sat back, nodded. "Safe in America."

"That's the problem," Brandon went on eagerly. "They settled in Bristol, maybe because Uncle Binh, trained in Nam as an military engineer, was given a cushy job at New Departure, General Motors. I don't know. According to my dad, they lost energy."

"Meaning?" Hank asked.

"Think about it, man. It was like they had it all in Saigon, and they still wanted *that* world. But, hey, it's America. Every step they took here reminded them of what they lost. Perfumed sheets and lotus tea. They still believe the Commies will crumble, all these years later, and they can go back. So they…they float in space. They wait. Hover over America like ghosts."

I summed up. "America as a way station."

"Exactly. They got no interest in America. It's just the country that once promised them a safe Vietnam, then broke *that* promise. Promised them a good life, and then broke *that* promise."

"But how did they end up in a housing project?" I asked.

He took a moment to answer. "As I said, no energy. And real bad luck. Fate. Buddha shopping at a different strip mall. Uncle Binh had some sort of accident at work, crippled, lost his job. His wife worked in a grocery store but got fired. So she and Uncle Binh live on disability in a dingy apartment down the street from the projects on Jefferson Drive."

"That's where Dustin's folks live?"

"Mother," he corrected. "Mother. His older brother, a jackass in his forties now, drifts in and out. A loser. Meth junkie, probably. Truck driver. Carpenter. Asshole—pardon my French. Drug dealer, so they say. Prison time. The younger brother married a welfare Rican and got a hundred sniveling brats."

"Father?"

"That's the interesting part of the story," Brandon confided. "You see, the whole bunch settled into poverty, food stamps and welfare and cash-under-the-table jobs on construction sites, but the lazy mommy gets pregnant when she's in her forties. Like—late forties. A big surprise. No one is happy. And one night, a snowy night, urban legend tells me, they were driving to the hospital on Federal Hill and daddy swerved to avoid a falling branch on Route 6, crashing into a light pole. Dead at the wheel. Mommy goes into labor with the help of a passing cop, and little Anh Ky is born in a squad car off School Street."

"Good God," Hank said.

"That's not the half of it. Ailing mommy is stuck with a squawking brat. She wants to watch *Let's Make a Deal* all day long on her crappy TV, but there's this little snot that took her husband's life. Sort of. Little Anh Ky, crapping his pants and wailing, his mommy too tired to walk the five feet to change him."

I shook my head. "Poor kid."

"Yeah, sure. He turned into this—real embarrassment. Look at him." Brandon sighed. "End of story. The winter apple."

"What?"

"My dad said that's what peasants in his village called such babies. The old sagging tree in the orchard surprises with a sudden apple. Out of season. In the winter of your life." He waved his hand. "That's Dustin. Gnarled, wormy, worthless. A winter apple. They never knew what to do with him. So they ignored him. He grew up by hiding away in the Bristol Public

Library." He grunted. "And the goddamned Lions Club pays for him to walk these expensive halls."

"But we still don't know the cause of the problem he's having with Professor Winslow," Hank concluded.

Brandon was stretching his limbs, yawning, preparing to leave. "Does it really matter, guys? There's something *wrong* with him. He wasn't supposed to be born. He's like a special ed kid or something."

"Enough. Brandon, maybe a little sympathy? It doesn't sound like he's had an easy time of it."

Brandon shrugged. "Guys, nobody gets a free ride in life."

"The fact that he's here at the college tells me he's doing something good."

"His family is a bunch of free-loaders, money-grubbing welfare frauds."

"You know, I spoke to him earlier," Hank said. "He was sitting in the lounge outside of one of the dorms, doing homework with another kid."

I was surprised. "A friend?"

Hank shrugged. "I don't know if he's a friend. I don't know him. A dark kid, bushy hair. Wearing a frazzled sweater, the kind immigrants from East Europe, like East Germany, wore. Or the Middle East. You know, like decades old and…"

Brandon spoke up. "Oh yeah, Darijo Delic. That retard. One of the Bosnian students here. A Bosniak, whatever the fuck *that* is. Two or three. Scholarship kids from Hartford. Boo-hoo refugee or maybe the son of refugees from the Balkan wars of a few decades back."

"I don't know him," I said.

Brandon, brimming with information, said, "Because you're not savvy to the collection of nerds floating around this campus. Information Technology Systems creeps. Computer Science. Nerdville."

"That's charitable, Brandon."

"That's me."

"Hank, maybe you should invite Dustin to the party on Thursday night."

Brandon protested, "No. He won't fit in."

"I'm the guest of honor, Brandon. Right?" Hank said gleefully. "State cop on campus. The Asian-American Alliance—what do you call them?—for *Asians*."

Hank shredded the rest of his Styrofoam cup, the jagged pieces strewn on the table. Brandon couldn't take his eyes off them. Resigned, he said, "Hey, you are the cop here. I follow the law of America."

Hank smiled at me. "I already invited Dustin when I saw him earlier."

I caught Hank's eye—a look that said *maybe I did, maybe I didn't*.

Brandon laughed. "And he said no way, right?"

Hank went on, "I told him I was a state cop. People tend to obey state cops. Without question. That's the reason I became one. So people would listen to me. Remember that, Brandon. Dustin has to show up."

"And he said?"

"He'll be there. He doesn't want to be arrested."

"Christ." Brandon got up, slung his backpack over his shoulder. As he left us, he rapped his knuckles emphatically on a table. "Christ Almighty. The shit I gotta deal with."

Chapter Five

Snow began falling early Thursday morning. I spent a few hours at my office in Hartford, pulling together the rudiments of a new investigation for Cigna. Then my partner, Jimmy Gadowicz, stumbled in, remarking it was nice to see me make an appearance at the office so early.

"It's ten o'clock," I told him.

My cell's sudden signal, a split-nerve buzz, always startled him. "I don't see why you can't use a real phone."

I showed him the text from Hank:

> Don't be late for party at Silo.

He grumbled, "Why are you going to a party on a Thursday night?"

Another dental-chair buzz a second later:

> You know how you are.

"Goddamn him," Jimmy said loudly.

"It's snowing out, Jimmy."

He squinted at me. "And now you're the local weatherman?"

I waved goodbye as I gathered my laptop and briefcase. "A real old-fashioned nor'easter, they're predicting."

He called after me. "The problem with you is you was born in a tropical climate. You don't have real weather there."

"Monsoons? Typhoons? Tsunamis?"

"I was in Nam protecting your people. Lot of thanks I got, by the way. Never saw one monsoon." He waved an unlit cigarette at me, then settled back in his chair. "Just lots of bullets headed my way."

As I drove back home to Farmington, swirls of light snow drifted along the curbs. I found myself thinking about Jimmy. The crusty old man, a wisenheimer by his own definition, gloriously overweight in his uniform: a Patriots XXL sweatshirt, appropriate pizza stains on the collar, a drizzle of brown sauce from General Tso's chicken takeout from China House down the street. A man who, as far as I know, only made one professional concession at my behest—he no longer smoked those stink-bomb cigars he got from the bodega on the corner. At least in the office. Okay—he'd sneak a cigarette now and then. His battered Ford Escort was another matter altogether, the ashtray a wonderland of discarded butts. He was the Vietnam vet who took me in, trained me when I fled life as a traumatized cop in Manhattan. The grumpiest man I ever met—and the kindest.

Gracie Petroni, my landlady, trailed after me as I climbed to my second-floor apartment. Fresh from a walk to the post office one block over, she was dressed for the Arctic Tundra in an ankle-length Persian lamb coat from four decades earlier, a fuzzy knit cap emblazoned with an outrageous cloth hibiscus, and a scarf so flowery it belonged on the swaying hips of an Hawaiian wahini. "Snow coming," she announced, breathing down my back.

"I know."

"You going out?"

"I have a late class—and a party."

An octogenarian ex-Rockette who owned the canary-yellow Victorian house I lived in, Gracie believed she needed to protect me—a fortyish man with a job as a PI—from the elements. All the elements. She danced up a storm at Radio City Music Hall back in the fifties, then moved with her husband to the quaint Connecticut town, lost him early, started renting out the second and third floors of her home, and enjoyed bossing her tenants around. I let her because she was a woman easy to love.

Now, frowning, she wagged a bony finger at me. "Nobody goes to a party on a Thursday night."

"I already heard that from Jimmy."

Her eyes got wide. "Now and then the man makes sense. As I say, now and then."

She followed me into my apartment, unraveling her clothing. As I hung up my coat, Gracie strolled around—"This rug looks new, Rick. Salvation Army again?"—and gazed from my windows down into the street. "Yes, snow. Lots of it." A heavy sigh. "Dreams of Florida again."

"Never," I insisted. "What would I do without you, Gracie?"

"You got a point there."

Shuffling around my kitchen, she put on the teakettle, rummaged in my cabinets for the Chinese white lotus tea that I drank, arranged cups on a table, and sat down, watching me. "What's with you?"

Bewildered, I glanced at her. "What?"

"You're not in focus."

I sighed. "Things on my mind."

Suddenly her eyes settled on Ben Winslow's new book that he'd inscribed the other night. I'd tossed it on an end table.

She pointed. "They mentioned this guy today in the *Hartford Courant*." She reconsidered. "Indirectly. I mean, that lunatic minister out in Bristol is on the rampage again." She chuckled. "The old saying is that any press, even bad press, is good for folks in the spotlight."

I got interested. "Tell me, Gracie. What did he say?"

She shrugged. "The usual nonsense. Threats of lawsuits against your friend. His church is the word of God. Divine inspiration. Your friend—a stand-in for Satan. You know the drill."

"What do you think, Gracie?"

Her voice got low, slow. "I'm a Catholic, Rick. God-fearing, of course. I'm not into frenzy and waving hands in the air like I'm swatting mosquitoes away. We talk about that Reverend

Simms at our Confraternity of the Rosary, you know. He's on local TV." Gracie broke into a rumbling, thick voice, "'You place your dollar bill on the TV right now and say the name of Jesus. Put that bill in an envelope and'...You know the rest. 'Jesus is the golden key to your hidden riches. Send your dollars, you poor folks, and the gospel of prosperity will magnify your donation into...millions.'"

I laughed. "Does it work?"

"I wouldn't know." She tapped the back of the book jacket, her fingers on Ben's cherubic face. "This here guy is Simms' mortal enemy. Of quackery, sham, all in the name of religion."

I glanced at the cover. Hardly a glossy best-selling cover— stodgy blue, discreet lettering, typical university press.

"Last time Ben received death threats when he wrote about Reverend Simms."

Gracie grumbled, "Yeah, nice touch. Kill in the name of Christ."

She pushed the book away and headed into the kitchen to quiet the whistling teakettle. "Who reads this crap, anyway?"

• ● ● ● •

Though I usually walked the five streets to the Farmington College campus, I decided to drive. The snow was falling steadily now, blanketing the bushes and sticking to the asphalt. The wind picked up. A rough night, and I needed to drive to that student party after seven, although that idea was losing any appeal. On snowy nights I relished my cozy home, the old Victorian rooms creaky and whispering from the drafts, the cast-iron radiators buzzing and clanging. A good book. Reheated pizza that I'd forget to eat.

The campus was dizzy with the possibility of class cancellation. A snow day, everyone a school kid again, nose pressed against the window. The commuting students scurried in, backpacks slung over shoulders, their shoulders crusted with flakes of snow, but the dorm students, lazily drifting in twos or threes, seemed eager to curl up on the sofas in the Student

Union. Anything better than class. My students, Criminal Justice stalwarts, were ex-marines and army grunts and high-school tough guys who never missed class. They narrowed their eyes in disapproval if I walked in minutes late. Punctuality was always a good idea when addressing steely-eyed students who kept guns in their glove compartments.

Stopping in the faculty lounge on the way to my office, I spotted Sophia Grecko sitting in one of the deep-cushioned side chairs, a closed art history text on her lap. She had her head tilted to the side, facing the wall, and as I passed she shuddered. The text slipped to the floor. I reached for it, and she offered me a wan smile of thanks.

"What's the matter, Sophia?"

Fingers splayed, she made an it's-nothing gesture, but her face tightened. She glanced around the room. Two or three other faculty members were clustered at the other end, lost in an animated conversation. Sophia mouthed one word: *Ben.*

I slipped into a chair next to her. "You okay?"

She drew in her breath. "We had words."

"Everyone in love has words."

"We never do."

"But…"

"He's a different man the last few days. That's what we fought about. I don't like secrets. In my marriage, a hundred years ago, that's all we had—secrets. I never want that again."

"What happened?"

She puffed out her cheeks. "You know, I wander in and out of his apartment. The nag from upstairs." A beguiling smile. "Usually he likes it. But I surprised him because he was lost in thought, gazing at the computer screen in his workroom. I peeked over his shoulder."

"And you saw?"

A quick breath. "He was on the FBI site."

That surprised me. "Research, Sophia? He's a sociologist. Who knows what he's…?"

Her hand flew up in my face. "I glanced down at a pad by him. 'FBI,' it said. And a phone number. To report a crime. *That* phone number."

I was silent a moment. "Still and all..."

"Yes, yes," she said, panic in her voice. "But he shut down the computer so fast, put his hand over the pad, and...and accused me of being a snoop."

"Maybe you surprised him."

A cynical laugh. "I certainly did." She grabbed the thick art history book, cradled it to her chest, and stood. "I'm sorry, Rick. His mood lately is like a cancer that touches everyone. You saw it on Saturday, right? It's been a week of—hell. Me—now I spread it to you."

"We're all friends."

She threw back her head and echoed, "Friends."

Headed to my class in the Dodgson Building, I swung by the College Union to get a cup of coffee. Dismissed students were flocking into the cafeteria, bustling, gleeful, on holiday. As I maneuvered around chatty students, I saw Dustin Trang standing by a bank of windows and staring out at the snowstorm. As students rustled by him, he never moved. His ungainly parka was draped over a chair near him, a book bag on the floor, but around his neck wound a bulky scarf. Strangely, he was wearing a T-shirt and those ridiculous rolled-up jeans. A boy dressed for any number of seasons.

"Hey, Dustin," I said to the back of his head.

He jumped around so quickly I stepped back.

"Hey."

"I didn't mean to startle you. You like staring out the window?"

He turned his head back to the window and placed his hand on the ice-cold glass. For a moment, concentrating, he ignored me, his face close to the glass. His head didn't move. Frozen in place, quiet. I debated what to do.

"I'm making you uncomfortable."

Suddenly he faced me, a blank look on his face, then he turned back to the window. "Snow," he said slowly. "I love when it snows."

I pointed out to the snow-covered quad. "And we're gonna have a lot of it, they say."

He still didn't look at me. "When it snows, everybody gotta stay inside."

"You like that?"

His palm moved against the glass. "No one can see you in the snow. It's like the world becomes wiped out."

"Some think it's pretty then," I said lamely.

He glanced back at me. "That's when the world looks best. When you can't see it."

Still holding his hand on the window, he arched back his head, gazing up to the heavens. A thin smile on his face, he shut his eyes, then popped them open. "What do you want?"

Startled, I stared at his stretched-out arm pressed high on the window. Such a skinny arm, exposed in that faded white T-shirt, a thin pole of bone and almost no flesh. No bicep. A stick of dark wood. His head above that oversized scarf looked disconnected from his body. A bobble head in Barney Google eyeglasses with those emphatic black frames.

"I thought I'd say hello."

He didn't answer.

"You going to class? Don't you have Professor Winslow's class in a bit?"

He shook his head. "No."

"But you drove to campus on a snowy day?"

When he faced me, his look was distrustful, angry. "Where else do I got to go?"

"You could go to class."

"What do you want?" But he seemed to regret his sharp tone because his eyes flickered. He rapped on the window, then dipped down to retrieve his book bag. He slung it over his shoulder and pushed by me, brushing my sleeve. Startling himself, he squeaked out a feeble "I'm sorry" but kept moving.

He forgot his coat so he had to step back, pull it off the chair. He kept his head bowed.

I watched him walk away, not in a straight line, but, peculiarly, a crooked wobble, shifting left, then right, as though he were desperate to escape gunshot.

Across the room, sat Brandon Vinh, his legs up on a chair, his arms folded over his chest, his head resting against a wall as he followed Dustin's curious departure. When he caught my eye, he nodded and pointed a finger at me, a gesture that communicated camaraderie, a mutual understanding that the skinny boy fleeing the Union was crazy. A young girl walked in, stepping aside as Dustin shuffled past her, and she waved to Brandon, who called her over. Laughing, she gave him a hug. When I walked by them, Brandon gave me a conspiratorial wink. I ignored him.

· ● ● ● ·

By six o'clock the weather app on my phone declared a full-fledged blizzard striking Connecticut, so I dismissed my class and watched them flee. Other instructors did the same. I went looking for Hank who'd be in the seminar room two buildings over, but when I read my texts I discovered his seminar had been cancelled earlier. He'd texted:

No class no party no fun tonight.

I texted back:

Where are you?

His reply:

Home where everyone belongs on a night like this.

A quick smart-aleck coda a moment later:

Did you notice it's snowing?

Ben Winslow, bundled up and loaded down with books, was leaving his office, but he spotted me. He darted back inside, closing the door. Strange, I thought, but not surprising. Since last Saturday he'd hidden out in his classrooms or office, avoiding the faculty lounge, even turning away when I approached him on the quad. Talking with Liz one night, telling her how bothered I was, she summed up: "Embarrassment, Rick. As long as we've known Ben, he's the hail-fellow-well-met kind of guy, the campus clown. 'Like me, like me, like me. Please like me.' The activist who is afraid to hurt anyone's feelings."

"He didn't hurt my feelings."

"I talked to Sophia after the party. He was…down. Really down. Not the perfect host. After that Dustin kid skedaddled down the porch and into the cold night, he got so quiet. You were there. That awful silence. All of us gathering our toys and going home. He feels he offended us."

"He's hiding from us?"

"Yes."

So now I considered knocking on his door, but I didn't. Instead, I dropped a book at the library, chitchatted with a graduate student manning the circulation desk, and headed to the faculty parking lot.

A wail of wind swirled sheets of snow across the lot. Already the remaining cars were covered with three or four inches of snow. I stood on the landing under the overhead lights that threw shadows across the lot. A hiccough of streetlights dotted the parking lot. Staring up into the lights, I saw snow blowing almost horizontally. As I pulled my gloves on, tightening my scarf, I watched a car deep in the lot maneuver its way out, beams of cloudy headlight lost in the swirling snow. I shivered—my car was at the back of the lot.

Suddenly, standing, mesmerized by the whirr and hum of wind and snow, I heard a distinct *pop*. My eyes shot to that corner of the lot. Then another *pop*. But this time I caught the flash of brilliant light.

Pop pop.

In the eerie quiet night with the hiss of wind and slap of snow against my cheeks, I understood, thanks to my early years as a beat cop in Chelsea. Hell's Kitchen. New York.

I ran, zigzagging through the cars, slamming against bumpers, slipping on the pavement, weaving my way. I watched another car screech out of the parking lot, its headlights illuminating the snow. It slid, braked, sped up, then disappeared around the corner.

I staggered to a car with its motor running. The driver's window was rolled down and already snow was blowing inside. A head was slumped over the steering wheel, resting there, turned to the side. A smudge of dark red covered his neck. A wash of blood on his left temple. A recognizable hole. His head was turned so that I could see one bulging, horrible eye.

The engine hummed and the windshield wipers moved slowly back and forth. Clumps of snow splashed off the front hood.

I reached into the car, hoping for a sign of life that I knew was not there.

Ben Winslow had died the moment he was shot in the head.

Chapter Six

The police picked up Dustin Trang for questioning late the next afternoon.

Friday began as a white-out day, a morning of fierce wind and an assault of two feet of drifting snow. I'd slept fitfully all night long, most of the time bundled in blankets on my sofa that faced the front windows, staring out into the blackness and shivering from the drafts that seeped through the old wood. I'd spent three or four hours the night before at the college, huddled with the Farmington cops who arrived on the scene after my 9-1-1 call, then with the state police crime machine that appeared. Sitting in the empty faculty lounge, repeating my sparse statement, I relived that awful moment when I realized gunshots had been fired in the parking lot.

What I also kept telling myself—something I did not admit to the cops—was that as I ran through the parked cars I knew, deep in my soul, that I'd discover the body of Ben Winslow. How do you tell that to the police? Psychic hotline for Rick Van Lam on one? My gut instinct, coupled with days of worrying about the metamorphosis of Ben Winslow from jovial backslapper to morose irritant, had plagued me, warned me. No powers of ratiocination there, but old-fashioned worry. Pick a card. Any tarot card. The hanging man.

Late that night, headed home in the blinding snow, a matter of blocks that seemed an endless journey into outer space, I planned to snuggle in with a cup of tea and leftovers—that emptiness in my gut was also for want of supper, a few Ritz crackers not sufficient—and bed. A narcotic sleep with no dreaming. But Hank was texting madly, even as I climbed the stairs to my rooms. Midnight: he'd heard the news through social media and cop hotline.

True? Tell me.

I texted back:

Yes. True. Tomorrow morning talk with you.

But the storm raged on throughout the night, and sleep was impossible. In the morning, switching on the TV, I realized that the governor had closed down the state. Only essential personnel were called in. Schools closed. A persistent crawl at the bottom of my TV chronicled not only schools and public places but also the closing of gymnastics studios, book discussion groups, holistic medicine sessions, yoga studios. On and on. Bizarrely I thought: what about the closing down of a lifetime? What about that? A man sits in his car and switches on his windshield wipers, probably sat for a moment contemplating, like some variation of Robert Frost's pioneering farmer, his car hood piling up with snow. Between the woods and frozen lake…promises to keep…

And then…then, I realized, he must have rolled down his window. He must have recognized his attacker. Maybe. A knock on the window. *Help me, sir. My battery is dead. Yes but…*Or: *What do you want?*

Drowsy from a lack of sleep and food, my mind roiled with spitfire associations that led me to bury my head under the blanket.

The college was closed for the day, of course, dorm students hunkered down in their rooms playing cards and smoking weed. But the announcer noted that the police allowed no one on campus. Grainy footage showed Ben Winslow's lone automobile circled with flapping yellow tape, a ring of cop cars surrounding it, flashing blue and red lights, and in the distant background, the blinking lights of the state evidence van.

TV coverage intermingled all day long with local weather forecasts. Both forecasting doom. At one point, mid-morning, dressing in jeans and flannel shirt after a long, cruel hot shower that did nothing to revive me, I heard Gracie rapping on my door. She was delivering fresh-made muffins. I gave her a quick peck on the cheek, a hug. Manna from the Gods, I told her, eyeing the blueberry muffins, breathing in the warm yeasty smell.

"Don't know about manna, but you got the goddess part of that right."

I hugged her again.

So the two of us sat with coffee and muffins and stared at the TV. I filled her in on what happened last night.

She held my eye. "What now?"

"What do you mean?"

"You—there?" She pointed to a wispy footage then on a loop on TV that showed the lone car in that parking lot. "You found the body of your friend."

"I know, Gracie."

"But I also know you. You're in this now."

I shook my head. "No."

A slight chuckle. "Why do you lie to yourself?"

"I don't." Then a thin smile. "Sometimes—a little."

She shook her head back and forth. "You're watching the screen with this look on your face. You're waiting for something. I'm watching the coverage out of curiosity, the ghoulish wonder we all have when people do horrible things. You're watching... waiting...for an *answer.*"

I smiled back at her. "It's the detective in me."

She shook her head more vigorously. Muffin crumbs drifted down her housedress. "Simple fact—this murdered man was a friend of that Manhattan beat cop."

I nodded. "Bingo."

But the incessant tape loop that played on every local station told me nothing. After Gracie went downstairs I lay back on the sofa and talked to Hank, then Liz, and finally Jimmy. Hank was on duty, given little time to talk with the chaos on the interstates that occupied his time, but he wanted me to retell the events I'd witnessed. But I had so little: the *pop pop*, the second one accompanied by that flash of light, running through the parking lot, a speeding car whose headlights cut the night and out onto the street.

"One car?"

I paused. "Another just before. A minute before maybe."

"Connected?"

"I doubt it. Faculty fleeing the snow."

"Timing," he said. "The killer was taking a chance. Other faculty—even you if you learned how to walk faster than a Saigon snail—could have approached that car in the snowstorm. The killer could not have seen who was nearby."

"True, and he had to wait until Ben was in the car, not walking up to it. Sitting, windshield wipers switched on. Maybe he counted on the darkness and the snow to shield him."

"He knew Ben's car."

"This was an ambush."

"Planned because of the snow?"

I considered that. "How do you plan for that? Yes, you can know Ben's teaching schedule, especially if you watched him for days. But he let his classes go early."

"So did everyone," Hank said.

"So he lays in wait, parked nearby, car running."

Hank concluded, "Gun at the ready."

My mind wandered—*Is this a dagger I see before me, its handle turned toward my hand…Come, let me clutch it…*

"Rick? Earth to Rick. You there?"

"I was thinking of Hamlet."

"You need more coffee."

"I always need more coffee."

"Vietnamese coffee. Potent, sit-up-and-notice coffee. The only gift the French gave to the Vietnamese. Not that namby-pamby stuff you drink." Then, quickly, "They're gonna pick up Dustin for questioning. The grapevine here."

"I figured." I drew in my breath. "The chatter on Facebook. The college page. Comments. Someone brought up the YouTube video, this time identifying Dustin by name. A frenzy. The second altercation caught on Instagram—all over the place."

"Yeah, hundreds of hits, Rick. The cops are monitoring that. Wild fire—Dustin and Ben's names."

"Twitter madness," I added. "Kids at the college revving up, crazy. Everyone has a story. I caught one tweet." I checked my phone. "'Snowstorm hit—you got more than a Dustin.' #DustinTrang. #ProfWinslowshot."

"This is only the beginning."

My landline was ringing. "Gotta go," I told him. "Liz is calling."

"I can't talk anyway. I'm on the way to another fender bender on I-84. Folks drive like it's the middle of August." The line went dead.

Liz was calling from Sophia Grecko's apartment, her voice a faint whisper. "I'm staying with Sophia. I finally got her to lie down. I don't know what happened. The news says you were there."

"Yes," I told her. "Ben Winslow. Poor Sophia."

"We were out to dinner last night, close by because of the snow, but when we got back around nine or so, there were squad cars everywhere. My heart stopped."

"Were they in Ben's apartment?"

"Yes, all the lights on. Frightening. At first I thought he was in there, but a detective—Harry Manus, known him for years—spotted me and filled me in."

"How did Sophia take it?"

"What do you think? Hysterical, frantic. I had to hold her up."

"Did they interview her?"

"A little, but she was not making sense. We were up in her apartment. Then she kept walking in circles, unable to settle. It broke my heart."

"Christ," I whispered. "What did she tell the cops?"

"Well, not much. They left us alone. I told them I'd sleep over. They'll be back here soon."

"Any scuttlebutt?"

She made a clicking sound from deep in her throat. "Rick."

"Tell me, Liz. I can always tell…"

"You are reading an ex-wife's simple mind?"

"Tell me."

"Sophia said little, but what she did tell Detective Manus was…Dustin Trang's crazy pursuit of Ben. The fights, especially his mysterious visit here Saturday night."

"Christ, she won't be the last one to give his name to the cops."

"Exactly. Phone lines buzzing at the station—his name surfaced. The state cops are involved. Where's Hank?"

"Staring down fender-benders on the highway."

"I called to tell you they're on the way to pick up the boy."

"Yeah, Hank just told me."

"Some nut tweeted #ArrestDustinNow. Channel 3 picked up some YouTube video—running with it. Even one of his professors tattled on him."

"This isn't good," I said into the phone.

"No, it isn't." A pause. "Do you think he shot Ben?"

An image rose of that odd student tucked away in the corner of the College Union. Those absurd rolled-up jeans. Those goggle glasses. The narrow pinched face of a lost boy.

"I hope not."

"That's not really answering my question."

"I don't know much about his life, Liz."

She waited a heartbeat, then I heard her sigh. "But you will, Rick. I know you. All parts of your being come into play here. Personal. Professional. Nosiness. Peskiness. Orneriness." A slight laugh. "But most of all a sense of justice."

"I don't want that boy to be the killer."

"We can't always get what we want, Rick."

"I said that to you a hundred years ago in Manhattan. Remember?"

A low ripple of laughter. "How can I forget? You used to sing that Rolling Stones song over and over as we sat in the West End Café."

I rolled my head to the side. "'You can't always get what you want...'"

She finished for me. "But you can 'get what you need.'"

"Even that was a lie, Liz."

"It wasn't a lie, Rick. It's just that the song forgot to tell us that what you need is not guaranteed to last forever."

"Call me if you hear anything."

"I always do."

• • ● • •

At noon the skies suddenly cleared as the last wisps of snow drifted to the ground. The world went suddenly quiet, that stillness after a raging storm, immediately broken by the grinding snowplows crashing through the streets.

When I answered the phone, Jimmy was already in the middle of a sentence. I could also hear him chomping on something, the crinkle of cellophane. A bag of potato chips?

"What?"

"I'm trying to do two things at once."

I laughed. "Eat and talk?"

"Don't be a wise guy. Potato chips ain't food. I mean, watch TV and talk to you." He swallowed and cleared his throat, a loud cigarette smoker's rasp. "You're on TV, Rick. At least they say the blur running through parked cars like a dizzy girl is you. Witness to a murder."

"Not quite a witness. Seconds after the fact."

"Ain't that the way it always is." The crunch of a potato chip, another cough. "Your usual bad timing."

"If I'd been any earlier, I wouldn't be a witness—I'd be the corpse."

He held the phone away from his mouth. "Anyway, what the hell is going on? Liz just called me."

"Tattletale."

"She's your wife. If someone can't blab about your bad behavior, who can?"

"Ex-wife, Jimmy. Ex."

"Yeah, keep telling yourself that. The two of you are meant to be together like…well…pork and beans."

"More food imagery, Jimmy."

"She's worried about you."

"She's always worried about me. When I was a cop, she worried. Then we got divorced. She still worries."

"That's what people in love do. Don't you know nothing?"

"You're a rank sentimentalist, Jimmy."

"Yeah, I'm a lot of things, but it sounds to me like you're in the thick of things. Liz tells me about this misfit, this Dustin kid. Christ, can't the boat people stay outta trouble?"

"We like to be noticed."

"Yeah, especially on a post office wall." I heard him rip open another bag of something. "Is this kid a murderer?"

"I don't know."

"Well, that's a good beginning. Jumping off a cliff without a parachute."

"That makes no sense."

"I'm hanging up now. They're mentioning you on TV again. I may have to ask for your goddamn autograph—if you ever choose to come into the office."

The police released the surveillance tapes, though I wasn't certain why. A number of cameras, various rooftop angles, one of which showed Ben Winslow sauntering slowly off the landing and headed to his car. Another showed me—"Professor Rick Van Lam, PI with Gaddy Associates in Hartford"—contemplating the snowstorm and then—you could hear the crack of gunfire, the *pop*, then another *pop*—darting toward it. Another camera angle showed the back of the lot, a dark car screeching out onto the street. Worthless tapes, the newscaster commented, quoting undisclosed police sources, because the dense snowfall made visibility nearly impossible. What one snippet of tape did show, however, was jerky movement by Ben's car, a grainy figure, shadowy, and two rapid-fire flashes of light from a gun. But far away. Out of the camera's limited range.

Given the prominence of the murdered man in the Hartford metropolitan area—and the horrific nature of the crime—local TV stations suspended broadcasts of *Dr. Phil* and *Judge Judy* and *Dr. Oz*, treating the viewership with endless loops of the same meaningless footage. Other than the sensational murder, a slow news day—snow and more snow. Schools shuttered. Even the criminals stayed at home—except, of course, for that one volcanic explosion last night. I got tired of seeing my wispy self, and hearing the mispronunciation of my name. Americans preferred "lamb," not "lam" that sort of rhymed with "bomb." So be it.

Then the cellphone YouTube footage—seconds long—of Dustin exploding at Ben in the hallway.

That was riveting.

Suddenly the broadcast went live as cameras zeroed in on a caravan of squad cars, local and state police, moving up Terryville Avenue and turning into Jefferson Drive. A rambling, decades-old housing project, two-story frame complexes that, even with the softening patina of new-fallen snow, came off as tired, desolate. Channels 3, 4, and 8 flooded the yard with cameras. Real-time reportage: A door opens. An old woman stands with her arms folded over her chest and gestures to a cop. We watch this scenario from a distance, the reporter's narrative accompanied by a cameraman whose angle is impeded by a cop's cautioning hand. The woman points away from the house, then, dramatically, slams the door. The cops look at each other, stupefied.

The caravan circles out of the projects. Channel 3 breaks for a commercial about Toyota End-of-the-Year Marathon sales. When the coverage continues, the newscaster, breathless and jittery, tells us that the police have pulled in front of Sullivan's Diner down on Route 6. For a half-hour nothing changes as the camera focuses on the eatery. A Dumpster next to two Ford pickups. One cop is visible standing outside his squad car. A cigarette between his lips. Nothing else.

We wait. I wait. I don't move.

Then a flurry of craziness as the front door opens and a cadre of cops, state and local, escort someone out. I step near the TV, hoping to get a better look, though I know my behavior is foolish.

Dustin Trang, taken in for questioning. "Routine," the newscaster intones. A person of interest.

Interesting. A person.

Shooting from the sidewalk, a photographer zooms in crazily, off-angle, at first catching a Help Wanted sign in the window, then focusing on Dustin's face—that tiny face magnified by those enormous glasses, a face now bewildered, his chin trembling. It's a horrible sight, that boy jostled between the hustling cops.

His mouth is moving, though we can't hear what he is saying. But it's clear to me, the old-time cop who spent years hauling off suspects who yelled the familiar refrain: *I don't understand. I didn't do anything.* Or, more authentic, *I ain't done nothing.*

Dustin, to his credit, speaks the president's English—that is, some of our presidents.

Then he stops, dips his head into his chest, as he is bounced into the back of a squad car.

The newscaster tells us in a thick, funereal voice: "This young student made death threats against Professor Winslow."

That was news to me. But possible, of course—what did I know about this boy?

Nestled on my sofa, my eyes riveted to the TV screen, my laptop opened to the college Facebook page, the comments piling up, I dropped into a stupor. So little sleep last night, nightmares plaguing my early morning nap. Though the TV droned on and the laptop slipped onto the floor, I found myself, drifting, nodding, assailed by a fierce headache. I was vaguely aware that TV stations had abandoned the sensational murder, and sensed rather than watched the canned laughter of *Big Bang Theory* reruns. The Barenaked Ladies' theme music jolted me back and forth through history—and dropped me unceremoniously into the present. And then a flood of nightmare visions: a field in

Vietnam, kilometers from Saigon, a hot scorched field, voices jeering, voices mocking, a boy crucified on a bamboo cross, a helmet so heavy every voice I hear echoes, the hot sun, taunts hurled my way—*mau di di*, the bastard boy—the sweat, the sunburn, the bugs crawling up my legs, the itching, crying... *mau di di*. Keep moving. Hurry up it's late. Now now now.

Now.

I woke with a start, stunned to feel a draft and to see ice and snow collected on the outside of my windows. I expected tropical heat. The sun a garish red fireball in the sky. Sunburnt flesh, aching.

The American boy. Lonely. Dust boy.

The bittersweet taste of chocolate on my lips.

I closed my eyes but fought with images of Dustin. Anh Ky. His hand touches the cold windowpane. Snowfall covers the whole world.

Shivering, I found myself ignoring the phone, text buzzes, a Facebook alert doubtless from Hank, even the insistent but gentle rapping on my door. Maybe Gracie, concerned. Echoes: *Rick Rick Rick*.

But the ten o'clock evening news stunned me—an on-the-spot interview with the Reverend Daniel Simms of the Gospel of Wealth Ministry. Caught as he hustled to a waiting Cadillac town car, a chauffeur with a ridiculous ribboned cap bowing him in, a reporter thrust a microphone into his face.

The Reverend Simms actually grasped the microphone, his instinctive gesture, surprising the reporter. A short man, round as a bowling ball, a parchment face with Crayola crimson cheeks, a fur hat, a billowing Chesterfield overcoat, open to show his dark black suit and the gilded gold-speckled vest, he took a deep breath.

What did he think of the murder of Professor Winslow, a man who'd criticized and mocked Simms' mega church? About an upsurge in publicity the past few days with Winslow's new book that perpetuated his stand against Simms' evangelical religion. "What say you?" the reporter asked.

Simms had issued a public statement condemning left-wing opportunist professors who were atheistic and communist. The added *coup de grace*: he'd called Winslow an unrepentant adulterer.

"Yes, I said those things. I stand by them." He pulled the microphone closer to his lips. "We see here the workings of a just but vengeful God."

"What, Reverend?"

A sliver of a smile. "This is the work of God who smites the godless, the satanic, the workshop of Satan that we call higher education."

The reporter broke in: "They picked up a young student for questioning, Reverend. A Vietnamese lad named Anh Ky…"

Simms held up his hand, a strange smile crossing his lips. "If he is the murderer, then he is the hand of Almighty God. Misguided perhaps, confused by the godless texts he's forced to read, but an angel of the Lord." He spoke into the camera. "I met this young man, you know. Dustin, he calls himself. He sat in my church, listened to me preach. He is one of my children of God…"

The reporter broke off the interview, addressing the viewer— "That's a revelation, wouldn't you say? Perhaps we have just learned a motive for the killing. Thank you, Reverend."

The station broke for a commercial.

I sat on the edge of the sofa and realized my mouth had gone slack.

Dustin, a child of a sadistic God who totes a gun.

I didn't buy it.

Chapter Seven

On Saturday at five, the streets dark, we met at Zeke's. It was Jimmy's idea, true, a powwow, but something I was anxious to do. After a sequestered Friday, I spent an aimless Saturday morning helping Gracie shovel out. At twilight Gracie and I walked on the sanded sidewalk the few blocks to Zeke's, my arm tucked under her elbow.

"It's this Dustin boy, right?" Gracie had whispered. "And your poor friend. It bothers you."

"What?"

"You don't answer my simple questions, Rick." She shook her head. "I had a husband who did the same thing. Stared right through me when I talked to him. Aggravating as all hell, let me tell you."

"I didn't know I was doing that."

"Neither did he. Until I hammered home the idea." She leaned her head into my shoulder. "All men are built the same." Her fingertip pushed into my side. "Imperfect."

I tightened my grip on her elbow. "I got Ben on my mind. I got Dustin on my mind. A friend murdered—a boy I scarcely know maybe the murderer."

We joined Jimmy at a back table, and for a while we said little. "Marcie and Vinnie are stopping by later," I told them. "The rest of my army." We talked about the snowstorm—"It's New England," Gracie groaned, "why do we always talk about the weather?"—and the sloppy cleanup. We were waiting for Liz, who was late. Liz had told me earlier that Sophia, distraught and rambling, had been taken to John Dempsey Hospital. She had no family, at least in Connecticut, so Liz stayed at her side. Ben Winslow had been her romantic discovery after a messy divorce and an impulsive move from Kansas to Farmington—and she had tucked all her dreams into his life. Sophia lay in a hospital bed and wept.

Gracie looked into my eyes. "Do you believe this—this Dustin boy is innocent? I mean, could he kill your friend?"

I didn't answer, though I sensed Jimmy's disapproving glare. Gracie looked up. "Thank God. Liz is here."

Liz was shaking her head as she slipped into a seat opposite me. We waited as she signaled the waiter for a coffee, then Gracie reached over and patted the back of her wrist. "Tell us, Liz," she said quietly, "are you all right?"

Liz was surprised. "Me? Yes, Gracie. As well as I can be having left the bedside of a shattered woman."

Jimmy, fidgeting with a Bic lighter because he wanted a cigarette, muttered, "Why is it when someone we know—not somebody *I* know this time, but the rest of you—is murdered, Rick here is always ready to find the accused killer innocent?"

"What, Jimmy? Nonsense."

He drummed his fingers on the table. "You don't remember when that little boy they called the Saigon Kid was accused of killing my old army friend Ralph?"

"He *was* innocent."

"But you didn't know that until you proved it."

I laughed out loud. "That's why we're investigators, Jimmy."

Jimmy sat back as he scratched his head, and the enormous sweatshirt rolled up his belly. "No, *you* investigate murder—and mayhem. I investigate simple insurance fraud in the Insurance Capital of the world. Cigna, Aetna. Travelers. You name it. Paper trails—not blood spatter. Embezzlement—not bloodletting."

Gracie was frowning at both of us. "Why are we sitting here then?"

Jimmy smirked. "I came for the corned beef sandwich. The special of the day."

"There's nothing special about it, Jimmy."

He shot her a withering look, which she ignored. "The truth of the matter is that this guy Ben Winslow got himself shot to death, and yeah, he was a friend of Rick's"—he stared into my face, unblinking—"and Liz here, I guess, was his friend, and so I know exactly how the story is gonna play out." He snapped his fingers at the waiter who scurried over. "Now add the missing ingredient—this Dustin Trang kid who's all over TV. Is he innocent, Rick?"

"I have no idea."

Liz was waiting to say something. "I don't like the way the TV reporters condemned the boy. All that footage of him being taken in for questioning. Those horrible close-up shots of his face. He looked so—vulnerable. Frightened."

Gracie added, "Baby-faced folks kill people, Liz."

"Yes, they do. But local TV is so—intrusive. One reporter on Channel 3 actually called him an 'angry student.' Hardly objective. Another talked of the rash of school-related shootings across America."

A loud voice greeted us from the doorway as Hank joined us, taking off his coat and pulling up a chair. Out of uniform, off duty, he was dressed in a camouflage flannel shirt hanging loose over his khakis, a smallish diamond stud in his right ear, colorful plastic bands on one wrist.

"Hey, folks." He grinned at Jimmy. "Miss me?"

Jimmy reached over and fingered the bands. "What cause are you representing today? Save the whales? Save the rain forest? Save your black bears?"

Hank's face lit up. "Save your breath."

"I think he looks very handsome," Liz said, sending a teasing look Jimmy's way.

"You know," Jimmy went on, "in the old days real men only got an earring when they crossed the equator."

Gracie drew her tongue into her cheek. "Well, you can head off now, Jimmy. There's still time to stow away on a freighter."

Jimmy pulled at an ear lobe. "I don't need decoration on my body." He squinted at Hank, who was beaming at him. "We Nam veterans wear our Purple Hearts…"

"Not quite on your sleeves." From Gracie.

"Anyway…" I pleaded.

"Anyway," Hank began, settling in, "I have something to say about Dustin Trang. I'm a little woozy from doing a double shift because of Storm Fred, but running over every news feed on my tablet made me realize that Dustin Trang is suspect numero uno. Tweets galore. Even a Snapchat alert from a kid in my seminar." A dramatic pause. "Folks, Dustin Trang is innocent."

I sat up. "Tell us."

"Yeah," Jimmy said. "I gotta hear this."

Hank's gaze took us all in. "Simple. The party that wasn't. The Christmas get-together of the Asian-American Alliance that I was invited to, a special guest." A half-bow.

"Which," I noted, "was cancelled."

"Yeah," Hank agreed. "Exactly. So said the slightly ungrammatical cancellation email sent out to all from Brandon Vinh." He made a half-bow. "Received, it seems, by everyone but little Anh Ky Trang."

"Meaning," I pushed him, "what?"

"It means, simply, that at exactly 7:15 p.m. I was on the phone with Dustin Trang."

"What? How?"

Hank retrieved his iPhone from his pants pocket, switched it on, brought up his Call history, and there it was: "7:15 Dustin Trang."

Hank was smiling. "He wanted to know where everyone was. He was sitting in the lounge at The Silo waiting for the party to begin. He said he'd been there for some time. He drove over in the snow from the college."

"But it was cancelled."

"True, but no one—like Brandon—reached him. Probably because he didn't have Dustin's email address. Or phone."

"And he had your phone number?" Jimmy asked.

He nodded. "I gave it to him. 'Call me if you ever need anything.'" I started to say something but Hank held up his hand. "Hey, I was concerned about him. When I told him there was no party, he said, 'You told me I had to come.'"

Liz winked at Hank. "The authority of the state police. Especially in uniform."

Hank preened, a wide grin on his face. "I have super powers. He was afraid not to come."

"But how do we know what time he arrived?"

Hank was ready with an answer. "I stopped at The Silo, minutes ago, talked to the manager on duty that night. The place was empty. They were getting ready to close for the night because of the storm. Dustin kept pacing the lounge. He remembered him." He made a funny face. "And not because he had blood on his coat. Or traces on his face."

"But," Gracie said, "he still could have shot this Ben fellow and rushed over."

I was thinking out loud. "Dismissed classes. My phone call to 9-1-1 was registered at 6:47. Ben was shot a minute or so before."

"Dustin could get to The Silo in a few minutes. It's down the street." Liz watched me closely.

"But in the snow? Speeding? With a smoking gun?" I counted the questions with my fingers.

Hank was shaking his head emphatically. "You know why? In our short conversation he was relaxed, even a little funny. He kept repeating that I told him to be there. I joked, 'Do you listen to everything someone tells you to do?' He said 'Yes' with an exclamation point. When I laughed, he sort of laughed back." Hank sat back, arms folded. "Listen, gang, this was not the conversation of someone who just shot a teacher twice at point blank range."

"Unless he's a sociological monster." Jimmy was nodding.

"Do you believe that?" I asked.

"I don't know the kid."

I concluded, "I agree with Hank. Dustin was not the killer."

"Which means," Hank finished, holding my eye, "you and I have a job to do."

"Hank, there is a police force in town," Jimmy said. "And the state police. Last I heard you were a state cop, notorious for pulling over speeders going one mile over the limit on I-84."

"I talked to my superiors," Hank told us. "Yeah, I'm a little too close to all this. I know the suspected perp." He emphasized the words by providing air quotation marks with his fingers. "The Vietnamese angle, I guess. But he said—what I do in my own time is my business."

Jimmy rolled his eyes. "How did I know we'd end up with this conclusion?"

"You're a mind reader," Gracie joked.

"So now, are we gonna eat or do I have to waste away in this dump while all of you yammer on and on?" He snapped his fingers at a waitress leaning against a counter.

So we ordered, Jimmy relishing his corned beef, Hank and I with our cheeseburgers, Liz with her chicken Caesar salad, and Gracie the grilled cheese-and-tomato sandwich she always ordered. As expected, Jimmy remarked that grilled cheese was something you didn't order in a restaurant—every fool could make one at home. Gracie ignored him, as she always did. They went back and forth with their familiar banter, which Hank once labeled "early-bird-special foreplay," but we all knew that the senior-citizen flirtation was played with intricate unspoken rules only Gracie and Jimmy understood—and savored.

Vinnie and Marcie walked in as we lingered over coffee, none of us ready to leave. They stood in the doorway and peered into the dim room, finally spotting us. I waved them over.

"We're headed to the hospital to see Sophia." From Marcie.

Vinnie put his arm around her shoulder. "We still can't believe what happened."

Liz commiserated, "Who can? Really."

"Do you two know this Dustin from the college?" Jimmy asked.

Both shook their heads. "I've seen him around," Vinnie said. "He sort of stands out. A loner, no?"

I nodded.

Marcie added, "Everybody seems to know him now. David Laramie has a lot to say about him."

That surprised me. "What are you talking about? I know he hates—hated—Ben."

"The professor everyone loves to hate. Sooner or later everyone on the faculty butts heads with him."

Marcie spoke over Vinnie's words. "It turns out he's Dustin's advisor. Computer Science. But he's a real showboater when it comes to the press."

"Like what?" I asked.

"He told one reporter that Dustin made a death threat against Ben."

"So that's where that came from." I slammed my fist on the table. "Goddamn it."

Marcie went on. "But he's walked back on that inflammatory statement."

"What do you mean?"

"We caught him on the local news before we got here. Now he's saying Dustin *implied* a death threat. Sort of. As in—he really didn't like Professor Winslow. Quote: 'He did tell me in my office that Winslow could get in trouble the way he treats students.' Unquote. Whatever that means."

"He spoke too quickly," I said. "Now he's sorry." But I was curious. "This interview…"

Marcie was smiling as she pulled a tablet from a carryall she'd placed on the floor, switching it on. "I recorded it for your viewing pleasure." Her eyes danced. "I figured you'd want—ocular proof, Othello. It's short, and classic Laramie testosterone speaking, but what follows is more interesting."

She pressed ON as we all leaned in. The reporter commented that she was following up on her interview with Laramie earlier that morning. She'd corralled him as he stepped from his car in the college parking lot, Laramie blinking his eyes rapidly as though unused to lights and attention. As Dustin's advisor, he noted that the young man was "brilliant," a "whiz," "a pleasure to have in class," but one "haunted by Professor Winslow's cruel harassment." Then, as Marcie noted, he stepped back from his earlier comments on death threats, though the reporter seemed unhappy he was now hedging. He told her he'd seen Dustin around six o'clock, right after he'd dismissed class because of the snow, spotting Dustin in the hallway as he chatted with his one friend on campus, "a Bosnian lad named Darijo Delic."

"Christ," I mumbled. "The man has no boundaries."

"What were they talking about?" the reporter asked.

Laramie looked away from the camera. "The snowstorm."

"How did they seem?"

Again Laramie avoided looking at her. "Like they were going home."

I sat back. "Well, hardly troubling."

Marcie held up her finger. "Wait for it."

A break in the sequence, the reporter back in the studio now, breathlessly noting, "Breaking news. Just one hour ago." She'd driven into the south end of Hartford, into Barry Square, an area called Little Bosnia, where she located Darijo Delic working as a waiter at his father's restaurant, Sarajevo Café. She and her photographer surprised the young man as he stood outside, taking a cigarette break, Darijo leaning on a snow shovel.

A camera thrust into his face. "What about your friend, Dustin Trang?"

Surprised, the cigarette dropped to the pavement as he turned away, then back. "I don't know. He's not…my friend. Sometimes we study together, that's all." He stepped back.

"You were with him just before Professor Winslow was shot to death. Did he tell you anything?"

Silence, confusion. His fingers gripped the handle of the snow shovel.

The reporter hammered home the question. "What do you know about the murder? What did Dustin confide in you? You must have talked?"

"Nothing." A thick Slavic accent, trembling. A scared look on his face. "I…"

At that moment a beefy man stepped quickly into view, pulled at Darijo's arm, and dragged him out of camera range. "*Odlazi,*" he shouted to the reporter. Then in a gravelly voice, "Leave now. Yes."

A quick glimpse of Darijo hustled back into the restaurant. The young man glanced back over his shoulder as the camera zeroed in on his frightened face.

The reporter, unfazed, spoke into the camera, "Darijo Delic's father, justifiably concerned that his son is involved in a murder investigation."

"Christ," I said again. "Who hires these idiots?"

"Give the people what they want," Jimmy grumbled.

Marcie switched off the tablet. "This is not good."

Hank rolled his eyes, unhappy. "What we're left with, folks, is the impression that this…this Darijo might know something about the murder. Hanging with Dustin minutes before."

I breathed out. "And what's worse is the possibility that the real killer, maybe watching that news snippet, might believe that Darijo does, indeed, know something."

"Which means," Liz concluded, "poor Darijo has to watch his back."

Chapter Eight

Liz watched me carefully over the rim of her coffee cup, not saying a word. When she finally placed the cup back in the saucer, a smile covered her face.

"What?" I asked her. "Somehow this has to do with me, right?"

She was grinning. "It always does."

We were sitting at noontime on Sunday in Rafi's Eatery a block away from her apartment in the south end of town. Her idea: "Meet me for a quick lunch after my workout." I'd been sitting in a booth, nursing a second cup of coffee when she rushed in, a loose-fitting lavender sweat suit under her unbuttoned winter coat, her long black hair tied into a careful ponytail. Sneakers with brilliant red stripes. "I didn't have time to go home. Shower. Forgive me." She'd dropped into a chair and caught her breath. "Although you've seen me look a lot worse."

I'd waited as she ordered coffee, rubbing her palms together. "So cold out." Finally, her hands circling the warm cup, she took a sip and watched me with wide, lively eyes.

"What do you mean it has to do with me?"

A sly smile, barely there. "The fact that you were eager to meet me here." She reached for her phone and scrolled through it. All business. "You want—information. According to police reports, the 9-1-1 call came in at exactly 6:47. Just as you said. From someone who was mightily out of breath."

"Not fair. I was running through snow—and chaos."

"Too much coffee." But she got serious. "And you found disaster."

"God, yes. I called the moment I realized Ben was dead. Maybe a half a minute later."

"Which is why I'm sitting here now—to provide you with the timeline as worked out by the police. This morning I spoke to Detective Manus who's shepherding the case with the state cops. The Farmington Police Department is all a-buzz. People don't get murdered in this fancy town. Their fat wallets and stock portfolios stop the bullets."

"And Dustin?"

"I'll get there." She signaled the waitress for a refill. "Despite the snowstorm and miserable driving conditions, the cops arrived within minutes."

"I know, Liz. I'm the one who waved them over." I tilted my head and smiled at her. "I *was* there, you know."

Another glance at her phone as she scrolled text. "Forensics is doing due diligence, of course. As of now we suspect that the gun most likely was a Glock 26, a convenient pistol to pack a wallop."

"Recovered slugs?"

"Two."

"What else did they find?"

She waited as the waitress poured coffee, then slowly took a sip. "Preliminary search of Ben's apartment came up with nothing. No threatening letters, no death threats nailed to the kitchen cupboards. No threatening notes pieced together from letters clipped from *Guns and Ammo*. Nothing in his office. Only one name surfacing. Dustin Trang. That boy a one-man plague. But only this last week. A new, uncommon wrinkle in his life." She sucked in her breath. "And of course Professor Laramie's now-disavowed comment didn't help."

I slammed my fist into my palm. "That's the mystery, Liz. A quiet student, hidden in shadows, friendless, it seemed, suddenly became Ben's nemesis."

"But a pleasant shadow, according to unnamed sources. Ben encouraged his students—and that recently included Dustin—to hang out, joke, follow him to the ends of the Earth. He liked that student attention."

"But something happened."

She fiddled with her napkin, bunching it up. "I'll say. Everything went south. Dustin's over-the-top anger. The YouTube video going viral. Ben's distractedness."

I shook my head. "Christ, it doesn't sound like Dustin."

Her voice was sharp. "C'mon, Rick. You don't *know* Dustin. Don't sentimentalize him."

I forced a smile. "I do that?"

Her return smile was warm. "All the time. Or, at least, when we're talking about the Vietnamese. Your guilt or shame or—or whatever you carried from that orphanage—is baggage you never checked at the station."

I tried to change the subject. "Okay, okay. So the police want to nail this on Dustin?"

She reached over and grasped the back of my wrist. "I'm not condemning you, Rick."

"I know."

For a moment we were quiet, watching each other, both of us with unaffected smiles. Finally, with a wistful twist of her head, she said, "Public Enemy Number One. Dustin Trang."

"A tight timeline, no?"

She tapped the screen on the phone, scrolled down. "According to the manager at The Silo, Dustin walked into the restaurant the moment the regulator clock at the reception desk chimed seven. He remembers that. Also, a bus boy, headed to the kitchen, recalls Dustin rushing in." She hesitated. "Unfortunately he told the cops Dustin seemed—frantic, disoriented."

"A snowstorm, a party he's not looking forward to, a new place."

"Excuses, Rick. But whatever. The Silo is five or six good minutes drive from the college parking lot. Of course, it's also snowing. Treacherous."

"All right. So Dustin had time to shoot Ben—maybe at 6:45 or 6:46, seconds before I ran to Ben, then jump in his running car and make it to the restaurant down the street."

"Yes, the cops like that timeline." She appeared to be in thought for a minute or so. Then another glance at her phone. "No gun at Dustin's home. Certainly not in his beat-up barely running Toyota."

"Dumped in a snow bank?"

"Possibly. Let's hope for a spring thaw in December."

"But his clothes...other...forensics?"

She held up her hand. "When Dustin was taken in for questioning the next day—a live melodrama on local TV—even live streaming on Facebook—that rivaled O. J. Simpson's meandering Bronco chase across the highways of that free-love state—they checked for gunshot residue on his hands. A day late, of course, he's working in a diner, handling God-knows-what. Nothing. Wearing gloves—it's winter. Who knows?"

"Ben was shot through on open window at close range."

"Which suggests that he might have recognized the assailant. I stress—*might*. But, more importantly, the likelihood of blood splatter patterns. A lot of blood when you shoot someone from a few feet away."

"And nothing?"

She shook her head. "They took the clothes from his closet, but he was also wearing his winter jacket when they grandly escorted him from the restaurant. A coat still damp from the snowstorm. No blood spatter. Nothing."

I sat back. "All good news."

She shrugged. "More or less. The problem is his recent spitfire battle with Ben. It's hard to put that in any context. And the death threats—most likely that didn't happen."

I grumbled. "David Laramie. Not to be trusted. He's walked back those comments."

"Yeah, but in another interview with Manus, Laramie said he detected rage in Dustin. Someone bumped him in one of his classes, and Dustin flew up, made a fist, beet-red face." She held my eye. "Laramie said he was afraid of the boy."

"True, I've seen that. An angry boy. Not good. You know what Buddha says, don't you?"

She rolled her eyes. "Here it comes, Confucian boy. What?"

"Anger is like holding a burning coal that you plan to throw at an enemy. But you're the one being burned."

She saluted me. "There is a lot of that going around these days. All directed at Dustin."

"And there's Reverend Simms of the Money Bags Church, or whatever it's called. He's angry at everyone but God. That damning statement on TV."

Liz was nodding her head up and down. "Yeah, we talked about that. Good for Dustin if he killed that atheist scumbag. Dustin as Gabriel with the sword of God. Vengeance is mine sayeth the bored."

"Is that in the Bible, Liz?" I asked, a smile on my face.

"Everything's in the Bible."

My cellphone buzzed. "Hank." I switched it on. "I'm sitting with Liz at Rafi's."

"Some of us are working," he answered. "Put me on speaker-phone."

Suddenly Hank's voice filled the booth. "Liz, is Rick wearing that horrible ski sweater he sometimes wears—the one with the enormous snowflakes?"

Liz leaned into the phone. "He knows better when he's with me."

"Do you know how often I have to apologize for his appearance?"

"What are you, Hank?" I interrupted. "State cop or fashion police?"

"I'm on my way to a shift, but the weirdest thing happened this morning. I'm coming out of the shower, maybe six-thirty or so, like the crack of dawn, and my phone is ringing. I hear this small, distant voice, like someone who's been awake all night long and…"

"Dustin," I broke in.

"You got it. It took me by surprise."

Liz leaned into the table. "What did he want?"

Hank's voice sounded weary. "A sad conversation that lasted less than a minute. 'You said to call you if I needed anything.' That's what he said. 'Okay, tell me,' I told him. A long silence, and then in a hesitant voice he goes, 'I don't know what to do. The police came again last night. I got fired from my job. I didn't shoot Professor Winslow. I never even had a gun in my hands. I never even *saw* one close up.' I mean, he went on and on, a little crazy, until I asked him, "'Who's home?' 'My mother. Only her,' he said. 'What does she say?' Then it got real strange. He whispered, 'She doesn't care what happens. She wants it to go away.'"

"His mother?" Liz asked.

"Then he said, 'She doesn't even know I'm in the house.'"

"Good God." From Liz.

"What does he want from you, Hank?"

For a moment he didn't answer, then quietly, "He didn't do it, Rick. I told you that. I don't know for a fact, but I know it. That call from The Silo."

"But the police..." I began.

"I'm the police." His voice rose, agitated. "You're the police. Sort of." I could hear him swallow. "Rick, nobody's his advocate. It has to be—us. You, mainly. You knew Ben, the others. The school. Even Dustin—a little. You gotta take this on." A pause. "I gotta run." Another pause. "Promise me, Rick."

I waited. Liz watched my face, an enigmatic smile on her lips. "I'll ask around."

Hank broke off the connection.

Liz said, "I knew we'd come to this."

"I'll ask around."

"Hank's instincts are always on target. Yours—sometimes. Mine—always. Do this."

"I said I would." I sat back, took a sip of my cold coffee. I spoke to myself. "Where to begin."

"I know where," Liz said. "One last thing I didn't get to. Manus interviewed Ben's ex-wife and their kids. The daughter gave the cops an interesting interview."

"Ben always called Melody...scattered."

"Yeah, she was focused enough to talk about the last meeting with her dad. She said he was pacing the floor, nervous, and he told her he was facing the most difficult decision of his life."

"Did he say what it was?"

Liz's voice was dark. "Only that it involved one of his students who confided something horrible to him and he didn't know what to do with the information."

"Good Christ," I said. "Dustin."

"He didn't tell her a name."

"Dustin," I echoed myself. "What secret could that boy have?"

Liz sat back and ran a fingertip across the rim of the cup. "Here's your starting line. Charlotte Winslow, bitter ex-wife, and the son and daughter that Ben always mentioned with a sad shaking of his head."

Chapter Nine

Charlotte Winslow wasn't happy to hear my voice. When I repeated my name, she broke in, "I know who you are, Mr. Lam. A friend of Ben's from the school."

Yes, I told her, and I offered my condolences to a woman who'd not been married to Ben for over fifteen years.

"What do you want?"

"This is a little awkward, Mrs. Winslow."

A raspy laugh. "Call me Charlotte. I hate that last name."

"And yet you kept it after the divorce."

"Because of the children." A deep intake of breath. "What do you want?"

"One of Ben's students, Dustin Trang, is a suspect in his murder," I began. "As you probably know. Everybody knows. The whole world who watches TV—or refreshes their tweets. I'm a PI, and…and I'm concerned that there might be a rush to judgment."

An artificial laugh. "And you're trying to clear his name?"

"I'm trying to find out what happened. He maintains his innocence, so I want to follow up on it. No one wants an innocent young man charged."

"I don't really care. I'm assuming he's guilty."

I caught my breath. "And why is that?"

"What do you want, Mr. Lam?"

"Your daughter Melody had a last talk with Ben. He told her he was dealing with the worst decision he ever had to make." I stopped because I could hear her gasp. "What?"

She barked out her words. "The worst decision he ever made happened fifteen or so years ago. An annoying social worker intern from UConn who sliced our marriage into pieces."

I waited.

Into the silence she said, "I suppose you gotta do this."

"Yes." Then, quickly, "Is it possible for me to talk with Melody?"

That surprised her. Suddenly she muffled the phone with a hand, and I could hear unintelligible, whispered voices. Then she came back on the line. "She says it's her decision. Not mine." A gruff laugh. "When have I ever been allowed to make any decision?" Again the muffled voices. "Come here at four, Mr. Lam. But I'm not guaranteeing a pleasant visit."

"Thank you," I told her. "You live over Avon Mountain, right? The address…"

But I was talking into the drone of a dial tone.

Her Dutch Colonial on a side street off Route 44 was the faded beauty on a quiet street of modest homes with well-shoveled sidewalks and splendid Christmas lights cascading off roofs. Reindeer on lawns glistened under blankets of snow. Plastic blow-up Santas dotted the landscape like a redundant circus parade. Crisp Cape Cods and Colonials sparkled and shimmered with the season. Jingle bell music tinkled from a corner house where guests flowed onto the driveway. Except for the Winslow homestead. Peeling paint, a lopsided black shutter, untrimmed evergreen bushes blocking the front windows. The only house without decoration and illumination. At twilight it was dark except for the hint of light peeking out the front plate-glass window. The outside light was not switched on, which caused me to calculate the house number by the process of elimination. The one to the left—the one with the rocking Santa with the pervert's grin—was number 110. The one on the right—the Cape Cod with the illuminated sleigh on the roof, Frosty the Snowman in Santa's seat—was 114. So Charlotte Winslow lived at 112.

I was always good at math.

Charlotte answered the doorbell, stepping back, her eyes narrowed. "I'm sorry. I forgot the light. I have no manners."

"It's all right."

She turned to walk into the living room. Although she hadn't invited me, I followed.

She swung her head back to look into my face. "I don't know why I'm doing this. My son Martin tells me I'm crazy." She pointed to a sofa. "All my life I've been crazy."

A remark I had no response to, of course, but thought that maybe she was. She plopped down into a chair, her body hunched over, and suddenly faced me.

"Mrs. Winslow."

"Charlotte, for God's sake." A slight laugh. "And I'm not really crazy, Mr. Lam."

"Rick."

She rocked in her seat. "Ah, old friends already. How easy it is to make friends."

Again, stupefied, I watched her, uncertain what to say.

"You know why I'm here."

She waved a hand in my face. "Let's get his over, okay? The last few days have been—unpleasant. I can't believe someone shot—I mean, *shot*—Ben. He was a lot of things, but a man who would get himself shot was not one of them."

"Agreed. His murder was a shock."

She rushed her words. "More than a shock. A—a horror show. My children will live with the idea that their father was murdered." She sighed deeply. "How do you talk to people you meet after that?"

"Mrs.—Charlotte…"

"Coffee? It's ready."

She rushed into the kitchen, returning with a tray of coffee, cups and saucers. Sugar bowl, milk pitcher. She'd gotten everything ready, waiting for me. Rushing, she nearly dropped the tray, the milk slopping over the edges of the pitcher, the cups rattling—fidgety, like a woman unable to settle herself.

Ben's ex-wife surprised me: sixtyish, a little plump with wide chipmunk cheeks, a short woman, a drab face with a hint of pink lipstick. But her hair was styled in some sort of pin-curl chestnut-burr cut, all tight corkscrew and curly fries. Mixed metaphors here, to be sure, but the dyed blond configuration was out of sync with the baggy pantsuit she wore.

She poured coffee, her hand trembling. "This has all been so horrible. Horrible. My children…Melody locked herself in her room."

"May I speak with her, Charlotte?"

"That's why you're here, right?" Then she seemed to regret her abruptness. "Melody," she rang out, turning toward the staircase. "Melody. Come down."

"I do appreciate…"

A hand up in my face. "The Vietnamese kid. I saw him on the news. Such a skinny little…man. A killer?"

"Or not."

"Everyone says he did it." She held my eye. "But why would he do that? Ben lived for his students." A tilt of her head. "That's *all* he lived for. Students and his books. Marriage was a secondary major in his college career. They voted him the most popular teacher year after year. Try bringing that factoid up in divorce court."

"When did you divorce?"

"Oh, fifteen or so years back." For a second her eyes got moist. "A mistake, you know. *My* mistake. Ben stepped out of heaven for a moment, tempted by that snake of a girl. A nameless flirt who bedded him and then moved on. It must have surprised Ben himself, that stay-at-home play-with-the-kids dad. He confessed the indiscretion to me almost immediately, but I…I went mad. Threw him out of the house, demanded a divorce. I burned with fury." She laughed lightly. "I was one of those maddened women you hope never to meet."

"No reconciliation?"

Her lips trembled. "I always thought we'd end up back together. Yes, I was cruel at first, turned the kids against him.

Martin was around fifteen, Melody thirteen or so. Vulnerable, horrible ages for parents to run amok like that. I bad-mouthed him. I made them hate their father. Horrible of me. Yes, I know that. A casebook study of what not to do." She shivered. "Today on *Dr. Phil.* The spurned housewife and the children who listened to her. I made them hate him, but they didn't—finally. Slowly they crept away to see him, never telling me. But even that didn't go well."

"Why not?"

A strange look in her eyes. "I filled them up with anger so that even his kindness to them translated into bile."

"But you hoped to get back…"

"Together," she finished. "A secret. I loved him." A sob escaped her throat. "No matter."

"But…"

"But then five years ago my daughter comes back and whispers that he discovered this…this…Sophia, brazen, loud, flashy, his bedmate." She shuddered. "I hated him all over again."

"I know Sophia," I told her. "A friend."

"Hah!" The word flew out of her mouth. "Oh, I know that. I can't believe I even allow you in this house. *His* crowd. I know a lot of things. Spies in the house of love. My children as spies. Isn't that a kicker? Good parenting on my part. But at that dreadful moment I knew there was no future, no reconciliation, no nothing. He'd lost himself to that woman."

"What about his celebrity? His attacks on local religion?"

She raised her eyebrows. "That lunatic preacher over in Bristol? A carnival show. You know, I think Ben secretly enjoyed the attention, the notoriety, the denunciation on TV by a God-smitten crackpot preacher. A scholar like Ben slumming in the tabloids."

A rush of steps down the staircase. Melody Winslow stopped at the bottom step and looked back upstairs, as if contemplating flight.

A woman in her late twenties, she seemed younger because her face was so childlike—small, oval with a tiny mouth and large, blue, watery eyes. Her hand fluttered to her chin, dropped back down to her side, like a little girl surprised at a birthday party. She wore her thick, yellowish hair straight, clipped at the shoulders, a slight bang over her forehead. A woman who was never pretty but probably was considered cute. They'd be calling her that when she was in her sixties.

"Mr. Lam, I presume. My father talked about you."

"Hi, Melody, thanks for…"

She moved rapidly across the room and dropped into a chair. Immediately she drew her knees up to her chest, and stared at me. "I'm not used to the police."

"I'm not the police."

She shook her head. "That's not what I mean. I mean, yesterday, the interviews."

"That's why I'm here."

"I know. My mother told me." She glanced at her mother who was frowning at her, eyes nearly shut. "And I listened from upstairs. My mother telling you the family history."

Charlotte started to say something but changed her mind.

"I'm sorry about your father," I told Melody.

Her eyes got moist and she brushed at them with the back of her wrist. "We were getting close again. He'd come into the library to look for me."

Charlotte explained. "Melody works three or four hours a day over at the Avon Public Library, shelving books." She rolled her eyes as if Melody were involved in illicit drug sales.

Melody, I knew from her father, had led a drifting, unhappy life. The divorce shattered her, a teenaged girl caught in the marital wars of her parents. After high school she'd taken community college courses, then skedaddled to California where she knew no one. "An actress," Ben told us one night. "A goddamn actress. I always told my kids to express themselves but…an actress?" Four or so years in a donut shop on Santa Monica Boulevard, then she drifted back home where she hid in her mother's home, unmarried, refusing her high schools friends' phone calls, her nights locked in her bedroom.

"My fault," Ben always said.

Melody went on. "Years ago I was so mad at him I wouldn't talk to him. Then"—a furtive glance at her mother—"I would sneak out to visit him, take two or three buses down the mountain to his apartment—and never tell Mom." Another glance at her mother. "Rebellion long after the years when you're supposed to do it. The last two years we started to be father and daughter again."

"Secrets." From Charlotte.

"War maneuvers," Melody corrected.

Charlotte was clenching and unclenching her fists.

"I'm here," I started, "because you told the detective that your father mentioned a decision."

Her lips quivered. "I didn't think it was important at the time. Maybe I should have asked more questions."

"But what exactly did he say?"

She looked over my shoulder, gazing toward the outside. "You know, with Dad his students always came first. Them, us, Mom. Then them, not us, not Mom. Them. He loved to talk about his students. The applause at the end the semesters, unheard of."

"Melody," her mother prompted.

She shot a look at her mother. "The last time he said that he had to make the toughest decision of his life. A student had told him something but exacted a promise for silence. Some boy scout pledge of trust. Nonsense." She laughed and turned her head to the side. "I was barely listening to him. 'What?' I asked him. "This is a horrible thing I'm going through, Melody. Someone's life in my hands.' He kept talking but I stopped listening. Then he stopped. Just like that. 'I'll deal with it.' That's what he said."

A door at the back of the house opened. Footsteps moved around the kitchen. A cabinet door slammed. Charlotte jumped, jerked her head toward the kitchen and seemed ready to say something. Melody, momentarily startled, shut up.

I went on, sensing the conversation was ending. "A student? He didn't mention a name?"

"No."

"Dustin Trang?"

Her voice clipped. "I said—no. He never mentioned that name. I never heard it until the TV coverage. Him being dragged off to jail."

"For questioning," I corrected.

"Whatever."

"Whatever!" A booming voice exploded from the kitchen doorway. A fist pounded the doorjamb.

"Martin," his mother screamed. "Do you have to barge in like you're a bull?"

He was frowning. "I told you this was foolhardy. Why are you talking to this man?"

Charlotte took the question literally. "Because he asked me if he could."

Martin stepped closer, his hands folded over his chest. Dressed in a ski jacket, unzipped over an Eddie Bauer T-shirt, he was the outdoorsy version of his hothouse sister: similar blond coloring, oversized blue eyes in a long oval face, but with his father's squat physique. Martin's cheeks were ruddy, as though he'd walked into fierce wind, his hair tousled, his swagger across the room an athlete's practiced gait.

"I told you not to come," his mother said, resigned.

"And miss this show?"

Charlotte surprised me. "Mr. Lam was just leaving."

On cue I stood, leaned toward Melody. "Thank you."

But Martin wasn't finished. "Dad mentioned you."

"We were casual friends."

"Good for you. The only person he couldn't be friends with was his kids."

"Stop, Martin." From Charlotte.

"I mean, I tried to see him." He tossed a bitter look at his mother. "I mean, after years of hatred and exile in this penal colony called home, I'd reach out, he'd reach out, lovey-dovey, dumb friends on Facebook, would you believe—and then we'd do battle."

I waited a second. "You saw him just before he died. He mentioned that. Right?"

The question threw him off as he considered his answer. "Yeah, we fought over my divorce coming up"—a throaty rasp—"strike two for the family heir. My goddamn job at the high school. He called me a loser."

"Martin." From Charlotte.

"Words that hurt! He coddled his students. Spanish Inquisition for his little boy and girl."

"You're not a little boy," I said, perhaps unwisely.

For a moment he sputtered, "He was not a complex man, this man everyone loved."

"What do you mean?"

He debated what to tell me. "He made snap judgments and you had no way to get him to change his mind."

"About you?"

But he was through. "Are you my analyst, Mr. Lam?"

"You seem to be feeding me material."

His mouth went slack as he swiveled on his heels. "Love hate. Love hate. The yin and yang of Ben Winslow. Which one will we experience today? I'm sure you never saw the real man, Lam. His students flocked to him and unloaded their five-and-dime problems on him. A sympathetic ear."

"Which was the problem," Charlotte noted, her head nodding vigorously.

He pulled in his cheeks. "I heard about what he said to little sister here. The biggest decision of his life. Bullshit. His biggest decision was turning his back on his family. But you know, he probably paid a price for his—openness. Give me your tired, your poor, your…foreign exchange students. God, he loved immigrants." A sneer. "Probably why he liked you. Or that Dustin murderer."

"We don't know if…"

"Or maybe not him." For a second his voice shook. "But it had to be a student who shot him."

"Why?"

"Because I used to joke with him—those times we weren't at each other's throats—joke that someday a student would kill him."

That surprised me. It made little sense. "You said that?"

"It was a dumb joke. 'Dad, you get so involved in their lives that it could backfire. You don't know how psychotic some of your students are...'"

"And he agreed with that?"

"It obviously happened. Tick tock. Tick tock. Destiny is a bitch."

Chapter Ten

"He doesn't want us to visit," Hank said as I drove into Bristol.

"He has no choice, Hank," I answered. "This case won't disappear by hiding away."

We were headed up Route 6 late morning, stalled behind clogged traffic, inching from one traffic light to the next. A congested avenue of cheap burger joints, drive-thru car washes, pizza restaurants, Chinese fast food, discount insurance agencies. A cluttered, helter-skelter world of Jiffy Lube, Pizza Hut, Hometown Buffet, Friendly's Ice Cream Parlor, and a tiny, grimy-looking façade that called itself the Wok Inn. A Vietnamese storefront, Hank pointed out with glee—Simply Pho You!

"Pho crying out loud," he roared. Then, shifting in his seat, "I don't know this town. I love it. There," he yelled out. "That sign."

Up ahead was a massive billboard mounted on the roof of a sprawling lumberyard: Gospel of Wealth Ministry NEXT RIGHT All Welcome. Blessed Are the Lost.

"Yeah," Hank grumbled, "the loss of your weekly paycheck."

"Let's make a detour."

I followed a hiccough of bigger and bigger signs, some with spotlights blazing in daylight, that finally led into an old industrial part of town. Abandoned nineteenth-century red-brick factories, windows smashed or boarded up. Rusted chain-link fences with warning signs to KEEP OUT. Junked cars, stripped, rusted, snow-covered. A sharp turn off the dead-end road and there it was: a gleaming amphitheater with white columns and a huge illuminated cross that pierced the clouds. Not a gigantic theater like those mega churches you see on TV, those super-bowl coliseums of the saved, the ecstatic Southern preachers with their hands waving Bibles at the multitudes. But—big for Connecticut. Not big enough to eclipse Bristol's other claim to fame—the sprawling sports complex of ESPN with its moon-walk satellite dishes dotting the landscape. But a far cry from the white-steepled Congregational Churches of the founding fathers. Cotton Mather wouldn't be happy. But then he never was happy anyway. I could bet on that.

"A hymn to money," Hank said.

A neon signboard, oversized letters, flickering brightly in the daytime sun: "God has a pot of gold for YOU! God gives you the key."

The You capitalized. And flashing. With an exclamation point.

"I didn't know it was so easy."

"Buddha would have a lot to say about this," Hank said.

"Buddha wasn't against wealth, Hank. He just didn't want it to cloud your real purpose in life. Suffering."

"Thank God for America," Hank laughed. "We reorganized man's priorities. We believe in happy endings. No suffering—life is a TV Sunkist commercial."

I cut across a side street, turned down another poorly plowed street, banks of dirty snow blocking unmoved cars, and found the entrance to the housing project on Jefferson Drive.

"You could walk to the church of money bags from here," I noted. "Perfect placement."

"Opiate," Hank added.

The projects were stunned structures from the fifties: long, two-story white vinyl-sided homes that mimicked the garden apartments that popped up after World War Two. But decades later neglect gave them the patina of rock-bottom despair—sagging roofs, windows loosed from frames, the faded siding a crazy-quilt patchwork of brilliant graffiti, probably gang related. Keith Haring hieroglyphics. One generation of gang-bangers layering their new violent or ego-bloated messages over the scribbling of older gang-bangers most likely doing time. Though not for desecration of private property.

Dustin opened the door before we knocked.

"Nobody's home."

I teased him. "You are."

His eyes widened as he stepped back. "I mean, like my mother."

"Can we come in?" Hank asked.

Dustin blinked his eyes quickly, as though struck by sudden sunlight. "You're not in your uniform," he said to Hank.

"I'm not on duty." Hank pulled at his sleek winter jacket. "I'm advertising the latest fashion from The Gap."

Dustin hesitated. "I was afraid you'd wear your uniform."

"I'm here as your friend, Dustin." Hank purposely lowered his voice. His words sounded warm. I smiled at him. Hank smiled at me. Dustin didn't smile at anybody.

"I thought your mother would be here," I told him.

"I told her. She will be, I guess. Shopping." He seemed at a loss what to do. Finally, shrugging, he pointed to the small living room. "I guess you should sit down. Is that what you want to do?" Helpless, he waved his hands in the air. "You gotta take off your shoes."

"We know that," Hank said.

Dressed in a T-shirt that was too small, he could have been a bony child. A tear under his left arm showed surprisingly white skin, a contrast to his dark face. He was wearing baggy cargo shorts, but he was barefoot. As he sat down opposite us, rocking on the edge of his chair, I noticed scratches on his shins. Absently he dragged his nails down a leg. A bead of thin blood appeared. "What do you want to ask me?"

"A couple things."

Hank zeroed in. "Your relationship with Professor Winslow."

The abruptness surprised him. "No relationship."

"That's not true," I said sharply. "A week before he died you suddenly went to war with him."

"I don't want to talk about that."

Anger in Hank's voice. "You're gonna have to. Especially if you want our help."

He slumped down, uncomfortable. "I was his spy at the Gospel of Wealth. I wrote this paper. I told him my mother—others in my family—go there. I could be a spy. Maybe. He promised not to tell anyone. But he wanted to meet my mother..." It was a cockeyed story, sloppily rehearsed in his head, that finally sputtered to an end. He sat back, closed his eyes, a thin smile on his face.

It was a lie, I realized. A bright boy, he'd expected the question from us. Of course. And he thought he was ready.

"Dustin, I don't believe that nonsense."

His lips quivered. "It's true. He—promised me. I went there—I talked to that Reverend Simms guy, you know. But he was gonna break his promise. I mean, Professor Winslow, like—tell people my name." But even now the words sounded false. He closed his eyes for a moment. When he opened them, he whispered, "There was no other relationship."

"But the fire in your voice. I *heard* it, Dustin. And going to his home."

"I told you the reason."

Hank was frustrated. "No, Dustin."

"And more than one person gave your name to the cops. That kid filmed it—loaded it onto YouTube. Bad taste, yes, but..."

Dustin stood up. "Yeah, I was real mad at him. Stupid, I know. But it had nothing to do with—like murder. I mean, murder. *Real* murder. That blew me away. Like, you know—guns. Just because I didn't *like* him any more, I'm not gonna kill him." A strange, faraway laugh that broke at the end. "That would never cross my mind."

I said nothing for a bit, then, "I believe you."

"You do?"

"I do. I don't think you shot Ben Winslow. But I also think you're lying to us."

"Because it's got nothing to do with murder."

"So you admit you're not telling us the whole story." Hank threw the words at him.

Dustin toppled back into his seat. "You're trying to trick me."

"We're trying to save your skinny ass," Hank yelled at him.

This line was getting nowhere, so I shifted my approach. "Talk about your family."

His eyes got cloudy. "Nothing to say. I live with my mother."

"How is she dealing with this?"

For some reason he gestured toward the kitchen, a bony shrug, as though his secreted mother would suddenly leap out and surprise us. I followed his hand. In view: a forties red enamel table covered with stacked dishes. A carton of Lucky Strikes half out of a brown bag. On a far corner wall, high up, a small shelf with a shrine to Buddha. A porcelain statue surrounded by joss sticks. Artificial flowers. A bowl of water. Something dark red. Maybe oranges. A small cardboard box. Beneath it a calendar from an Chinese restaurant.

Dustin followed my glance. "We're poor."

"I was looking at the shrine. I'm Buddhist."

"I'm not." Hank's contribution.

Dustin smiled at Hank. "I'm not either."

"But you go to Reverend Simms' church a few blocks over?" I asked.

Dustin rustled in his seat, uncomfortable. "Yeah, I saw him talk about me on TV. I don't know why. That was real stupid of him."

"You go?"

He swung his head back and forth. "No, like never. A few times I gotta drive my mom. Like in bad weather. Otherwise she walks. They all walk from the projects. It's like a…a pilgrimage of the poor. Everybody here thinks he got the key to millions. She and my Uncle Binh go. My Aunt Suong." He shuffled out of his chair and took a pamphlet off a sideboard. "Here. Protestantism meets the great Buddha. My mom thinks they belong together."

I scanned the glossy pamphlet. The usual pitches about seed money, instant wealth, promised riches, God's blessings. The keys to the kingdom.

"Dustin, he knew your name. He knew who you were."

He faltered. "I told you. I was—like a spy. I…"

"Stop it," Hank demanded. "Don't bullshit me."

Dustin rolled his eyes. "Mom dragged me up to him one time. Another time he talked to us. But I won't go any more. He's a scary dude. Really. All that shaking and hallelujah stuff. I went to please my Mom." He made a face. "It didn't work. I've spent a lifetime trying to please her, but I never win." He scrunched up his face. "Strike three."

Hank leaned in. "She's your mother. She must love…"

His words hot, furious. "You don't understand, do you? I was the mistake boy. That's what Uncle Binh calls me. The mistake boy. I'm eighteen and my Mom is sixty-five or something. Do the math."

I did. I was good at math."

"But…" Hank protested.

He tightened his face. "No buts, man. You know I got two brothers who look right through me. The scuzziest is Hiep— Hollis to the authorities. He hasn't said more than a few words to me in ten years. Maybe more."

"I don't understand."

"You don't get it, Mr. Lam." A thin smile as he faced Hank. "Hank?"

"Tell us."

He debated what to say. Then, quietly, "Everything stopped when I was born. My dad killed in that car crash on the way to the hospital. They blame me."

"But that's ridiculous," Hank said.

"Yeah, tough shit. Since when does ridiculous stop people from thinking dumb thoughts?"

I laughed out loud. "True. But surely your mother…"

He kept checking out the front door. "Everything was perfect in Saigon. Before the Commies. A paradise. I don't know—crap talk like that." The words hung in the air like a painful lament. He waited a moment. "The clock stopped ticking when my family was dropped into Fort Pendleton in California."

"They had to get out of Vietnam, Dustin." From Hank.

"What do you know about the war?" I asked.

That surprised him. "Nothing. Nobody wants to talk about it. Mom—she like cries. So I shut up. I don't care anyways."

"Another lifetime." Hank watched the boy's face closely.

"What they have left is a postcard. In their heads. A hope to go back. Look around here." His index finger shot out, pointing here and then there, aimless, a scattershot gesture. "A dump."

Life in the projects: a small, tight living room with peeling white walls, scuffed and battered wood floors covered with grimy throw rugs, a large plastic potted plant near a cabinet, an oversized flat-screen TV on a stand, on the wall the obligatory clock in the shape of Vietnam. I stared at it. The time was wrong. He saw me looking. "It's set to Saigon time from a hundred years ago."

A stale, rancid smell hung in the rooms: old wood, decay, perhaps mouse droppings in the walls, water bugs and cockroaches underfoot, the lingering hint of old cooking oil and onions and ginger.

A sarcastic laugh. "It was the world's fault—the Americans— that they had to abandon the lake villa I always hear about, shade from a goddamn banyan tree in the backyard, the overripe mangoes hanging outside their windows, a French Citroën in the street, country girls to do the cooking. Bougainvillea blocking the scent of napalm. *Da da da dum da dum.* Drum roll, please. The same story over and over. All my life. A bedtime story. That story, yes. But the war—taboo city. The Americans promised this and promised that—and then forgot about them." He stopped, out of breath. "Sorry."

"They flew them out. Your family. Uncle Binh and his wife."

"Yeah, sure, big deal. Forced into purgatory. Handouts. Welfare. This"—his voice got shrill—"this stopover on the road to wealth."

"You're a bright young man. You've thought about things. That's evident. You found your way to Farmington College."

"A charity case. We're all charity cases. But I won't be here forever."

"So your family stopped...living?" Hank questioned.

That same laugh. "No, they still *live*. But back in Vietnam. In their dreams. The past but never the present. Or the future. America is money. Right behind door number something is the key to the gold mine. I got a druggie brother Hollis who stumbles from one get-rich scheme to the next—and falls on his face. Lives with this girlfriend or that. Shoplifts cigarettes and lottery tickets. Does time in county. I got another brother Thang—a loser named Timmy—who is married to a Puerto Rican woman who lives down the street. They got two kids and he got no job. She goes to work—McDonald's." The laughter stopped suddenly. "But someday we'll be living on easy street. Living large."

I didn't know what to say to this rant. But then he shut up, regretting his words, biting his lip, switching to "Do you want anything to drink?"

The polite young man who wanted to please.

Hank and I both shook out heads: No thanks.

He sighed, relieved.

"You got your mother," Hank said.

His lips in a razor-thin line. "A monthly check until I turn eighteen. Which just happened."

"What does that mean?"

"Hey, we'll find out, won't we?"

"Dustin, Rick and I want to help you. You called me. But what can you tell us about the murder? Anything. Some clue. You and Professor Winslow. Let's get the police to stop thinking it's you."

Color rose in his neck. "It got nothing to do with murder. Okay, yeah, I got a temper. Yes, I made a fool of myself with the professor—he made me so mad."

"I believe you," I repeated.

Suddenly his face fell as he brushed away tears. Embarrassed, he shielded his face with both hands. He slipped down in his seat. "What's gonna happen to me?"

The front door opened, the sound of laughing voices filling the room. An old woman, a younger man and woman. The laughter stopped when they noticed Hank and me sitting with Dustin. The man grunted, nudged the old woman who tottered, leaned on her cane, but shot him a mean look.

"Company," the man said.

Dustin whispered, unhappy, "My Mom. Brother Thang—Timmy. His wife, Rosie." He jumped up, performed almost a benedictory half-bow, then rushed away. Within seconds we could hear a door at the back of the apartment closing quietly, the sound of a latch.

"I'm Rick Van Lam," I said to the old woman.

His mother, doubtless. A woman in her sixties who appeared much older. Small and skinny like her son, but shriveled, her prune face a continent of deep wrinkles. She stepped closer, squinting through myopic eyes concealed behind thick magnifying glasses as she balanced herself on a cane. Wobbly, she grasped the edge of a shelf. Close-cropped white hair mostly hidden beneath a frayed knit cap. When she looked at me, she offered a slight, confused smile, and I noticed a missing front tooth.

"He told me you would be here," she said in thick Vietnamese I had trouble understanding.

"If we could talk…"

But the man interrupted, his voice gruff. "The police been here. *He* explained." The *he* was Dustin.

Dustin's fortyish brother was no reflection of Dustin—nor the mother. Short but thick, a flabby stomach over spindly legs. Close-cropped military hair with the hint of a light green tattoo on the side of his neck. He glanced at the woman with him, also short and chubby, with long uncombed hair, an enormous winter parka doubling her size. She mumbled something to him in Spanish and he rolled his eyes.

"We're not the police," Hank explained, which of course was not exactly true…

The couple had walked in loaded down with packages. Christmas shopping, I could tell. A board game sticking out of the Toys R Us bag. A Sears bag. Target. Long rolls of wrapping paper—cartoonish Christmas trees, snowflakes, jolly Santas. Dustin's mother motioned to a side table, and Timmy put down the packages, sighing as he did so. For a moment mother and son talked in broken English about something that happened while shopping, with muttered interjections from Rosie. Some insult, some muttered slight by a cashier. "Piece of trash, she was," Rosie commented.

Hank and I exchanged looks, uncertain what was happening. Then, almost on cue, the three turned as a body and faced us. "He didn't kill no one," the old woman said loudly in English.

"I believe that," I began, "but…"

"So it should be over." Flat out, a dip of her head.

"It's not that easy," Hank added.

She held up her cane, punctuating the air with it. "Over. We want to be left alone." She muttered in Vietnamese at us, *"Khong phai chuyen cua an."*

This was none of our business.

"What would you have us do?" I asked in English.

"It'll go away." She sighed. "He brings trouble, always." Then in Vietnamese, *"Khong ra gi."*

Good for nothing.

"Always?" From Hank.

That same weird smile. "Always." Then back to Vietnamese. "The day he is born out on the highway. That night I dream of a life that stops."

"What she saying?" Rosie asked her husband sharply. "You know I hate it when she does that."

He puffed out his cheeks. his eyes flashing anger. "It ain't nothing. The kid, that's all."

"He ain't a kid," Rosie told him.

"Timmy," I interrupted purposely, "what do you think about Dustin's problem? You must have given it some thought, no?"

"No." He acted surprised that I addressed him, question in his voice.

"No?"

"I don't know nothing about it. He hides in his room."

"You want his name cleared, right?" From Hank.

"She"—he pointed at his mother—"says he ain't done it." He shrugged his shoulders. "I don't know nothing about him."

Rosie's voice ran over her husband's words, glancing first at me, then at Hank. "You see what he did? He's a ghost here. Hides in his room."

The old woman mumbled, "We don't want to see us no more on TV." She pointed to the big-screen TV.

"The Reverend Simms named him."

She shook her head sadly. "A good man, that one. But a mistake to do that. Neighbors knock on our door. They throw stones on the doorstep. Reverend Simms is a child of God. Blesses us. He says Anh Ky is touched by the devil—that's why it all happened." She leaned toward Hank, confidential. "A foolish boy, a liar. He was supposed to know what to do. I ask him one time." She stressed the words. "One time. Behave—no trouble. The boy who broke my body. One time." She actually screamed out. "Good for nothing. Breaks the dreams in half."

"What are you talking about?" Hank asked.

She waved a dismissive hand at him. "Nothing. Trouble in the house. He walks around like trouble."

With that she turned and hobbled into the kitchen. Timmy and Rosie followed, picking up the packages from the side table. From where I sat I could see them peering inside, emptying the contents onto the kitchen table, commenting, even laughing.

We were forgotten.

"Time to leave," I told Hank.

No one said a word as we walked out, Hank fuming and looking back over his shoulder. "What the hell's the problem with them?"

I flicked my head back toward the doorway. "Dustin *is* a ghost it that house. That was one of the truest things told to us."

Hank spoke bitterly. "That's why he hides away."

"A mother's love."

"Mistake boy."

"Sad." I shook my head. "The winter apple."

In the car he blasted the heater. "What did we learn?"

"First off, we learned that Dustin is lying to us."

"True. But why? We're helping him. What good does it do to lie about his relationship with Ben Winslow? Ben is dead. Possible murder charges against Dustin. Why lie to us?"

"People lie for all sorts of reasons."

"A cliché, Rick." He punched the dashboard. "They're not gonna be any help to us."

"Maybe she told us something important. I mean, her strong dislike of her own son. Her—cold indifference."

"God, you're hearing voices. Talk about ghosts." He punched me in the arm.

"That's a clue to something, Hank. Maybe that explains the anger under the surface of his life. His striking out—maybe those confrontations with Ben—were meaningless. Misdirected anger that got out of hand. He doesn't know how to deal with people."

"That's because he hasn't lived with any. No one ever gave him a road map."

"A little cruel, Hank. They have their own battles, Hank. Uprooted from Vietnam…"

He broke in, not buying it. "So have a million others." He blew out his cheeks. "Lots of questions from this visit."

I lowered the heat and breathed out. "When we have those answers, maybe everything will fall into place."

Chapter Eleven

I sat with Marcie and Vinnie in Marcie's office, the three of us sipping coffee from Styrofoam cups. A reading day at the college, and I'd planned to spend the afternoon at my Hartford office, finishing up an insurance investigation, perhaps catching lunch with Jimmy. He'd called a few times, leaving the identical message each time—"You're either there or you're not, but if you're there and you don't pickup, you're a damned fool"—and I kept meaning to get back to him. After all, he was my partner.

Vinnie wore a pinched look. "What surprised you this morning, Rick? Anything?"

I waited a heartbeat. "David Laramie."

That morning the college had held a memorial service for Ben—mournful, sad, a succession of students talking of Ben's being their favorite teacher. His influence on their lives.

I'd spotted David Laramie sitting five rows behind me. Why was he there? The last person I'd expect at Ben's memorial. Stony-faced, eyes unblinking, sitting with rigid posture, he looked right through me. It gave me the chills. He was the final mourner at the funeral, come to make certain the body is buried. For some reason Vietnamese words popped into my head: *Buoc qua xac chet cua toi da.*

Over my dead body.

That intrigued Vinnie. His brow furrowed as he pointed out the door in the direction of Laramie's office. "The pain-in-the-ass

IT prof. Farmington College's contribution to the waste bin of floppy disks in the town dump."

"Yeah. The fact that he showed up. He hated Ben."

"And how," Marcie noted. "Yeah, I was surprised to see him there."

"To make certain Ben was really dead?" Vinnie wondered.

I tossed my coffee cup into the basket. "I found myself checking out his face."

Marcie frowned. "I never liked him, you know."

"That's because his politics are to the right of Attila the Hun."

"That's true."

"But why Ben, in particular? I never understood it."

"Tenure committee," Marcie told me quickly. "Laramie was up for full professor and Ben was on the committee. Laramie's application touted a book he'd written on using computers in elementary school."

"And?"

Her eyes twinkled. "And Ben pointed out that, yes, Laramie had written such a welcome tome, but he'd run off a dozen ungrammatical copies at Staples. More of a class handout. The vote went against Laramie, and Ben became persona non grata for life." She shivered. "Until death, as it turned out."

Vinnie scratched his chin. "It was more than that, Rick. Ben spouted his atheism as well as his jaundiced view of tent-city religion. And Laramie is deeply religious."

"An evangelical?"

He shook his head. "Nah, not like Reverend Simms crazy, or televangelist crazy, but a charismatic Catholic. Ben's place in a classroom was an affront to Laramie's personal beliefs."

"So personal *and* profession antipathies?" I summed up.

"Yeah, the whole package." Marcie pushed papers into a briefcase. "Laramie saw Ben as everything that was wrong with the school—maybe society. He was Dustin's advisor, which surprised me, though he was assigned the task. He does *not* care for scholarship students, especially ones of color."

"Really? That's a serious charge," I told her.

"Make of it what you will." She stood up and shrugged. "A narrow man with a narrow agenda."

• • ● • •

Headed out of the building, I spotted David Laramie balancing a tray of food as he maneuvered the key to his office. Alone in the hallway, he was humming some tune to himself—and that annoyed me. So I'd lingered in the hallway, giving him a chance to spill his tuna melt with fries onto his lap, then knocked on his door.

I heard rustling inside, then the voice of someone with a mouthful of food. "Office hours aren't for an hour."

"It's Rick Van Lam."

Silence. Then the sound of a squeaky drawer opening and closing. "Come in."

Laramie was seated behind his desk, no food in sight, though the aroma of oily French fries was unmistakable.

"Did I interrupt your lunch?"

He glanced toward the drawer of a cabinet near him. Slightly ajar, he leaned forward and shut it quickly. "No. What's up?" Nothing friendly in his tone.

"Do you mind if I talk to you a bit?"

He hesitated, then bit his tongue. "Have a seat." He motioned to a chair opposite his desk. "I'm not gonna like this, am I?"

I'd never been in his office before, no reason to, and found myself surveying a wall of heavy-duty oak shelves. A collection of early computers, bulky and archaic, a museum wall of a PC collector's dreamscape. Brands I'd never heard of: TRS-80 from Radio Shack. Altair 8800. The IBM SCAMP. An Olivetti Programma 101. A wall of gadgetry. I leaned in to check one out. "My God, one of my first computers. This Zenith. Nobody even knows that they…"

He half-rose from his chair, his voice cold. "What do you want, Mr. Lam?"

I stared into his face. "Dustin Trang. I want to talk about him. I'm convinced he's *not* involved with Ben's death."

His mouth was set in a hard, tight line, his eyes flickering. "And you're doing this—why?"

"I don't like to see innocent people railroaded."

He swiveled in his chair, glancing out the window behind him to the snowy landscape. "Fair enough. But I still don't see…"

"I was surprised to see you at Ben's service."

His eyes widened. "Why not? A colleague of mine. The whole college community was there. Something called—respect."

I was shaking my head. "But you had your battles with him. You didn't like him."

He sucked in his cheeks. "I don't like a lot of people—in fact, I could write a book"—he laughed to himself—"but I know when to pay my respects. I wasn't raised in a barn, you know."

I said nothing, watching him. He kept his eyes on me, his pupils focused pinpoints, and he rocked in his chair, his fingers intertwined in front of his chest.

An unlovely man, almost purposely so. The way he put himself together. Average height, a little overweight with puffy jowls and charcoal bags under his eyes, a man in his early forties, my age, but a man who probably assumed middle-age when he was in college. A slapdash moustache that needed trimming, wispy hairs drifting over his upper lip. A blondish buzz cut that he probably sported since adolescence, with just the hint of sideburns. A sloppy shave job. The sad sack father trailing after his kids at Disney World. The physiognomy of someone you'd never be able to pick out in a police line-up. If it ever came to that.

And his clothing: a baggy sports jacket with leather elbow patches. A simple white dress shirt. A poorly knotted red tie. A look he probably appropriated from watching the cool guys in *Revenge of the Nerds*. His cardigan-clad heroes.

"What are you smiling at?" he said sharply.

"Sorry. I didn't realize I was."

"Are you hired by his family?"

I shook my head. "No."

"Then what business…?"

"Do you think Dustin killed Ben?"

The question startled him. "I haven't thought about it."

"Well, of course you have," I insisted, a little testy. "You had a lot to say to the cops about him."

He rolled his tongue over his upper lip. The ice-cream parlor moustache twitched unhappily. "They asked me questions. I answer. That's what good citizens do."

"But you seem to have shifted your stories, no? To the cops. Even to the press. Your face on TV."

He waited, deliberated what to say. "Not really." He fidgeted. "I'm not used to microphones thrust into my face."

"So you make things up? The first reports—the one that probably sent the cops to his door—mentioned that he'd threatened Ben's life. That you heard him say that. Then you walked back from that statement."

Clearly rattled, he scanned the wall of old commuters. Absently he reached out a hand, brushed his fingers against the keyboard of an old Atari model. He stammered, "I never thought it would come to...this."

"To what? A boy suspected of murder."

"Well, Dustin is my advisee. He sits in the chair you're in, you know. I asked him how things were."

"And he told you he was going to kill Ben?"

He swallowed. "No, not exactly. But he...he mentioned problems with Ben."

"Like what?"

Suddenly he sat up, his face flushed with anger. "Look, Mr. Lam. I listen to what my students tell me. I'm not a fool. Ben wasn't *good* for students. He poisoned their minds. Lies. Godlessness. I'd see him walking in the hallway, followed by a gaggle of fawning students. Vulnerable minds. Weak kids. He turned them against... There should be no place on a college campus for...subversion."

I waited until he sputtered to an end. "Maybe he saw the world differently from you."

"To put it mildly." Nervous, he pointed a finger at me. "Dustin was troubled. I could see that. And the trouble was Ben—suddenly."

"But what? Dustin won't talk about it. No one knows."

A moment of camaraderie, his voice softening. "You know, I asked him. The day before the murder. 'Tell me.' Nothing. But that boy has fire in his belly. A time bomb. He made me nervous. More than nervous—frightened. A whiz with computers, a quick learner, but I expect bad things from him." He paused. "And maybe that's what happened here. Bad things." He drew in his breath. "A bad thing."

"But maybe not from him."

"Who's to say?" A heavy sigh. "He did tell me that Ben failed him. That was his word. Failed. There might be"—a deliberate pause—"trouble. I didn't understand."

"What exactly did he say?"

He deliberated. "'He failed us.'"

"Us?"

He slammed his fist down on his desk. "I don't know. Stop this…badgering. I barely listened to him. It was like he had to tell somebody something."

"And he chose you?"

He drew his tongue into cheek. "Weird, no? I'd expect you to say something—snarky. I made it clear to him that I didn't—well, care for true confessions."

I circled back. "But why talk to the cops?"

His eyes glazed over. "Right after the murder, I panicked. The cops confronted me—everyone. I…I don't know. I read between the lines."

"That's a dishonest answer." I crossed my arms and glared at him.

My words infuriated him. He bristled, drew his lips into a razor-thin line. "You have a hell of a nerve coming in here and accusing me."

"I'm only trying to help Dustin."

"I'm sorry I even spoke up. People look at me now, question in their expressions."

"No," I said sharply. "People look at *him*." I raised my voice. "Tell me, David, do you like Dustin?"

A thin, wavering smile. "Not really."

"Why?"

A smug look on his face. "If you must know—and I feel you are cut from the same intrusive cloth that dominates this campus—the college has evolved into a kind of…Salvation Army approach to education. Especially in my computer science classes. They dump scholarship students from other countries. Accents so thick I have to keep saying—What? What? What? I go home with headaches."

"But Dustin speaks perfect English. An intelligent student. Born here."

He didn't answer. He rustled some sheets on his desk and glanced toward the door. "I have office hours shortly."

"What about Darijo Delic?"

"The Bosnian kid? He identifies himself as a Bosniak. What the hell is that?"

"A Muslim from Bosnia." I waited second. "Maybe a friend of Dustin."

"Dustin has no friends. Look at him."

"What do you think of Darijo?"

He squinted. "Yeah, a Muslim who leaves my lab to pray in the hallway."

"You're a religious man, David. You should applaud that."

A harsh rasp. "I know who God likes."

The answer stunned me. "Really? Isn't that presumptuous?"

He half-rose from his chair. "You better believe it."

"But…"

He stood over me, pointed to the door. "Goodbye, Mr. Lam. I had nothing to do with Ben's murder. So this is all stuff and nonsense."

"Not until a murderer is caught."

"Knock your socks off."

I stood. "David…"

"This conversation is over."

Chapter Twelve

Glistening slivers of carrot and pickled daikon piled up on the cutting board. Chopped Thai basil and mint sent waves of sweetness throughout the kitchen. Peanuts, pounded into specks, rested in an enamel bowl. Lettuce leaves rinsed under a faucet, sparkling on the counter. Thin strips of pork, pounded wafer-thin and marinated in a slathered mixture of shallots, garlic, dark soy sauce, sesame oil, lemongrass, sizzled and popped on the grill. *Nuoc mam*, the aromatic fish sauce, ladle at the ready. Water boiling, ready for vermicelli noodles, firm but not too soft. Just right. Always just right.

Hank's grandmother and mother were making *bun*.

Hank and I sat at the kitchen table, watching. Hank might be used to artists in his family kitchen, but I wasn't. To me, wide-eyed, this was wonder. Vegetables dripped their color onto the counter. The barbecued pork glistened with a caramelized luster.

Outside light sleet pinged the windows. Wind snapped a tree limb against the siding. Inside the old cast-iron radiators clanged and hissed.

"Mom," Hank said, "I'm hungry."

His mother stopped peering into the boiling water. "All my life you're hungry. A baby reaching for my milk."

Hank held up his hand in mock shock. "Mom, Rick's here. He's delicate. Family secrets."

Grandma was chuckling as she reached over to tap him with a wooden spoon, and said in her melodic Vietnamese, "*Meo khen meo dai duoi.*" A bird likes to hear itself sing. Then she added, "Rick has seen more of life than you ever will."

Hank protested, "Grandma, I'm a state cop. We see it all."

Grandma twinkled. "You see the underbelly of life."

"And what does Rick see?"

She deliberated. "He sees the stars in the nighttime sky."

"Grandma, you're not making any sense." He stood up and gave her a quick peck on the cheek. "I see stars, too."

His mother smiled softly. "Yes, when you bang your head into a wall."

Hank danced around his mother. "I do that to get attention. No one listens to me."

Grandma laughed. "When you were little, at the New Year's parties, you'd stand on a table and sing. Jumping up and down. *Chao chi. Chao chi.*" She mimicked a little boy's voice in English. "Hello. Hello. Hello." Back to Vietnamese. "Like a parrot."

His mother added, "I feared we'd brought a trained monkey into the house."

Hank feigned horror. "I never did. Grandma, Rick will think
- less of me." He made a face. "Besides, the Connecticut State Police would never hire a trained monkey."

Grandma smirked. "Yes, the trained monkeys run for political office."

Hank laughed out loud. "Grandma has a jaundiced view of American politics. She watches CNN and then Fox and then gets confused."

Hank's line was said in English, and Grandma, not fully grasping the meaning, was rocking on her heels, disapproving. Then, a wide grin, "Somebody in the family has to know what's going on in this country."

"It seems to me…"

Grandma wagged a finger at him. "Quiet, you chatterbox."

I loved the Nguyen kitchen in East Hartford. Small, cramped, three or four calendars from different Asian markets gracing the walls, a sink that always dripped, a refrigerator that announced itself with a startling *bang bang bang*, but it was haven, warmth.

Salvation. Years back when Hank was my student at the college, he'd been leery of me—me, the *bui doi*, dust boy, mixed blood Vietnamese, anathema to the cult of pureblood so beloved of Vietnamese. But once we found each other as friends, he'd integrated me into his close-knit family, slowly and sometimes painfully. Grandma embraced me immediately, this loving woman, although Hank's father and irascible grandfather still harbored Old Country biases, especially when his dad has a little too much to drink downtown. But nowadays I was at home there—I ran to that room for shelter.

"We won't wait for the others," Hank's mother said, glancing at the clock.

Hank's father and Grandpa. Since her husband retired as a factory laborer at Manchester Tool & Die, he'd discovered other cronies at Minh Le's Bar and Pool Hall on Park Street in Little Saigon, a dusty old tavern where he talked for hours with other retired Vietnamese, Laotian, and Cambodian foundry workers. Never a social man in his working days, in retirement he'd found a crowd. He'd forget to look at the clock.

So the four of us sat at a kitchen table covered with a slick, pristine oilcloth, crinkly at the corners but now loaded down with bowls of *bun*. Grandma served *goi cuon* first, prepared earlier, luscious cylinders of shrimp, pork, chives, and mint encased in a thin rice wrapper. Dipped in thick hoisin and peanut sauce, the summer rolls thrilled with each bite, the taste of mint taking you away from the winter outside your door. Hank used chopsticks to stir a dollop of hot sauce into his dipping sauce. I never did.

"Coward," he threw at me.

"You leave him alone." Grandma smiled at me. "When Hank was a boy, he put hot sauce on everything. Even…what do you call that bread? Wonder Bread?"

"I did not," Hank laughed. "Only sometimes. Rarely." A pause. "Only when I *had* to."

"The house is quiet now," I said to his mother. "Now that the kids are gone."

She looked sad. Hank's younger siblings were at school—his sister finishing a scholarship program at a prep school, preamble to her first year at the Rhode Island School of Design. His younger brother was now a freshman at the University of Connecticut. This week his major was chemical engineering. Last week it was biology.

Grandma answered. "A house needs young folks running around. Now all you hear is my old bones cracking and the wheeze of old men."

"Grandma," Hank began, sitting back and placing his chopsticks across the top of his bowl, "tell Rick about the Trangs. I told him you know them."

"Know *of* them," she corrected. "I know them the way we all know each other. All of us fleeing Vietnam. All of us dazed as we met each other in the marketplace." She smiled. "All of us shell-shocked from the bombing, suddenly standing in the aisles of Stop & Shop and"—she changed to English—"crying because we didn't know how to buy a chicken."

"But you met Uncle Binh. Even Anh Ky's mother?"

Hank's mother was making a *tsk*ing sound. "His mother. Ngo Thi Mai. A sad story, that one."

Grandma sighed. "You have to understand how it was back then. The end of the war. Here we are—1975 maybe, up to 1980, one horrible year after another. We are in America—scared of the streets. But the Trang clan was"—again the drift to English—"how you say, celebrities." Back to Vietnamese: "Uncle Binh, the hero. The decorated hero of the South Vietnamese army. He walks around the camp in Guam in his uniform. The stars on his shoulders. His head thrown back. The man who worked with Westmoreland." She pronounced it: *Oet-mo-len.*

Hank was baffled. "But I don't understand what happened to them?"

Grandma clicked her tongue. "You stop living."

"But why?" From Hank.

Grandma fiddled with her chopsticks, tapping them on the edge of her bowl. "You see, the rush of folks out of Vietnam—the craziness of that April day in 1975—helicopters and planes and boats—screaming, crying. We struggled out, we paid gold coins for a boat to Hong Kong, we all ended up in Guam, stunned, numb. But folks like the Trangs were taken out without—without tears."

"But they must have been sad to leave," Hank said.

"Yes," Grandma said hurriedly. "Of course. Tears to leave behind the only world you know. We all cried—we're human. Tears from panic, fright, gunshots, bombs, limbs lost. But the Americans flew out Uncle Binh because he was a high-ranked man. He and his family. His wife. His brother and his family. That is, Anh Ky's father."

"How did they make it to Hartford?"

Hank's mother answered. "Most went to California, of course. Camp Pendleton, the first stop. Some to other camps. But so many...everyone tried to get sponsors. We had cousins in Connecticut. So, I guess, did the Trang clan. Connections."

Grandma added, "They lived for a while on Park Street. Little Saigon. But...how do I say this? They weren't in America."

"I don't understand." I stared into her face.

Grandma shook her head back and forth. "Their souls stayed behind in Vietnam. The meat of their bones. A rich, good life there. Mangoes fell from the trees into their palms. The servant girl hands you lotus tea. You get used to that life. A good life. And the American military there added this pleasure to their lives, that reward, this bit of candy and spice and beautiful silk *ao dai*." She chuckled to herself. "But here in America they got frozen dinners and people who pointed at them and cursed."

"But I still don't see how they fell—I don't know—from that kind of grace." I glanced at Hank.

Grandma's voice got soft. "You see, they sat in America and waited for the Communists to fail in the homeland. They believed they would go back when Uncle Ho's cruel world ended—when the Viet Cong found God. Wisdom. Penitence. Jesus. The better nature of loving Buddha. Their eyes long for the old village."

"So they waited…"

"And waited," Grandma went on. "Uncle Binh would fly to San Jose, to the big Vietnamese colonies on the West Coast. He'd wear his uniform and march with the other military men in a parade, the South Vietnamese flag flying. The red beret on his head. The men marched while the women stood on the sidelines and cried. Vietnam on the Pacific."

"Or applauded," Hank's mother added. "The women applauded."

"There was even a rumor that Uncle Binh was somehow involved in the invasion of Vietnam through Thailand by some refugees and American military. All secret. All failing. Men captured, tortured, killed."

"I know," I said. "A number of attempts to invade or to find MIAs. American congressmen led campaigns, dropping leaflets. Vietnamese-based operations from America. Exiled soldiers moving through the mountains. A disaster."

"Yes, a sad time. The Communists stay in power."

"But I still don't see why the family ended up in a housing project. In poverty."

Grandma's voice got sad. "I told you." She said in English. "Frozen."

"Frozen?"

"America is not a country they live in. They live under America. Their dreams are all back in Vietnam."

"But decades have passed."

Hank's mother summed up: "After a while, doing nothing is all you know how to do."

"And the government pays you to do that," Grandma remarked. "Look at other Vietnamese refugees. Look at their children. One generation. Harvard. Yale. Doctors. Lawyers. These are children of poor people who carried nothing with them to America." She paused. "Except hope."

Hank's mother made a face. "And some become state police, so that their mothers toss and turn in bed all night long."

"I carry a gun, Mom," Hank said with a smile.

"And this is supposed to make me feel good?"

Grandma was listening closely. "No matter. These children make their own lives."

"But Dustin's mother, Ngo Thi Mai, even Uncle Binh, had misfortune."

"Yes, that car crash. Yes, Uncle Binh works at a factory and a machine falls on him. But the car crash was—what? Two decades ago. When little Anh Ky was born. That's twenty years or so after they arrive in America. The stunned life began right away. The accident just gave them a reason to curse God."

Grandma nodded at the shrine high on a kitchen shelf: porcelain Buddha and the Plaster-of-Paris Virgin Mary, fresh blood-red oranges, joss sticks, a few dried palms from Palm Sunday Mass. A bowl of water. A family of Buddhists and Catholics living under one roof.

"What about Dustin's older brothers?" I asked.

Hank jumped in. "Yes. Hiep and Thang."

"They gave themselves American names," Hank's mother said. "Hollis and Timmy. Who know where they got those names? Even Anh Ky became Dustin. A name no one has ever heard of."

"I met Timmy. Thang. Married to a Spanish woman."

Grandma nodded. "The gossips in A Dong talk of them. A drifter, that one, but I understand a decent father. His wife, a woman called Rosie, she's had to raise their kids on her own salary from McDonald's. A struggle."

"And the other brother?" I asked.

Grandma actually shivered. "Hiep. Hollis. A petty thief, I hear. The gossips in the market whisper—drugs. He was caught once or twice. In jail. Or out of jail. Out of jail now but not for long. His mother is afraid of him, so they tell me. He stole from her purse. She won't let him in the apartment. At A Dong market she was crying in the aisle."

"And what about Anh Ky?" I said.

"The baby nobody wanted," Grandma said sadly.

"And I bet he was told that over and over."

Grandma dipped her head into her chest. "When he was born and her husband was killed, she was alone with Hiep and Thang. Two wild teenagers, out of control. A little baby that cried all night. Grieving, she slept all day. The baby lay in its filth all night."

"How do you know this?" Hank asked skeptically.

Grandma's voice rose. "You think we all didn't talk then. Uncle Binh's fame in Saigon—the way he strutted in Guam—made them the subject of talk—jealousy at first, then...then mockery. 'See how they fall in America?' That kind of remark."

Hank's mother frowned. "She asked the state to take the baby away."

My jaw dropped. "Adoption?"

She waved her hands in the air. "It was a scandal we all talked of. She called people I knew, other mothers in Little Saigon. Childless families. A baby for you. Come, take him. Like you had a litter of puppies."

"No one took her up on it, I bet." Hank's face was red.

His mother nodded.

Grandma poured more tea, stared into the cup. "One time I saw her, it must have been fifteen years back, a Tet Festival at the VFW Hall. They show up, Uncle Binh in his tattered uniform. He marches in. His wife in a stained *ao dai* dress. Little Anh Ky was maybe three or so, tagging after his mother, pulling at her hem. Burying his scared face in her dress."

"Trying to get her attention?"

"I guess so."

"What did she do?"

"She ignored him. She made a joke to other women that made no one laugh. She pointed at her boy. 'Ah, the morning sickness that stays with me forever.'"

"Good Lord," I swore.

Hank summed up, "And he's probably still trying to get her attention to this day. To please her. Trang Anh Ky, cipher in the corner. 'More gruel, Mr. Bumble.'"

"And it never works," his mother said sharply. "Little Trang."

While we were talking, the kitchen door opened, and Grandpa and Hank's father walked in. They paused on the threshold, watching, listening as Hank's mother repeated her lament—"Little Trang"—and I heard Grandpa emit a low, muttered "Damn." But that was his gift to me, I knew, though it was said less convincingly than had been the case for years. Just as Hank's father had softened his dislike of impurities gracing his homestead—sipping blackberry wine on a hot summer night, we'd have long, aimless talks about homeland politics, the homeland being Vietnam—Grandpa would nod at me, acknowledge me, and one time even shook my hand. The earth moved. Planets spun out of their orbits. Hank gurgled with pleasure.

Saying nothing, Hank's mother immediately began assembling bowls of *bun*, rushing to the counter and dipping vermicelli noodles into a pot of water kept at low boil.

Grandpa, shaking his head, mumbled something about not being hungry and began shuffling toward the hallway.

But Hank's father wore a faraway look. "Trang," he echoed.

His wife's brow furrowed. "We are talking of the…accusations against the boy. The story in the paper."

He cleared his throat. "I heard you. Why do you talk about failure?"

Grandma spoke into the silence. "Rick is trying to save the boy from jail."

"Maybe he belongs there." He slid into a chair, hunched over the table, and fiddled with a pair of chopsticks. Under the overhead light his balding head gleamed.

I hesitated, but spoke up. "I want to make sure he's judged fairly."

He scoffed. "Fairly?" He punched the air. A chopstick fell out of his grasp, clattered to the floor. He pointed to the refrigerator, and his wife scurried to get him a Budweiser.

"How well do you know the Trangs?" I asked.

He waited a second, watched his wife pop the tab. "Years go by. Nothing. A chance meeting at a Tet Festival maybe." Then he shrugged his shoulders. "Uncle Binh. The evil patriot."

"What?" From Hank.

He took a swig of Budweiser, grunted his satisfaction. "The hero in the uniform. Captain from the military. Each time he talked about it, he was closer and closer to Westmoreland. An acquaintance, a friend, a loyal confidant." A harsh laugh. "Blood brothers maybe. Slicing a finger and watching the blood flow into each other's life."

"Dad," Hank began, "you don't like him?"

"A schemer, that one. How to get your hands on the gold. You know what we called him. I was in the army, too, but lowly, a grunt. We called him Buddha for Hire."

"Meaning?"

"Pockets filled with gold coins. 'A gift from Buddha,' he whispered. 'Because I honor him.' The best persimmons in the marketplace. The only slab of dried beef during the lean days at the end. 'I work for Buddha.'" He swallowed. "Buddha for hire. A greedy man."

A rustling from the hallway, Grandpa shuffling in, his face set in a scowl. He'd been listening to his son's condemning words.

"A hero," the man began. He eyed his son, his gaze hard. "To speak like you do." He spat out, *"Im di!"* Shut up.

His son faltered. "I was in the army with him."

The old man shuddered. "I don't care. A man who fought against the Cong. Uncle Ho's torture." Now he faced me, his face trembling. "Easy to forget the ugliness. Hanging by your feet. Bleeding. Scrunched in bamboo cages that wouldn't hold a small monkey."

"Grandpa," Hank broke in, "that was long ago."

He yelled at his grandson. "That was yesterday. Today."

"You knew the family?" I asked, curious.

"Uncle Binh and his wife were from a village a few kilometers from Vung Tau, two hours from Saigon. His brother's family, too. We—we—were in Saigon, but when the North overran us like animals breaking free in the barnyard, Binh went and got his brother's family. Americans swept through there, then the Cong. Bloodbath. A burnt-out village."

"And now?" I asked him. "What's left there?"

He debated what to answer. Then, quietly, "Cousins and aunts, maybe an old aunt, now living in one house. The Commies gave them *one* house. A meager farm. Binh sends money back. What little he has. We all do. We send money back. He has to. We have to. Packages of medicine. Bayer's Aspirin."

Hank questioned his grandmother. "That's what you mean—their eyes still long for that village?"

But Grandpa answered. "They think it's still a place with jack fruit toppling into your lap. The lazy afternoon eating chicken and crunching the bones underfoot. Peace. You know, when I saw Uncle Binh in Little Saigon, maybe four, five years back, he talked of the village, of wanting to die there. His dust mingled with his ancestors. But I felt sorry for him. What about the present? I wanted to say—you live like a mole under America. You are a hero. You fought…"

Hank's mom was in a hurry to say something. "I don't understand about the boy. The trouble now. Anh Ky. This…Dustin."

Grandpa blew out his lips in a dismissive gesture. "He made the mistake of being born in a world they didn't live in."

"What does that mean?" From Hank, frustrated.

"It means, when they look at him, they see America."

"So what?" Hank said, furious.

"That's not a country they live in."

"But neither is the Vietnam of their memories," Hank said. "Try telling them that."

Chapter Thirteen

Something caught my attention as I stepped out of my car after I pulled into a space in front of Brasso's Luncheonette. A busy intersection, cars jammed at a light, but from one street over a squeaky *ka-clunk ka-clunk ka-clunk* from a passing car. Every few seconds, a rhythm. No big deal, but the sound, mixed with the other sounds of the street, made me realize I'd heard it earlier that day. Stopping at the market down on Main, rushing in, I'd heard that same annoying repetition: *ka-clunk ka-clunk ka-chunk.* I'd paid it no mind but now, already late for my lunch with Liz, there it was again.

Glancing toward a side street that ran parallel to where I parked, I caught the glimpse of an old car slinking by slowly. An unrecognizable dark car except for a right-hand passenger door painted with white primer. *Ka-clunk.*

Bothered, I hopped back into my car, steered into traffic, and rounded the corner. Cold out, I nevertheless rolled down my window and listened. Vaguely, I heard the sound up ahead. I followed. Nothing. Stuck at a light, I thought I heard it in the distance, but wondered: What am I doing? I tracked back, circled the block, but found nothing.

My phone beeped. Liz, texting:

> Where R U? I'm here waiting. Everyone's late. I saw you parking then nothing. Off you go.

I swerved out of traffic, did a risky U-turn, and got back to the restaurant. Alone at a front table, Liz waved at me through the window.

"Am I losing my mind?" Her first words to me as she smiled lazily. "Didn't I just see you…?"

"No, I *may* be losing *my* mind. I thought…never mind."

"Ah, the two words most remembered from our brief marriage."

I grinned. "I do?"

"Never mind."

I leaned in to give her a peck on the cheek.

"This is going to be interesting," she commented, pointing over my shoulder toward the entrance. Hank and Dustin were walking in, Dustin trailing a few steps behind Hank, who was nervous and kept looking back at the boy.

Hank had called me earlier that morning, checking in, and surprised me by saying that Dustin had become a regular caller. "A chatterbox," Hank had laughed. "In person he's quiet, morose sometimes, a goddamn Sphinx, but on the phone, late at night or early morning, he has a lot to say."

"Like what?"

"It's like he never had a chance to use his voice—or to have anyone listen to him—and so he rattles on like a faucet that won't turn off."

"I'm sorry."

"I'm not, Rick. He only reaches me when I'm not working, of course, but also when I want to talk to him. I think it's important…"

I'd interrupted. "And has he told you the true story of his battle with Ben?"

I could hear him laugh. "I ask him."

"And he says?"

"The same nonsense. A spy. Maybe a spy who changed his mind. The spy who came in from the cold. Variations on a theme—this boy is hard to rattle. He's like a smoldering firecracker. Impossible to read."

"He *is* aware the cops suspect him of murder?"

"It doesn't seem to cross his mind. It's because he doesn't believe anyone would think he's a killer."

"You better shake him up a bit."

Then he told me Dustin had agreed to lunch. "I told him we gotta talk."

Impulsively I'd said, "I'm meeting Liz at Brasso's at noon."

"We'll join you."

I'd hesitated. "Liz does want to meet him, but this may not be the best time."

"There'll never be a better time," Hank had said. "Getting Dustin to say okay to lunch was a monumental decision. I won't give him a choice. Maybe we'll learn something."

"Yeah, the sound of silence."

Now, settling into seats, coats draped over the backs of chairs, Dustin sat next to me and faced Liz, while Hank sat next to Liz. Only Liz was smiling. Hank was staring at Dustin's blank face, and I was nodding at Hank. Liz extended her hand to Dustin, introducing herself; his handshake was so tentative and weak he could have been checking the direction of the wind.

Small talk was engineered by Liz, funny and trivial, often directed at Hank or me, but with slight humorous and gentle turns with Dustin. He was clearly befuddled by the exchanges. Watching him with sidelong glances, I could tell he was interested, showing a twitch of his lips when Liz gave him attention. The upturned chin. The flicker of his eyes. The large ears getting a tinge of color. His fingers tapped the bridge of his eyeglasses. A slight hesitant smile when she teased him about the company he kept.

"Dustin," Liz began, "do you like this place?"

His head swept around the room, his eyes staying on a huge wall mural that depicted romantic landscapes from a sentimentalized Italian countryside. "I've never been in a fancy place like this."

Hank started to say something about Brasso's—a mom-and-pop eatery with red-and-white checkered tablecloths and dripping candles in wicker Chianti bottles, a giant clock over the ovens in the shape of a pizza—but Liz forestalled him. "Then I'm glad your first time is with us."

He smiled at her. "I'm used to…like Burger King. The diner I used to work at." He made a fatalistic whatever gesture. "They told me not to come in anymore."

She went on in a smooth voice, "Relax, okay. You're among friends."

He started at that word, peered into her face, but that sweet smile reappeared.

"You smell like flowers," he said abruptly.

"Lilacs," she said. "Do you know that flower?"

He shook his head. "I heard of it."

"You like it?"

"I don't know." Then he seemed apologetic. "Yes."

"You don't have to like everything about your friends," she told him.

"Yes, you do." A blunt, quick answer. Hank turned his head, surprised.

"He's wearing something." Dustin was indicating me with a flick of his wrist. "I don't like that."

Hank had been taking a sip of water and now, caught off-guard, sputtering, let the water dribble out of the corners of his mouth. "Old Spice," he laughed. "Rick wears Old Spice."

"It smells like old people."

I sat back, watching Hank's utter delight at Dustin's frankness. Finally, I said. "When I was first in America, maybe thirteen years old, I lived in New Jersey with American parents. My father wore…Old Spice. I liked it. It was American, and I was desperate to be American. So, sort of for sentimental reasons I sometimes buy myself a bottle of Old Spice at Christmas time. For old time's sake."

That seemed to make no sense to Dustin who stared at me, unblinking.

"Do you cook, Dustin?" Liz asked, shifting the talk.

He waited a bit, sizing up the question. "No. A little. I make rice. Sometimes a burger. At home."

"Your mom doesn't cook?" Hank asked.

He shook his head. "She makes a big pot of rice, you know, like in a rice steamer. It's always there. Rice, I mean. I help myself. She doesn't like cooking."

"What does she do?" Hank asked.

Dustin contorted his mouth. "She watches TV."

I noticed Dustin staring at Liz's hands—her slender hands with two small rings on her right hand. A red ruby and dark green jade. My presents, years ago. Manicured nails—once a week at Le Salon on Main Street—painted a delicate rose shade. His eyes drifted to her face, and he blinked slowly. She was dressed in a light blue sweater, a string of pearls around her neck. Dustin was obviously enjoying the look.

He sat in baggy khaki trousers, bunched over brown work boots. An oversized rust-colored sweater, so big it exposed bony shoulders. No shirt on underneath. Poorly chopped hair that convinced me he scissored his own hair, and not very well.

"Dustin," she said slowly, "I've never seen you at any Vietnamese functions."

That surprised him. "You go to them?"

She nodded quickly. "Tet celebrations at the VFW Hall in East Hartford. Every year."

"Why?" A puzzled look, then, "I used to go when I was small. With my mother. I don't remember much about them."

"You don't go any longer?"

He shook his head vigorously. "No."

"Hank likes to dance," she said mischievously as she poked Hank's arm. She mimicked a cha-cha-cha rhythm, and grinned.

"They don't dance there," Dustin said quickly. He glanced at Hank.

She laughed. "I know. But that doesn't stop him."

Dustin grinned.

"Liz can make a mean happy pancake. *Banh xeo*." I stressed the words. "She's a whiz with rice powder."

He squinted his eyes. "*Banh xeo*. You?"

"But usually it turns out unhappily."

He waited a bit. "How do you know...them." A pause. "Him."

The *him* was obviously me, given Dustin's quick glance at me. The *him* in question answered. "Liz and I were once married."

He shot a look from Liz to me, his neck jerking forward, an expression on his face that communicated disbelief that her radiant lilacs once flourished in the ethereal atmosphere of my old-folks-home Old Spice.

"Then why are you sitting here?"

"Because we love each other."

Dustin considered that but lifted his chin, a doubting gesture. "I don't understand."

Liz smiled at him. "Sometimes people find out they're better with each other when they're not married."

"We were very young," I added. "In college. Intoxicated. Bad timing."

Liz was watching me closely. "Yes, bad timing." A chuckle in her voice. "I couldn't deal with Rick becoming a cop..."

Dustin yelled, "You're a cop?"

"Not any longer."

"I am," Hank said.

"I know that. But I thought..."

"I'm a private investigator now. Former cop."

Liz laughed out loud. "And formerly married to me."

Dustin seemed puzzled. "But you love each other?"

"Madly," Liz beamed. "In all meanings of that word. Or— insanely. As in—animal crackers."

"Wild." Dustin's final comment, shaking his head. "I don't know if I believe any of this." He narrowed his eyes. "People make up stories all the time."

"I save my lies for insignificant things," Liz told him, then smiled. "What about you? Do you want to get married some day?"

He nodded. "Yeah, of course. I plan on it."

"Good for you."

But Dustin was already speaking over her words. "I've thought about it. I'd like five children." He counted them off on his fingertips.

Hank whooped it up. "Five, Dustin? You already planned…"

Dustin beamed. "Yes, it will happen." His fingers turned into a fist that he rested in his lap.

"What if your wife protests?"

He stared into Hank's face. "A wife has to do what a husband wants her to do."

The words hung in the air as Liz, Hank, and I exchanged glances. Liz, mouth agape, started to say something but stopped, stupefied. Hank, rocking in his chair, was flicking his eyes like a mischievous child. I waited for the next line.

"What?" From Liz, finally.

"Yes."

"Do you have a girlfriend?"

"No. Not yet."

She tapped the table, a rapid Morse code I could easily interpret. "You're gonna find it hard to find a wife who obeys your every command, Dustin." But her words were soft, smiling, gentle.

"I know. I'll go back to Vietnam."

"Still…" She persisted. "Dustin, women have a right to their own lives. You do know that?"

He was shaking his head, a little unsure of himself now. Quickly, like an agitated rabbit, he bit the corner of a fingernail.

"I suppose you can tell her what to eat?"

He nodded. "I order the food."

"If she wants steak."

"I choose what she eats."

Liz, frustrated. "Dustin, someday you and I have to have a long talk."

That pleased him, and he beamed at her. But Hank, grimacing, leaned into him. "Dustin, you gotta look out at the world you live in."

Dustin quoted something in Vietnamese, which perplexed Liz.

Hank repeated it, and then translated: "*Ong an cha ba an nem.* Sort of—men get the meat, women get the bread. My loose translation in the interest of personal safety." He nodded at Liz.

We ordered food in silence. Dustin pointed to spaghetti and meatballs on the menu. "With a Coke." Liz ordered the lunch special of pasta alla vodka. When it arrived, Dustin stared at the dish and then asked, "Whiskey?"

Liz laughed. "A little vodka goes a long way."

"People shouldn't drink." He scrunched up his face.

"Well, I'm hardly getting plastered at happy hour, Dustin."

His face reddened. "I only mean…not you. I mean, people. Drinking."

Out of the corner of my eye I watched as he ate his lunch. An incredibly meticulous boy, precise. He maneuvered his napkin under the knife and fork, positioning it so that it was straight. Then, when the food arrived, following our lead, he placed the cloth napkin on his lap, once again aligning it, smoothing the edges. Everything about him was ordered, mechanical. Sitting with an erect spine, he brought the fork to his lips with the precision of a submarine torpedo. Fascinating to watch, this routine, so careful an execution it seemed robotic—and alarming. He cut his strands of spaghetti into small pieces, measured, moving his way from one corner of the dish to the other with the frightful calculation of Sherman marching to the sea. We all watched him, surreptitiously, though I caught Liz's eye once or twice. Periodically, he would dab at his lips, a gentility that struck me as a gesture he'd appropriated from some TV show he'd seen. When he was through, he sat back, folded his hands on the table.

"Thank you." The words said to no one in particular.

Liz smiled at him and then, in a sudden gesture, reached across the table and grasped the back of his wrist. It was so sudden that Dustin jerked his hand back, let out a faint yelp as if hit by an electric shock and dropped his hand into his lap. Liz watched him closely.

She was smiling at him.

"What do you do?" Dustin asked her.

"I'm a psychologist."

He drew his mouth into a thin line. "So that's why you're here? To analyze me?"

She shook her head. "No, I'm here to have lunch with friends. I don't analyze friends." Then glancing at me, "Although I do psychoanalyze ex-husbands." A high laugh. "I have to—by court order."

I leaned into Dustin. "True. She has to. It's part of the Geneva Convention. Rules of war."

He seemed confused. "I'm not crazy."

"No one said you are," Liz noted. "I'd say you're a very intelligent young man."

"You think so?" Pleased.

"Of course."

"My brothers call me stupid."

"Your brothers?" she asked. "How many?"

"Two. A lot older. But they don't talk to me."

"What does your mother say about that?"

His eyes blinked furiously. "She doesn't care. She doesn't like them much either. One can't even come into the house anymore."

"Why is that?"

He didn't answer. But I could see him relaxing, his shoulders slumping, his eyes warm as he watched Liz. He was trying to please her. At times Hank and I seemed not there at all, the two of them chitchatting like old friends. She asked him about school, about Bristol, about the job he just lost, a rambling question-and-answer run that he had no problem with, but he recoiled when asked about his friends.

"I got none."

"What about Darijo?" I asked. "I've seen you with him. The Bosniak boy."

"We're not really friends. Like we don't hang out or anything."

"But I've seen you sitting with him."

A puzzled look on his face. "He's like…alone there, too. So we…you know, sit together. It's…" He shrugged. "I guess you could call him sort of a friend. But I've never been to his house or anything."

"He come to yours?"

He shuddered and let out a phony laugh. "God, no. He might bump into my brother or somebody. I wouldn't do that to…" His voice trailed off.

Liz turned to me. "I do have to go." She started to gather her purse, her gloves. "Dustin, could you walk me to my car? It's snowing."

In a body we all looked out the window at the wispy snow squall. Barely there. But Liz's words suggested we'd suddenly been dropped willy-nilly into Superman's Fortress of Solitude in the icebound Arctic. Towers of ice blocked her path.

Dustin jumped up, inordinately happy, beaming, thrusting his arm into the sleeve of his coat. Then, gentlemanly, he grabbed Liz's coat, held it out so she could slip into it. She took it from him.

"I can put my own coat on, Dustin."

Startled, he handed it to her.

"But thank you." She smiled at him.

He smiled back at her.

Liz waited a second, then said goodbye—"I think Rick is paying for lunch, right?"—and the two of them walked away. Dustin's eyes never left her face, his head nodding up and down.

I shook my head. "Liz has charmed another."

Hank's eyes twinkled. "She's already begun the re-education of that boy." He made a face. "No one is gonna walk me to my car."

"I'll do it, Hank. I wouldn't want you to get lost in the blizzard out there."

"Thanks, but I'm the one usually leading you around." He craned his neck to see Liz and Dustin. "Does Liz always solve all your cases, Rick?"

"Only the hard ones."

Chapter Fourteen

The voice on the phone squeaked, words swallowed so that I had to keep saying, "Who is it?" to the point of absurdity. Finally, I heard "Phan Binh Suong," followed by "Anh Ky's aunt." Uncle Binh's wife. Trang Ky Binh. "Yes. You know me?"

"I know who you are."

"It is important that we speak to you about the boy." A pause. "My husband Binh told me to call. He hears horrible stories."

"I understand. Dustin is in trouble."

"Trouble," she echoed. "No one wants trouble. We are quiet people."

"I understand."

"You will come here?"

"Of course."

A deep sigh of relief, a few muttered words as she covered the phone and spoke to someone nearby. When she came back on the line, her voice was more assured, louder. Carefully articulated English, a practiced inflection. "I will give you the address now."

Uncle Binh and Aunt Suong lived in the basement apartment of a three-family house two streets away from the housing project where Binh's sister-in-law lived with Dustin. A tired street of old three-family, pre-World War II carbon copy homes, lost in the shadow of the projects. A dead-end street that led to a chain-linked out-of-business auto parts factory where, if I could judge by the rusted metal shells dumped there, stolen cars were stripped and abandoned.

I pulled my car into the back lot of the Binh home, a haphazardly plowed narrow lot, parked it alongside an old Chevy up on cinder blocks. Rusted fenders and open windows—snow and old tires filled the back seat.

The house sloped down to the right, so that the owners had converted the basement into a walk-out apartment, its unshoveled sidewalk hazardous with packed-down snow and patches of frozen ice. A plastic snow shovel rested against a cellar doorway.

Aunt Suong opened the door before I could knock, a worried look on her face. "You are Vietnamese?"

"Yes, I am."

She was confused. "Yes, but those blue eyes. The…"

"My father was white."

"No one told us."

"Is it important?"

She faltered. "Of course not." A nervous glance over her shoulder. "Come in. Please."

A tiny woman, bony, stoop-shouldered, with a gaunt, long face with high cheekbones. Large dark eyes, alert and wary, clashed with her small mouth. A feeble smile revealed glittery false teeth. Salt-and-pepper hair pulled into a careless clump at the back, secured with a red ribbon. She shuffled as she walked, her shoulders rocking back and forth. Maybe in her mid-sixties, maybe older.

"Sit here." She pointed to a worn sofa under the South Vietnamese flag tacked to a plaster wall. Left and right of it hung tourist-market pastels of old Saigon. A small, dank room, low-ceilinged, with a run of exposed pipes overhead. I sensed the weight of three floors above this cavern. Only one lamp was on, which threw most of the room into shadow. Scatter rugs covered a black-and-white tile floor. A stingy world. Gorky's lower depths. Purgatory.

She called out. "He's here."

I looked toward a small hallway that led to a kitchen and a bedroom. Leaning against a wall was a wheelchair and a pair of crutches. She followed my gaze.

"My husband suffers still."

"I'm sorry."

She shook her head. "A moment in time and you pay for it forever."

I didn't know what to say to that, so I said nothing. But I soon heard the labored steps of Uncle Binh, a pitter-patter sound of a child learning to walk. He paused in the doorway as he held the doorjamb, caught his breath, and nodded at me. "Mr. Lam." He spoke in Vietnamese. *"Xin chao."* Hello.

I answered him, returning the greeting and adding my thanks. *"Cam on."* I waited a second. *"Ban co biet noi tieng Anh knong?"* Do you speak English?

Aunt Suong was surprised. "You speak…"

"A little." I shrugged.

"A language that breaks my heart." Her lips quivered.

Binh took small difficult steps into the room, finally settling himself slowly into a side chair. He grunted, exhausted.

"Some days are worse than others." He had a thick accent, almost impenetrable, and finally drifted into Vietnamese. *"Ai bao troi khong co mat."* A bitter laugh as he offered his own English translation. "It is easy to forget that God can see you."

Aunt Suong mumbled something about hot tea—"Of course, tea, of course"— and moved toward the kitchen. She returned with a tray and poured tea into small decorated Chinese cups. I thanked her. Jasmine tea, strong, fragrant. The whole time Uncle Binh said nothing, staring at me over tented fingers held in front of his chin.

Like his wife, Binh was tiny, barely five feet tall, with the same drawn look in his eyes. But he had a flat moon face, a round head on a skinny neck, so that he seemed in danger of having his head wobble, fall like a balloon loosed from a string. Cheap green work pants, a blue denim shirt. On his head the red beret I associated with soldiers of the failed republic. But battered now, stained.

"Drafts," he said, a wheezing smile. "I carried it with me the day we fled."

Suong shook her head. "Foolish."

He shot her a look that was more indifferent than angry.

"You live close to your sister-in-law," I said to Binh. "A few streets away."

Suong answered me. "Section 8 housing. Poor people."

Binh narrowed his eyes. "You got to live somewhere."

"Are you a close family?"

"Yes. Who else do we have?" Suong waved her fingers in the air.

Binh's voice suddenly got strong. "It's our hope to die in Vietnam. To return to the village of my father…"

Suong smiled. "All of our dream. Of course."

Binh continued, "It would be nice if, like Russia, the Commies fail."

"You can return now," I said. "Vietnam is open to travel—to returning…" I stopped because Binh was shaking his head.

"Ah, yes," Binh sneered. "But the Communists still rule, though they can't rule over a dead man in the family graveyard. My dead body has no politics."

"True," I agreed. "But…"

"Of course, I cannot wear my uniform." He pointed to a far wall lost in shadows, where I could see a green uniform hanging off a hook. "I can still fit into it." A laugh that dissolved into choking that went on too long. He straightened himself in the chair. "Somehow my uniformed body will thumb my nose at the Commies. A senior officer, you know. I worked with Westmoreland."

"When do you plan to return?"

They nodded at each other, and Suong answered. "Someday."

"Relatives there?"

"Everybody has relatives there." Peeved at the question, she looked at her husband. "Everybody. Cousins in his village. Near mine. Outside Vung Tao. Neighbors. A struggling life there, everybody in one house. The Northerners permit that."

Binh was fussing. "But…peaceful. Quiet. The water buffalo in the morning. Afternoons under the banyan trees. Laughter.

Families smile at each other, bring children into the world and then watch the old people die happy."

I waited a moment. "I hope you get your dream."

Suong's voice had an edge. "It isn't hope, Mr. Lam—it's fact. We will return."

Binh pointed to the kitchen, lost in darkness. "Buddha is the answer. We suffer here"—his hand swept the room—"suffering, suffering. The pain in my body from the American machine that fell on me. But Buddha answers." Again he pointed.

High in a corner of the kitchen, murky in shadows, an obligatory shrine to Buddha. A shaft of light from a window in the room illuminated the head of a plaster Buddha, disembodied, lost in clouds.

Suong smiled at me. "Our Buddha talks to us." She paused, lapsed into Vietnamese: "*Cai kho lo cai khon*. You understand?"

I nodded. "Suffering will bring wisdom." I sat back, sipped the tea. "Dustin." I paused. "Anh Ky."

"Madness." Suong threw out the word, her English shrill.

"Why are you doing this?" From Binh.

Flummoxed, I stared into his face. "You mean investigating?"

He fluttered his hands. "What is going on? Our family is caught in this…"

"Madness," Suong finished again, an English word completing his Vietnamese sentence.

"I want to prove your nephew innocent of murder."

"Murder," Suong screeched. "That boy? Are you crazy?"

Uncle Binh cleared his throat. "You know, we don't understand this…this thing. Who is this teacher that died?"

"Ben Winslow. And he was murdered."

"Yes, yes." Suong rushed her words. "But the police come to their house, and they scare her. She runs to us for help. They tear apart the place."

"Well, Dustin—Anh Ky—had been having a fight with the professor. Some disagreement."

"And you kill a teacher for that?" Binh's words ended in a raspy cough.

"Dustin won't say what the fight was about."

Suong shrugged. "Maybe it was nothing. A grade on a paper."

I sipped my tea. "Dustin has conflicting stories. He's lying to the cops. To me."

Binh swallowed. "A boy that's trouble." His eyes rested on the wheelchair as he sighed deeply.

"How?" A trace of anger crept into my voice.

He shrugged. "You know. He comes out of nowhere, born out of nowhere."

"His mother Mai goes into labor during a snowstorm, no midwife like before, the old days…and…"

"And her husband dies on the highway." Uncle Binh's fingers stroked his chin.

"Not Dustin's fault."

"A mistake baby." He shot a glance at his wife.

"I'm tired of hearing that," I said hotly. "He's an intelligent, clever boy."

Suong raised her hand in my face as she chuckled. "We were surprised he went to school."

"You mean the college?"

Binh spoke in English, his accent thicker now. "No one ever sees him."

I waited a heartbeat. "That's true. No one ever does see him."

Suong weighed my words, then said, "He runs from the house. School, he finds a job, he hides in the library all night. He locks himself in his bedroom. Like a criminal."

"He earned himself a scholarship."

Her wave dismissed that fact. "Yes, his high school pushed that for him. And now he is mentioned on TV. Like on *Cops*. The face of evil. In the newspaper we do not read. Pictures of the police at Mai's house. The world upside down."

"If you could get Dustin to tell us—tell the cops—what was going on."

A harsh laugh from Suong. "You think we got power over that boy?"

"What do you want from me?" I asked finally, finishing the last of my tea. "You asked me to come here today."

They exchanged looks, then Suong said slowly, "Make this go away. First, you stop…pushing that boy. With your questions. Your friend, the state cop. Police everywhere. His mother comes to us for answers. You—tell them to—*stop*."

"I can't do that." I waited a second. "Don't you want his name cleared?"

Suong squeaked out, her English almost unintelligible, "But he didn't do nothing. No name to clear."

"That's not how it works. The police…"

Smugly, a breathy voice. "Will find the killer. Not you."

"I'm not tracking a killer. I'm trying to clear that boy."

"What's the difference?" From Binh, agitated.

Soung's voice was sharp, her face contorted. "His mother, you know, is a fool. She expects a son to be a son. Dutiful. Good. Not…this." She stood up and disappeared into the bedroom, returning with a small sheaf of flyers. "This."

She handed me a flyer from the Gospel of Wealth Ministry. Expensive paper, glossy, a toothsome smile on the Reverend Simms' fat face.

"What?" I asked. "What are you telling me?"

Her voice rippled with laughter. "We go to this big church. The three of us. Mai, Anh Ky's mother. Us. We find strange comfort there. We are Buddhists"—a nod in the direction of the shrine—"and that is our heart. But the minister comforts. A whole lot of Vietnamese go, sit in a group."

"I'm not following this? You follow Buddha and Jesus Christ."

"The Reverend Simms says there is no problem. One the path to peace, the other the path to heaven. Suffering, then peace."

I stared at the flyer in my hand. "He said that if Dustin killed Ben it was the work of goodness, God's hand striking down the Satanic infidel."

"It has to go away." Finality in Binh's words. He closed his eyes as though it would all disappear. "Nobody knocking on their door."

"This!" yelled Suong, pointing to the words on the flyer. "This is what comes of that murder. Anh Ky on TV. This new flyer!"

I read: "The Enemy Outside, the Enemy Within: Satan's Henchman Slain by the Sword of God."

"Lord," I said under my breath.

"Yes, yes." Suong pushed the paper at me. "Take it, take it. You see what we mean? This coming Saturday night he gives a sermon on that teacher's murder. His enemy. A man who attacked him for years. Mocked his ministry." A weary sigh that was almost a sob. "We are afraid he will mention Anh Ky again. Our family dragged through the dirt. Fingers that point. We are afraid of that."

"Will you go?" I asked.

Binh flicked his eyes. "Yes, maybe. If he sees us—our faces—maybe he will not shame us."

I tucked the flyer into my breast pocket. "He promises to make the poor rich."

"Hope." From Binh.

Suong leaned into me, her palms out, a plea. "Disgrace for our family. We have so little but—pride. Do you see that?"

A sharp rat-a-tat on the door, but only I jumped. Neither moved, but the door swung open. Two men walked in. I recognized Timmy, Dustin's married brother. Another man behind him, shorter, but pushing against Timmy's back.

Without saying a word, both men slipped into chairs and focused on me. "You again?" From Timmy, a smile on his face.

"Timmy."

"You remember my name?"

"Yes." I checked out the other man. "And you must be Hiep."

A cigarette grunt. "Hollis." A cough. "Yeah."

Timmy grumbled at his aunt, "Didn't know you got company."

Suong's voice was wispy. "We called him. You know…to stop…"

"Bullshit." Timmy pounded a fist into his palm. "You fuckin' crazy? Butting in our business."

I kept still, watching the brothers. Timmy's enormous belly peeked out of his flannel shirt. A cheap plaid jacket tight in the shoulders. But Hollis was rail thin, wiry, with a ferret's narrow pointed face and dull dark eyes. Sallow skin, someone who shunned sunlight. A neck plastered with prison tattoos. Some sort of Chinese symbol over an eyebrow. He wore an unzipped parka over a T-shirt, and his wrists, exposed, revealed a wealth of zigzag tattoos.

"Your little brother…" I began, but stopped, alarmed by Hollis' contorted face.

"A piece of shit, that fucker." Hollis' voice was mechanical, dragging. Said, the words seemed to make him smile, and I saw broken teeth. He reached into a pocket and took out a cigarette, snapped on a lighter. Smoke covered his face.

"Hiep," Suong pleaded, "I told you—not in the house…no."

He ignored her. He blew a smoke ring into the air, watched it. "I ain't allowed in mom's house, so you gotta put up with all my vices."

Timmy waved away smoke that blew in his face. "Anh Ky is trouble. Always."

"Did he ever tell you about his beef with Professor Winslow?"

Hollis snickered. "Who the hell talks to that boy? I ain't heard nothing." Hollis widened his eyes. "Fuck him."

Suong was waiting to speak. "You see, Mr. Lam, what has happened in America? The children become godless. They curse." She shook her hand at Hollis who muttered under his breath.

"But not Dustin," I said purposely.

"The most godless of them all."

"He doomed this family," Timmy said.

Hollis was nodding. "Look around you, man. Look around this fleabag of a place. Some families is…like they're doomed. It's the way it is."

"I don't buy that."

He sneered at me. "I don't give a fuck what you buy."

Timmy spoke over his words. "They"—he pointed at his aunt

and uncle—"they rush to that money-bags preacher and think money will flow into their pockets. Look around you."

Suong protested. "Comfort, that Reverend Simms."

"If you want money you gotta get it yourself. God ain't gonna help you."

Uncle Binh was listening to all this, but nervously, his arm twitching, and his jaw kept dropping. His eyes watery, he breathed in. "Stop this. All of you. " He narrowed his eyes at Hollis. "Yeah, what you got—jail for selling drugs on the corner."

Hollis was unfazed. Idly, he blew smoke rings into the air.

Suong, flustered, stood up quickly, rocked left, then right, then said angrily, "A family is never doomed."

"You got that wrong." Hollis was actually smiling.

Suong was becoming increasingly nervous. "Maybe you have to leave now."

I stood up. "I still don't know why you asked me here."

For the first time her voice got ugly. "To *stop* this. You know the police. Tell them to stop talking to Anh Ky." Her voice broke at the end.

Hollis watched me. Absently, he scratched his chest through his shirt. His head jerked back and forth. Like a meth user, I thought.

He pointed a finger at me. "Doomed." He started to laugh.

Chapter Fifteen

Dustin Trang surprised me. Sitting in the adjunct faculty office, I'd been dreamily marking final exams, getting ready to leave to do some Christmas shopping, when I heard the tentative knock. Dustin was standing on one foot, balancing himself, adjusting the book bag on his shoulders, while curiously picking lint off the ratty sweater he wore.

"I finished my final exam with Professor Laramie."

I waited. He watched me, one nervous finger still picking at the fabric.

"Is that your last one?"

"They don't want me here on campus."

"Why do you say that?"

"Everybody looks at me, you know. People stop walking to watch me."

"Come in."

He moved by me and took a seat. Strangely, he kept his book bag slung over his shoulder, forcing him to sit awkwardly, his body tipped to the side. His winter coat was open, a pair of gloves protruding from one pocket, a knit cap stuck in the other.

He avoided me, his eyes sailing left, then right, unable to focus.

"What's up, Dustin?"

"You went to Uncle Binh's house." The declarative words were too loud, laced with question. "Everybody is unhappy."

"They invited me there."

"Why?"

"They didn't tell you?"

"Yeah, I know." A hint of a smile. "The on-going troubles with Anh Ky Trang, boy blunder."

I raised my voice. "Stop that, Dustin. For Christ's sake, don't put yourself down like that."

His eyes fluttered. "They think because you're investigating things—for me, I guess—they think it causes *more* problems. More TV crap. You know, more..."

"They want this all to go away."

He spoke quickly. "So do I."

"But it won't until Ben's murderer is arrested."

Dustin flinched as he looked back to the doorway as if someone were there, eavesdropping. "I didn't do it."

"I know that. But I also know you're holding back information." I counted a heartbeat. "Are you protecting someone, Dustin?"

He sat up, startled. "That's...like nonsense."

"Is it?"

He stood up, pulled his overcoat around his chest, though immediately it fell back open. "They're angry."

"Uncle Binh and Aunt Suong?"

He nodded. "They said you won't listen to reason. I had to go there last night and talk to them."

"I met Timmy again. Even Hollis."

A grunt. "Yeah, the ex-con."

"They're not nice folks."

A harsh giggle escaped his throat. "Yeah, like understatement of the year. I avoid them. Or they avoid me. Hollis was in jail for...like five or six years. Now he's back. Jackass of all trades. Low-rent heroin dealer in the shadow of Bristol Mall."

"Then he's gonna go back to jail again."

He made an invisible check mark in the air. "The sooner the better."

"And Timmy?"

"He's all right. Just dumb. The only thing that makes him happy is the all-you-can-eat buffet at Tokyo Szechuan, him and his fat wife. Two Buddha look-alikes gnawing at the crab legs."

I laughed. "He could be doing worse things."

He was through talking. "Whatever."

He backed up, bumped into the doorframe.

"Dustin, your family wants me to stop investigating. Me and Hank. Do you want me to stop?"

His tongue rolled over his lower lip. "No."

"Then I won't."

"I like Hank," he said flatly. "He listens to me."

"He's a good guy."

"I never knew a cop before. I was always afraid of them."

"Is that a problem?"

He didn't answer at first. Then, mumbled words, "And, you know, that…Liz. Your like…she was your wife. She's funny."

But suddenly he smiled, seemingly embarrassed by his sputtered words. Quick footsteps shuffled down the hallway.

David Laramie materialized, his hand on the doorjamb but his face peering down the hallway, doubtless tracking Dustin's departure. He wore a scowl on his face and seemed out of breath.

"He showed up for his final."

"And that's a problem, Professor? I heard he was enrolled in your class, no?"

Another quick glance down the hallway. A student passed behind him, and he started, flinched. "Don't you think he should be suspended?"

I stared into the petulant face. Haggard, a pale face not uncommon with instructors at the end of finals. But Laramie was squirrely, his hair sticking out in a brushy clump at the back, as though he'd napped in his office beforehand and neglected to look into a mirror. Idly, he brushed his hair back with his fingertips, a gesture that simply made other parts of his hair stand on end.

My fingers tapped my pile of exams. "He's not been arrested."

"But he will be."

"How do you know that?"

"I don't *know* anything. Frankly, when he walked into my exams, some students gasped. I didn't know what to do."

"What did you do?"

"I let him take the exam. I'm not a fool." He checked the hallway again, his head flicking nervously back and forth.

"What do you want from me?"

Another glance into the hallway. "I'm scared of him."

"There's no reason to be."

His voice boomed. "I saw him watching me once or twice during the exam. I swear, I got chills. That face. Those eyes. Like...like he was thinking of what I told the cops."

"And to the press. Don't forget that interview. Maybe you should have kept your mouth shut." I looked down at my pile of exams.

I stood up, dropped the exams into a folder, and gathered my laptop, my briefcase, dropping a book inside. I snapped it shut. He was waiting for me to say something. "What?"

"We have to see that he is removed from campus."

"I'll protest."

"You're adjunct." A nervous smile. "You got no vote."

"I still have a mouth." I reached for my coat. "Look, David. You stoked the fires with your hatred of Ben Winslow."

"That has nothing to do with what happened."

"I wonder how much you baited Dustin, dragged information out of him, stroked his insecurities, played a game with his life—just to get ammo to attack Ben Winslow." I walked past him. "What measure of guilt should you have in Ben's death, Professor Laramie? Think about it."

I brushed by him, our shoulders touching. He pulled back against the doorframe. I could smell his breath: hot, raw. A face filled suddenly with fear—of me.

"Maybe you should move." I looked back over my shoulder. "You're standing in the draft."

• • ● • •

Rattled, I walked into the College Union for a cup of coffee. Nearly empty at that hour, a few students drifting in and out, most in their dorms or finishing exams, two students loudly arguing over some terrorist incident, one electric-haired boy jabbing the other's chest to make his point. The other, an ex-marine I recognized from one of my classes, recently returned from a third go-round in Iraq, kept grunting in the other's face. Both were enjoying themselves, given the escalating heat of the argument.

I sat on a couch near the rec lounge and spotted Dustin knocking balls on a billiards table. Three pool tables, only Dustin in the room, slamming balls into pockets with exacting concentration, his small body leaning over the table, a careful assessment of a shot, then the whack of ball against ball. The *clack clack* sound of balls dropping into a pocket. He moved around the table slowly, occasionally pushing up the bulky sleeves of his sweater, though the sleeves kept slipping back down. He set up another rack, stood watching the table, and then broke.

"Lone wolf." A voice from behind me. Brandon Thanh Vinh, looking into the rec room over my shoulder. "Portrait of a killer at large."

I bristled. "All right, Brandon, cool it."

"A celebrity, that loser. On TV. An Internet meme nobody needs."

"Leave him alone."

Emboldened, he swaggered into the room and waited while Dustin, glancing up for a moment, ignored him, aiming his house cue at a ball and sending it into a pocket.

"Bam," Dustin said too loudly. He sneered at Brandon.

Brandon cleared his throat, glanced back at me, the unwanted Greek chorus witnessing this standoff. He reached for a cue on the wall, waved it grandly in the air, barely missing Dustin's head, and announced, "Eight ball. You and me. Now."

Dustin hesitated. "No."

"Coward. Mama's boy."

"You're on, Brandon."

"You a betting boy? Betting you won't be charged for murder? Maybe? One game. I'll play you for what you got in your pocket. If you're betting, you gotta post up your money."

Dustin reached into his jeans pockets and pulled out loose bills. A few nickels and dimes fell onto the floor. Slowly he counted out money, mostly dollar bills, wrinkled and wadded. He straightened them out with his palm.

"I only got nineteen."

Brandon threw a sidelong glance at me, and crowed, "Like I tell the world. Some people go through life a dollar short." He flashed a twenty-dollar bill and laid it on a side table.

Dustin placed his bills on top of Brandon's crisp twenty, evening out the edges. "Yes or no?"

"Play."

Dustin caught my eye—a sliver of a smile as he flicked his head toward Brandon. "Asshole," he muttered. He gathered the balls, feeding them into the rack and positioning it on the foot spot. He deliberated, adjusted the rack, squinted at it. He stood back, one hand gripping the cue stick, the other scratching his shoulder nervously. An antsy glance at the money on the nearby table.

Brandon circled the table, his eyes never leaving Dustin, a cruel smile on his face. "I'll spot you the break, killer boy."

Dustin breathed in, shot a glance at me. Again that quirky smile. His fingers trembled on the pool cue. He made a couple practice strokes, then threw his body into the break, a clean follow-through. The cue ball exploded the rack. He stood back, back arched, watching them spin chaotically across the green felt. A ten ball careened off the rails, lazily sailed back across the table, and dropped into a pocket.

"Stripes," he announced.

"Like the one down your back." Brandon bowed, happy with his line.

"Asshole."

Dustin eyed the table and squinted at a twelve ball, maybe three feet from a corner pocket. A clear shot. Easy. Straight line. With his slightly warped house cue, he named the pocket and, leaning in, he made the effortless shot. A lightning shot, the ball moving fast, banging into the pocket.

"Bingo."

"That's a different game," Brandon chortled. "That's for little old ladies."

Dustin tuned him out. "Thirteen." Dustin pointed to a pocket. A difficult shot, Brandon's solid five in the way, but Dustin's shot was calculated—the cue ball slammed the opposite side of the table, careened back dangerously, but nipped the right side of the thirteen, which wobbled, slowly inched, but miraculously fell into a pocket.

"Lucky stiff." Brandon had a little wonder in his expression.

"Fourteen." Dustin pointed.

But he deliberated, stiffening his back, walking around the table, watching, calculating, his arm extended as he gauged the direction, the speed. A mathematician's careful and logical estimation. Dustin, the orderly boy. Again the calculation.

Brandon erupted. "Shit, move it." Then in Vietnamese. *"Mau di."*

I jumped up, angry.

Dustin twitched and carelessly slammed the cue ball. It ricocheted, narrowly missed the eight ball, and crashed against the rails and drifted to a stop.

"The way it goes," Brandon announced. "Now I'll show you the ropes."

He glanced at me. I'd stood up, leaning against the doorway, watching, feeling protective of Dustin but keeping my mouth shut. Slowly, as though he were being filmed—I expected him to whip out his cell and snap a selfie and post it on Instagram—Brandon leaned his cue against the table. He pulled his sweatshirt over his head. He was wearing a white wife-beater undershirt more commonly associated, at least by me, with Mafia movies.

Tight, it accented his defined abs. He smiled a look-at-me expression and picked up his stick.

"These cues are cheap shit," he announced. "I got me a Southwest at home. Ten times better than this shit. And this table sucks."

"Shoot." Dustin's voice sounded tinny and faraway.

"Don't rush the master." He took his time. "Hey, Anh Ky, little boy, did your mama wear combat boots to the rice paddy?"

Color rose in Dustin's neck. His knuckles gripped his stick. From where I stood I could see a vein on his neck pop.

Brandon laughed loudly.

"Six in that pocket. Watch and learn."

He leaned over the table.

"Gotta keep at least one foot on the floor." Dustin's voice made him stop.

"What kind of shit is that?"

"There are rules, creep." Dustin stood back, head arched.

"Don't tell me how to play the fucking game."

"Shoot."

Brandon's ball landed in the pocket. He beamed.

"Seven."

But he miscalculated. The seven was wide of the mark, hitting the back rail and rolling forward, stopping inches from where Brandon stood.

"Fuck."

Slowly, mimicking Brandon's preening behavior, Dustin paused, setting his cue down and taking off his ratty sweater. Underneath was a baggy undershirt with a gigantic hole under one sleeve. It draped over his skinny body. Watching, Brandon burst out laughing. Dustin, watching him, purposely made a bicep that, to be sure, was nonexistent. His rail-thin upper arm was a matchstick. "Captain America." Dustin's voice was ragged. He repeated. "Captain Vietnamese-American."

Brandon stared, befuddled. "Jesus Christ Almighty," he bellowed. "You must have slapped a Cong woman in a previous life. Reincarnated as a...a stick figure."

Dustin named his ball. The nine in a pocket. But he seemed distracted now and his cue slid off the side of the ball. The ball moved two or three inches, stopped.

Brandon crowed. "Show you how it's done."

He named his ball, tapped the table with a finger, and slammed the ball in. Then he proceeded to run the table, banking balls, skirting by Dustin's remaining balls, each move more chance than skill, it seemed to me. But effective.

At each strike Dustin's body tensed. I sensed the anger building in him, though he kept himself under control. Each time Brandon landed a ball, he let out a yelp, almost involuntarily. At one point Brandon, moving to the other side of the table for a shot, brushed against Dustin, a purposeful move that knocked Dustin off balance for a second. Dustin said nothing, but I could tell by his posture that he was battling his anger. He gripped his cue so tightly it twisted in his hand, banging the edge of the table.

"Foul," Brandon cried out. "Ball in hand."

"Shoot the fucking ball," Dustin yelled.

Brandon, winning now, focused his eyes. "Sore loser, killer boy."

"Shoot." Dustin's voice roared.

"Ah, the money ball." Brandon took his time contemplating the eight ball, positioned a foot from a pocket. An easy shot, but he was not going to rush it. Dustin bristled.

Brandon rocked on his heels.

"Shoot." Both boys jumped because that word came out of my mouth. I hadn't taken my eyes off Dustin, concerned with his purple face, that throbbing vein in his neck.

"Yes, sir." Smiling at me, Brandon cavalierly struck the cue ball and the eight ball smoothly landed in a pocket.

"And that's how we do it in downtown Saigon." He bowed.

He reached for the cash on the side table, waved the bills in the air.

Without saying a word, avoiding eye contact with me, Dustin quietly placed his house cue against the table and grabbed his coat, sweater, and book bag. I started to say something but decided against it. He strode out of the room, stepping by me, headed through the College Union.

Brandon and I watched each other.

"I dislike wimps." He waved his hands in the air.

Suddenly Dustin flew back into the room, speeding past me and grabbing the stick he'd used. Brandon, startled, backed up into a wall, and put up his hands.

Dustin held the pool cue in front of him, then pulled up his knee. He crashed the stick down hard on his kneecap, snapping it into two jagged pieces.

Smiling, he held out the two pieces to Brandon.

"Hey, you fuckin' muscle freak, I think you know where to shove these."

Chapter Sixteen

Late afternoon, lost in paper work on a troublesome Aetna fraud investigation, staring at the garish pizza parlor neon light flickering across the street, I drifted off. My cell phone buzzed, Liz calling from Ben's apartment. "You sound groggy." In the background another woman's voice muttered, "Tell him to get over here. Now."

"Sophia?" I asked Liz.

"Yes. You free to stop in?"

"What's going on?"

A quick exchange of muffled voices, then she said into the phone: "Game changer."

"I'm in Hartford. At the office. I'll be right there."

"Ben's kids might be here, so don't ask questions of me."

Liz had volunteered to help Sophia break down Ben's apartment. Living upstairs, she could drop in and out, but the emotional journey, Liz told me, was treacherous. Still grieving, Sophia wept upstairs, dragging herself to campus for finals, but otherwise avoiding the doorway she passed whenever she left her building. Police evidence teams had torn the place apart—never a comforting sight—and Sophia, panicked, had spent nights putting it back together, obsessed with removing the stain and pain of their presence.

I also knew, by way of Liz's grapevine and our late-night chatter, that Ben had left his bank account—a paltry few grand, his equally scant life insurance, his retirement benefits, and the other smaller bits and pieces of his academic life—to his children, Martin and Melody. Yet he'd added a recent codicil that Sophia handle his estate in the event of his death. A simple bequest: his books to the school library. His manuscripts to the school's archives. A few token requests to old friends—like an early signed edition of *All the King's Men* to a college frat buddy in Manhattan. A few pieces of art he'd bought with Sophia on vacations. Sentimental depictions of the White Mountains where they'd summered, often with Marcie and Vinnie, at their rustic cabin. A gold-link chain she'd bought him that he never wore because he said it made him look like a Mexican drug lord.

A simple valedictory to a man who lived a modest though wonderfully examined life—and never expected to be brutally murdered.

"Sophia told Martin and Melody that they could take whatever they wanted from the apartment," Liz told me the night before. "Anything. Furniture, baubles, photos, anything. Martin told her he'd be there the next day—and that she'd better not throw anything out. Or hide anything. That surprised Sophia." Liz clicked her tongue. "She said he had a voice laced with anger."

"At her?"

Liz had sighed. "I think Martin is angry at the world."

"His newest divorce?"

"His being born. Maybe." Liz had laughed into the phone.

When I pulled up in front of the apartment, darkness was falling, a grainy twilight, the day bone-chilling with gusts of sleet. All the lights blazed in Ben's first-floor apartment. Liz's car was parked in front, and I pulled in behind it. A decade-old red Chevy convertible with a smashed left fender was parked in the driveway, in effect blocking access to the rear parking lot. As I walked by, I touched the hood: warm to the touch, crystals of glistening melted sleet. Martin's car, I figured.

Inside Martin was standing by the front window, gazing out at the street. With the shadows thrown by the fading light and the yellow glow from a lamp on a table next to him, he reminded me of his father: a short man, the bumpy nose on a round face, his fuzzy hair already receding.

"You look like your father."

"Yeah, I've heard that. It explains why women run from me."

"I meant it as a compliment."

"Well, thank you. Such proper manners."

I caught Liz's eye. She sat next to Sophia on the sofa by the back wall, the two women with shoulders touching, both with their hands folded in their laps. Still life of sisters with wonder in their eyes.

Liz spoke. "Martin is surveying the apartment."

Said, the words hung in the air, a sardonic judgment, and Martin, moving away from the window, shot her a baffled look. Sophia cleared her throat, ready to stand, but sank further into the lumpy cushions.

"Where's his computer?" Martin asked.

"The police took it. With his papers. His files. Anything that..."

"I want it back."

Sophia said in a soft voice, "I'm sure you'll get it. They're reviewing everything."

"He'd want me to have it."

Sophia drew her lips into a thin line. "And have it you shall."

He didn't look at her but spoke to me. "They ransacked his place."

"No," Liz began slowly. "This is a murder investigation and the State Police Crime Unit knows what to do."

"Did they find anything?"

"No one sent me a report." Liz shook her head back and forth.

Martin then swaggered around the rooms, pulling at drawers, lifting a blotter on Ben's desk, even tipping a wing chair on its side.

"What are you looking for?" I asked.

An edge to his tone. "I don't know what I'm doing here."

"Are you all right?" I asked.

He stopped in front of me. "Just why are *you* here?"

Good question: I had no answer. "Friend of the court." A wise-guy response he ignored.

The apartment had a starved look about it. Yes, Ben's ragtag furniture had been shuffled around, but his work area had been stripped of his papers and files. The computer stand empty. The life of an academic, stripped bare. Martin—maybe Sophia?—had begun emptying out his life there. By the front window five cardboard boxes were neatly lined up like railroad cars at the station, each filled with miscellany: I spotted a framed family photograph, a sports trophy, a Red Sox pennant, even Ben's Ph.D. diploma in a simple black frame. A copy of Ben's last book. *Evangelical Fury.*

Liz had a tickle in her voice. "Martin provided his own boxes."

"I want that computer." He was talking to himself.

In fact, Liz had told me earlier that Detective Manus had let her know that the State Police Crime Unit had found little of value—at this stage of the investigation. The only document that related to Dustin was a photocopy of his brilliant paper, with Ben's laudatory comments in the margins. Nothing else. No fingerprints of the boy, who'd obviously never been inside the apartment. I learned that Dustin had voluntarily submitted to fingerprinting the day he was questioned. No letters, notes, warnings, threats, reprisals. Nothing. A blank slate. Neither was there anything that pointed to another killer. Nothing at all.

Watching Liz's face, I mouthed the words: Why am I here?

A cautionary finger in the air. Wait.

Martin stopped fidgeting and pointed at Sophia. "What did you take?"

She waited a moment, rolled her tongue over her lower lip, and smiled. "Three small paintings." She pointed to a wall. Empty space, three small nails visible.

"They're mine."

"No, they're not."

"Why should you have them?"

She deliberated what to say to him. Finally, in a cool, low voice she said, "Bucolic scenes of the White Mountains."

"They're mine."

Her voice deepened. "Were you in bed with your father and me when we nestled in that rustic cabin and talked about buying them the following day?"

His jaw went slack. "That isn't funny."

"Yes, it sort of is."

His foot kicked one of the boxes. "I'm outta here." Then, swiveling around, "I want all the furniture." He pointed at the sofa they were sitting on. I was leaning against an armchair and his gesture pointed at that. "All of it. Since my...separation, I'm living in a fleabag welfare motel on the Berlin Turnpike, surrounded by white trash mothers with too many kids. I need this stuff."

She shrugged. "It's yours."

Sophia stood up and walked to a table. "Here." She held out her hand. "An extra key. Move it all out when you want. But by January fifteenth. So sayeth the landlord."

"What were you going to do with his stuff?"

A mischievous smile. "Full circle, Martin. Most came from Salvation Army on Route 10, and it was going back there. Life is a circle."

"Yeah, sure." He gripped the key, dropped it into his pocket. "I'm out of here."

The doorbell chimed, and Martin walked to the front window, peered out. "Oh Christ. Melody. She said she wasn't coming."

I opened the door and greeted his sister.

"I changed my mind," she said to her brother as he rolled his eyes. She smiled at all of us, each in turn, even at Sophia. "It would be...the last time, you know." She looked around the room. "Maybe."

Sophia stood up and grasped her hand. "Look around, Melody."

Her hand dropped to her side. "I don't know what to do here."

Martin reached into one of his boxes and took out a framed photograph: Melody in her high-school graduation gown, standing with her father, his arms around her shoulders. A broad smile on both their faces. "This." He thrust it at her.

She brought her face close to the photograph, and then held it to her chest. "I remember this photo."

"Yeah," her brother snarled, "he kept it on his nightstand. You notice there wasn't one of me."

"That's not fair," she began, but then stopped, a sidelong glance at Sophia and then me. "Not now."

A horn blew, shrill and long, someone leaning on it.

"Christ, what?" From Martin.

Melody whispered, "Mom's in the driveway." A heavy sigh. "She insisted on driving me over."

Sophia peered out the window. "Ask her to come in."

Martin scoffed. "You gotta be kidding. Her? In this place. Dante's inferno has more appeal."

"Nevertheless, a cold car..."

Sophia left the room and returned with a vase. She held it out for us to see. "Roseville." A light robin's-egg-blue vase, perhaps a foot high, clusters of faint pink roses circling the lip. "Ben said they bought it on their honeymoon. At an antique store in Buffalo."

"Buffalo?" Martin made a face.

Melody was shaking her head. "I don't know."

"Do you want to give it to your mother?" Sophia asked. "It should be hers."

Neither said a word. Finally, exasperated, Sophia cradled the vase in her arms and, coatless, left the apartment. We congregated by the front windows, watched Sophia slowly approach the car, her footfall tentative on the icy patch. We watched her knock on the closed window. Exhaust billowed behind the car, the heater on full blast. Suddenly Charlotte rolled down the window, muttered something to Sophia, and reached for the vase. Something was said, but Sophia didn't move. Then the window rolled up. Sophia stood still, though she glanced toward the apartment. Instinctively we all jumped back. Suddenly the interior light snapped on, and I could see Charlotte holding the old vase up to the light, turning it. From where I stood I could see her shock of bright yellow hair framing the blue vase.

Then the window rolled down again and Charlotte jammed the vase into Sophia's chest. Sophia staggered back, then watched as the window rolled back up.

Back inside, Sophia stood in the doorway, clearly rattled, shivering from the cold, her hands clutching the vase. Quietly, she placed it on a table. Her face was flushed. "She told me to smash it to pieces."

Martin laughed. "I'm surprised she didn't smash it on your head."

Melody whispered, "Mom is…filled with anger."

"Join the club." Martin grabbed his overcoat from a wrought-iron hall tree by the door, nodded at his sister, then Sophia. "This place will be empty in a few days."

"Take the vase," Sophia said.

"Yeah, of course. It's mine."

Melody mumbled something about the sad way things had turned out and she left, still cradling her graduation photograph.

Then we were alone. I sat in the armchair watching Sophia and Liz staring back at me. "That went well," I commented. Then, gesturing toward the departed Winslow family. "And the reason I was invited to this wake?"

They exchanged looks, conspiratorially.

"Houston, we have a problem." Liz's smile was melancholic.

Sophia walked to the hall tree and fumbled with a jacket hanging there. A brightly colored red brocade Chinese-style spring jacket. "My jacket."

"Yeah?"

"I always kept it here. If we ran out and I needed…anyway, I found this in the pocket." She showed me a folded-over white envelope, crumpled. She opened the envelope slowly, her fist closing on something. Two tiny microcassette tapes. "From Ben's answering machine."

"Game change," Liz said to me. "Ben must have purposely hidden them there."

My heard raced. "And they tell us what?" I caught my breath. "Dustin?"

"Yes, both of them," Sophia said. "Ben was getting scared. One is a partial conversation, as though he started recording it midway through a talk, probably sensing he needed to document something. The other is a full but brief conversation. Deadly."

"Deadly?"

"Like lethal?"

"For Dustin?"

Liz nodded. "You judge."

The answering machine was on an end table next to the sofa, an old-fashioned clunky apparatus Ben used for years. Sophia sat down next to it and pressed a button. We heard: "Hello, this is Ben Winslow. Please leave a message after the beep. Evil telemarketers beware." A beep, then nothing. Sophia snapped out the small tape and inserted one of the others. "A little shaky at first, like Ben didn't know what he was doing. But..."

A scratchy voice, Ben's. I leaned in to listen:

(Static, mumbled words, more static)

Dustin:...*hear me?*

Ben:...*about...*

Dustin:...*no...*

Ben: *No? You gotta make up your mind...*

Dustin: *Sorry I told you...*

Ben: *Why did you?*

Dustin:...static...*a nice guy...trust*

Ben: *I am.*

Dustin: *You can't do this. I mean no disrespect, sir.*

Ben: *You don't know the meaning of respect, Dustin. Otherwise you wouldn't do this. Do you know what this means? I keep telling you over and over...*

Dustin: (a shaky voice) *I'm confused...what to do.*

Ben: (loudly) *You know what to do.*

Dustin: *I gave my word.*

Ben: (furious) *Then break it, dammit. There's a higher truth here, Dustin. For Christ's sake. You're better than this. You're a bright boy and...*

Dustin: *I wish I didn't know.*

Ben: *But you do. You do. Hear me?*

Dustin: *No.*

(Click. The line went dead. The drone of a dial tone.)

"Good Christ," I muttered. "This is horrible."

Liz held up her hand. "Tape number two the next night—two days before Ben was murdered."

Sophia changed the tape. Her hand shook and it slipped onto the floor. She was sobbing.

"His voice," she said. "Ben's voice. It's...horrible."

"Listen." Liz watched me closely.

Dustin: *You told me to call you.*

Ben: *Decision time.*

Dustin: *No, I...*

Ben: *You have no choice.*

Dustin: *You have a choice.*

Ben: *No, I don't. But I warned you, Dustin—I will do something. I'll report you. I can't sit on this info and not do anything.*

Dustin: *It's not your business.*

Ben: *A dumb thing to say.*

Dustin: *Why?*

Ben: *This is serious. People—people live...they wonder... You have an answer.*

Dustin: *I made it all up.*

Ben: *Dustin, don't play games with me.*

Dustin: *I mean no disrespect, sir.*

Ben: *But you do, Dustin. Respect for others.*

Dustin: *I don't...*

Ben (a long pause) *Dustin...I get no answer from you.* (pause) *A life lost, Dustin.*

Dustin: *I know.*

Ben: *Dead.*

Dustin: *I know.*

Ben: *You know where the body is.*

Dustin: (pause*)* *No.*

Ben: *All right, you have a choice. You call the authorities or I do. But I want you to do it. You have to step up. I've given you two days to man up. The deadline is tomorrow. Tomorrow. Call me and let me know. Otherwise I drop a dime on you.*

Dustin: *You can't.*

Ben: *I will.*

Dustin: *You're headed for trouble, sir.*

(Click. The line went dead.)

Silence in the room. We stared at one another.

"You're gonna have to give the tapes to Detective Manus right away," I said.

Sophia nodded. "I know."

Shaking my head, frustrated, angry at Dustin, I reached for my cellphone, scrolled my contacts, found what I was looking for.

"Yeah?"

"Dustin? Rick Van Lam here."

"What?"

"You told Ben Winslow about a dead body."

Click. The line went dead.

I faced the two women. "I shouldn't have done that, but no matter. The cops'll ask him the same question."

"So now it really begins."

Chapter Seventeen

The next morning Liz texted me:

> Dustin in for questioning. Won't talk. More to follow.

Lingering over a cup of coffee, I texted back:

> Let me know. Telephone now?

The impersonality of early-morning texting—I wanted to hear her voice, gauge the tenor of her words. She replied:

> Can't do. Sit tight.

That wasn't easy to do. A restless night, flashes of those recorded messages dipping in and out of my brain, startling me awake. Dustin one minute tremulous and unsure, the next minute bold, demanding. Two sides of a coin tossed willy-nilly into the air. Ben's demands, a resolute tone in his voice I'd never heard before.

But then—I'd never known where a body was hidden.

A body? Murdered maybe?

The body in question…

Late morning Gracie knocked on my door. I smelled fresh-baked cupcakes under a dishcloth. But I also detected the questioning look in her face. Noontime: I was still in my flannel bathrobe, bare feet, hair askew because I hadn't showered yet.

"Good grief, you look like an unmade bed."

"I am an unmade bed." I scratched my head. "You look—like one of the lesser Andrew Sisters."

She strode past me. "I had more talent, of course. A high-kicker for the Rockettes needs to be—dimensional."

She was wearing a bright yellow dress with an elaborate lace design across the bodice. A tall, willowy woman who never lost her dance-school body, she stored trunks of vintage clothing in a back room—"and none of it needs altering." She eyed me sharply. "I'm headed to the market. Do you need anything? Shampoo?" A pause. "A new bathrobe?" A grunt. "A personal valet?"

"Yeah."

She laughed as she placed the plate of goodies on the table. "Ben Franklin wouldn't condone such laziness, Rick."

"He also demanded all of us imitate Jesus and Socrates."

"Good advice." She grinned at me. "Though I suppose you can throw your Buddha into the mix."

She went into my kitchen and put the teakettle on. Within minutes she was rattling in my cupboards, finding the white lotus Chinese tea we always shared. I sat on the sofa with my eyes closed, drifting back into slumber. Setting a tray on the coffee table, she nudged me. "You're bothered."

I told her about Dustin and the tapes. She leaned into me. "Snippets of tape like that probably can lead the police in a thousand different directions."

"What do you mean?" I sipped my tea.

She thought about her words. "You don't know what came *before* those conversations. Sounds to me like they're the tail end of a long story between your friend and that sad boy."

"But the police…"

"Rush to judgment." Her words overlapped mine. "Let the boy have his say, Rick. Make sure of that."

I saluted her, smiling.

She picked up the glossy flyer I'd been given by Dustin's aunt. Crumpled now, lying on my coffee table. A good Catholic parishioner, faithful, even on Holy Days of Obligation, Gracie fingered the sheet. "What's this nonsense, Rick? You trying to find God in all the wrong places? I told you what I think of that—huckster. Remember?"

"I learned that Dustin's mother goes to that mega church. Other Vietnamese." I reached for the flyer but Gracie held it close to her eyes. "Ben Winslow's symbol of evangelical fraud."

Gracie bit her lip. "Malarkey."

"People have a right to believe in what they want."

Her face tightened. "Who told you that?"

"It's America," I said a little feebly, reaching again for the flyer. She handed it to me. "You're talking to all the wrong people." But she laughed now. "That's because you come from a Communist country. You believe democracy covers all sins. Our politicians are Pied Pipers."

Standing up, walking to the front window, I stared down into the street. A peaceful Sunday—a young family hidden in bulky winter clothing walked along the sidewalk, headed home from the Congregational Church on the corner. A young boy danced around his parents. Noontime—the peeling of bells from the Catholic church one street over. The little boy paused, jumped up and down, one hand pointing to the distant bells.

"A reading from the gospel of the Gospel of Wealth Ministry." I deepened my voice as Gracie frowned at me. "The Reverend Simms' sermon is on Ben Winslow tonight." I pointed to the topic: "'The Enemy Within.' A parable of the atheist who got what he deserved." I shook my head slowly. "Beat a dead man when he's down. A shame." I folded the flyer. "I'm going. He's mentioned Dustin on TV, said the boy did God's chosen people a favor, so I want to see if he mentions him tonight."

Gracie took the flyer from my hand, stared at the print, holding it so close to her face I feared the colorful ink would smear her careful makeup.

"I'm going with you."

"Gracie, there's no need."

Her tone indignant. "Why do people deny me adventures? I traveled with Bob Hope in Korea, danced up a storm in the name of our country, and..."

I held up my hand. "And the war lasted another two years."

"Smart mouth." She grinned. "I can behave myself in public, you know."

"All right," I surrendered. "Six o'clock."

• • ● • •

A few minutes before six I knocked on her door and was mildly alarmed to discover Jimmy Gadowicz greeting me. "This calls for an experienced investigator." His first words to me, an unlit cigar bobbing in his lips, though I detected a few cupcake crumbs and pinkish sugar frosting happily settled into the wrinkles of his chin.

"Who are you again?" I asked. "This suit you stole from..."

Because Jimmy, in fact, had changed off his usual attire: an XXL sweat shirt emblazoned with a Boston Red Sox logo riding up a tremendous belly and displaying remnants of his last pepperoni grinder. And bulky sweat pants with the same gastronomic evidence, sadly worn brown shoes he bought in Walmart. Now he wore a Dapper Dan suit reserved for funerals and court appearances, shiny in the elbow, but presentable. A Stackpole, Moore, Tryon necktie from that tony shop in downtown Hartford—a gift from a satisfied client. And, the frosting on the cake, a tired metaphor that came to mind given his obvious sweet fest, hair slicked back and glistening with some oily confection in the same family as Jiffy Lube motor oil.

"I shine up real good," he announced, stepping back.

Gracie emerged from her bedroom and paused dramatically in the doorway. From her trunk of wonders—I admit I'd rarely seen her repeat an outfit, which seemed an impossibility given her constant surprises—she'd located a art-nouveau cocktail dress, flowing pastel chiffon, rows of bugle beads, cascading rivers of stitched sequins, a high lace collar. Dangerous high heels for the octogenarian. So many ribbons in her hair she could be a flower girl at a Polish country wedding.

"I thought I'd dress down," she hummed. "It is a church."

Jimmy was beaming. I'd be chauffeur for an evening of their idle flirtation with each other, both of whom would have been horrified if I dared suggested some sort of geriatric do-si-do was in evidence.

"You gonna stand there with your mouth open," Jimmy said to me, "or are you gonna get the car?"

Gracie sized me up. My spiffy Brooks Brothers suit, my oxblood dress shoes, a burgundy necktie with matching handkerchief. A black overcoat draped over my arm. The middle-aged lawyer on *Court TV*.

"He's dressed like he's going on a date," Gracie chuckled. "Prowling for a wife."

I grinned. "I decided I want five children and a wife who'll eat only the bowl of bran cereal I place in front of her." Then I quoted Dustin's curious remark: "*Ong an cha ba an nem.* I eat a hamburger and she eats bread."

"He's speaking in tongues." Jimmy pointed a finger at me.

"Here we try to blend in with our surroundings," Gracie went on, "and he blows our cover."

Jimmy laughed. "Our son was never properly disciplined."

"I tried," she joked in a high whine. "Oh, how I tried."

"I turned out real good." I danced a two-step.

"No parent ever believes that hogwash." Gracie shooed us along, waving her house key at me.

• ● ● ● •

Before I turned into the parking lot of the Gospel of Wealth Ministry, I cruised through the neighborhood. A pass in front of Dustin's house in the projects and a slow drift by Uncle Binh's apartment. Quiet, quiet. The shades down at Dustin's. Uncle Binh's eerily quiet with a flickering light switched on somewhere in the rooms, though the upstairs apartment was flooded with illumination as partiers crowded a front window decorated with multi-colored Christmas lights and a beaming plastic Santa Claus.

A few stragglers were walking on the side roads, single file, headed to the church. I strained to see whether they were Vietnamese, impossible with their faces shielded from the cold. By the time I parked the car, most of the lot was full, bundled-up folks scurrying in. Waves of laughter, exchanged greetings, gleeful "Merry Christmas" yelled across snow banks and rusted fenders. Two greeters at the wide front doors—an old whiskered man who kept saying, "God loves you," while an old woman, standing opposite him, intoned, "Have a good day."

Gracie frowned at her. "Some of us have made other plans."

"Gracie," I said, "play nice."

As a crimson-robed choir began singing onstage, I scanned the crowd, half-rising from my seat. We were seated in back, along an aisle that inclined down toward the front, but off to the side was a small group of Vietnamese celebrants, clustered together. And there, sitting in the aisle was Uncle Binh in his wheelchair. To his right Aunt Suong. To her right Dustin's mother Mai. They sat stiffly, eyes riveted to the stage, though Dustin's mother's hand waved hypnotically in the air. Two old women sitting behind them rocked back and forth.

I pointed them out to Gracie and Jimmy. "Seekers after gold."

I watched them and tried to imagine Dustin in this vast hall. When had he accompanied his mother to these services, especially the visit that resulted in the Reverend Simms singling him out, learning his name—ultimately rejoicing publicly in the boy as assassin?

A heavyset black woman in black flowing robes appeared and demanded the congregation hold up Bibles. Gracie rolled her eyes and mouthed the words: You were supposed to remind me, Rick. "Repeat after me: Oh Lord, let my prayers reveal the key to the glorious riches God the Father has set aside for me. Show me the sign that tells me I'm ready for gold, dear Jesus. In the name of the Father. Amen." The fevered chanting of parishioners swelled throughout the room, echoed off the rafters, punctuated by *hallelujahs* and *amens*.

Immediately an usher materialized in each aisle with what resembled a farmer's bushel basket, lifted in the air.

"Show your love to Jesus," the woman intoned.

Across the room hands waved envelopes and cash in the air. Dollar bills, fives, tens, even twenties. As an usher moved up our aisle, I watched the Trang contingent tossing in cash. I wondered how much, but couldn't see. When the usher approached the back row, Gracie pulled a five from a pocket.

Jimmy nudged her, "You'll get more bang for your buck at Popeye's Chicken."

Suddenly the Reverend Simms appeared on a darkened stage, a beam of foggy light trailing him. He stopped center stage before a microphone, his hands raised above his head. In a choked, thick voice he bellowed, "Bless the souls who love Jesus."

Show time.

His rambling sermon touched upon Judas, on the money changers—he seemed to be on their side—on Mary Mother of God, on angels we have heard on high, a chaotic mishmash that built with steady crescendo as congregants rose and roared and sang out. But nothing about the subject at hand—the heretic in the neighboring town. Ben Winslow.

Of course, that was the climax—a heated and almost euphoric depiction of Ben Winslow as exemplum of Satan's Godless power. "A man who took *my* name and God's in vain." "A man who maligned *me* and God in the press." "A man who listened to the false gods of Baal." Snippets of attack that finally resulted in a thunderous profile of Ben Winslow as agent provocateur of evil. "A teacher, and a Godless one. America's children." "But God has plans for all of us. If he guarantees us riches, he also guarantees us vengeance—which is His, sayeth…sayeth Himself." Momentarily rattled by his own chaotic sentence structure, he paused, then burst out, "Murdered, that man. Yes, murder is wrong. But like the Crusaders who besieged the heathen Muslins of Jerusalem, death can be the sword of the believer. This

Winslow was a minor character in God's magnificent drama, but a man who chose to take on God."

He paused, withdrew a white handkerchief from a pocket and ran it over his face. Dressed in a white linen suit with a white vest that barely contained his rotund body, his foot tapped as if to a gospel tune echoing in his head.

His voice suddenly became low, raspy, and confidential. "A teacher entrusted with the care of our youth." His eyes drifted over the congregation. At that moment his eyes settled on the small Vietnamese contingent, and he hissed, "An *innocent* child of God touched by that predator. Touched. A boy. Sullied, stained, violated."

I froze—was he accusing Ben of molesting Dustin? The reason Dustin killed him? All the harsh and unforgiving language of sexual molestation, insinuation.

Jimmy shot a glance at me and mumbled, "The man's dangerous."

I whispered back. "What's he trying to do?"

My mind swam as I gripped the back of the seat before me. The congregation roared and yelled out: *Monster. Sinner. Beast. Violator. Vermin. God's wrath.*

A child of God, violated.

A chorus that rose as the Reverend Simms kept saying "Amen, amen, amen."

Behind him the chorus began to clap wildly.

I sensed movement down the aisle. Something was happening. Craning my neck, I spotted Uncle Binh rocking in his wheelchair while Aunt Suong kept patting his shoulder, whispering something, trying to calm down the frantic man. As I watched, an usher appeared and began rolling the old man up the aisle, meekly followed by Aunt Suong and Mai, both shuffling, heads bowed, Dustin's mother hobbling with a cane. Suong's face was trembling, but Binh was furious. He kept glancing over his shoulder at the stage where the Reverend Simms, oblivious, ranted on.

I stepped into the aisle just as the three of them neared me.

Uncle Binh spotted me. He let out a horrid gasp. Startled, Suong and Mai followed his gaze. Suong cried out in Vietnamese. "*Ngung lai!*" Stop! Then, a hand held up to my face, she sneered, "*Nguoi my!*" The American! A curse.

But it was Uncle Binh's face that alarmed me. What I saw there was raw fear.

Chapter Eighteen

The next morning's news cycle headlined the police release of the audiotapes, followed by a laconic statement by Chief of Police Jeffries that Dustin Trang, interrogated at the station for hours—the televised remarks showed a pause here as the chief amended his words—"an hour before being sent home." The investigation continued. No arrests. And—no explanation of Ben's volcanic statement to Dustin on the phone: *You know where the body is.*

Newscasters got dizzy with the story.

Reporters banged on his mother's door, but were greeted by silence—and by a security guard for the projects who kept shooing them away in a melodious Jamaican accent.

Media frenzy, the rest of the day. The college's Facebook page crashed. Hundreds of comments, most nasty and inflammatory. Delirious students, hungry for information. The digital copy of the college newspaper had a banner headline: *New Clues in Murder of Prof.* A snapshot of Dustin being taken into custody. Students claimed they knew Dustin—had predicted the murder. A link to Brandon's web page, also flooded with infantile commentary, Brandon fueling the fires with his cautionary tale of the dangers of scholarship boys wandering through the ivied gates of Farmington College. A Facebook page—ArrestDustin-Now—that disappeared within the hour.

A rising tide of innuendo and blatant lies. Someone on Tumblr began a succession of short, unfunny messages that were immediately picked up by an anonymous student who kept repeating: *He killed my favorite professor.* Comments about Ben on the Rate My Professor website went on for pages. Hank kept retweeting the annoying tweets that claimed to provide information from police headquarters. #DeadBodyDustin. #Wherethebodyis. #ArrestDustin.

Liz alerted me to some quickly deleted Snapchat trolling of Dustin. Threats, warnings. Rapid-fire, in-the-moment blather. The complex web of social media exploded, judging, demanding, ultimately becoming a digital Circus Maximus. Millennial madness as fingers tapped on Smartphone keypads. And that YouTube cellphone video had thousands of likes, something that irked me. Likes?

Late in the afternoon I sat with Jimmy in our office in Hartford and fiddled with end-of-year cases I wanted to wrap up: those mysteriously disappeared files at Cigna, a falsified personnel file at Hartford Hospital, a simple welfare fraud case for Department of Children and Families. Tedious, but they paid the light bill. Across from me, Jimmy scribbled on yellow pads, occasionally eyeing me as I flicked through the laptop keyboard. The *Hartford Courant* rested in his lap. Now and then his grunt reminded me that old-fashioned shoe leather was best. After all, his name was above mine on the door. In fact, it was Gaddy Associates. I was one of the associates.

"This morning's *Courant.*" Jimmy indicated the daily newspaper. "Your name is mentioned. They didn't capitalize the 'v' in Van."

"I'm really Dutch."

Jimmy added, "Your boy seems to be placing himself in hotter and hotter water. I mean, those damn audiotapes. Sensationalism." He ran his fingers down a column in the *Courant.* "But that boy's got too many secrets. Rick, where *is* the body?"

"I don't know if there is one."

"Of course there is."

"You're so sure?"

"Don't bullshit me, Rick. You know there is as well as I do."

I nodded. "How do I break through to Dustin?"

"Maybe you can't. Maybe the cops gotta do it."

I shook my head. "Me or Hank. One of us. That boy has to trust someone in his life."

"That may be impossible." He turned away.

"I'm worried about Dustin." I stood up. "I'll catch you later."

Jimmy watched as I put on my overcoat. "Rick, what are you going to do?"

I didn't answer.

A little crazed, I drove to Bristol, turned into the parking lot of the housing project on Jefferson Drive. Dustin's home was dark, not even a front light switched on. A snow-packed front stoop, though a snow shovel rested against a railing. I rang the doorbell. Nothing. I waited. I banged on the door. I peered inside through the small window, focusing through the security bars that graced all the first floor apartments in the projects. A dead bolt on the door. Perhaps a police lock.

Someone had spray-painted graffiti on the front door, and through the dim light of a nearby streetlight I could discern a jagged word. "KILLER." Big block letters in red, though the paint trickled down, creating a waterfall effect. Blood spatter. I touched the paint. Fresh, sticky to the touch.

I rang the doorbell again. Nothing. A glimmer of light at the back of the apartment.

I got out my phone and scrolled my contacts, dialing Dustin's cellphone.

"Yeah?"

"It's me, Dustin. Rick."

"I know. Caller ID."

"You're home?"

He didn't answer. Then, "What do you want?"

"I'm outside your door. I rang the bell. Let me in."

A long pause. "Why?"

I yelled into the phone. "Just do it, dammit."

The line went dead. I waited. Finally, the door opened. Dustin stood in the shadows and stared at me. "What?"

I pushed by him and found a light switch. "We have to talk."

He backed off. "No, we don't."

I headed into the kitchen and snapped on a light. "Where's your mother?"

"Not home. Uncle Binh's, I guess."

"Sit down."

He didn't move, standing in the doorway, his eyes watching me. He was dressed in old boxer shorts and a baggy T-shirt, and idly he scratched his chest. Suddenly he darted out of the room. When he returned, he'd thrown on a pair of flannel pajama bottoms. Incongruous, vaguely funny—an iterated image of Mickey Mouse ran up and down his legs.

On the kitchen table a small bowl half-filled with dried rice, specks of stringy meat on top. An abandoned meal. A pair of chopsticks was dipped into the bowl.

I pointed. "Dustin, superstition says that chopsticks left in the bowl symbolize death. That's why folks lay them across the top of…"

He yelled out, "You here to teach me manners?"

"Good point."

I detected a sliver of a smile as he turned away.

He sat down opposite me at the kitchen table, arms folded. "People were yelling things at my door before."

"And they left you a message with spray paint."

"The whole goddamn neighborhood got graffiti."

"Ignore it—when you see it."

"You think I give a fu—?"

"You can say 'fuck,' Dustin."

"I say it in front of Hank."

I sat back and smiled. "He's a cop. Lots of folks probably use that word with him—but usually it's a choice two-word phrase."

He got serious. "I don't know why you're here."

"You know why I'm here. Those audiotapes need an explanation, Dustin. This isn't a game. You're in trouble."

"It's got nothing to do with that murder. I swear. Nothing!"

"Make me believe that." I breathed in. "You have to realize how you come off on those tapes. Help me out. Your fight with Winslow— maybe you *heard* something. Maybe you said something to another student. Maybe another student with a grievance heard your battle and…I don't know, Dustin. Maybe you're connected to a murder but you aren't aware of how."

"That's real crazy."

"Is it?" I banged my fist on the table. "Explain those tapes to me."

He bit the corner of a fingernail. "It was—stupid. Dumb shit."

I was frustrated. "A body."

He started. "*He* said that. *I* didn't."

"You're lying to me. What are you hiding, Dustin?"

"Nothing."

"You are, dammit."

I could see him shutting down. "Maybe if you think back to kids you talked to. At school. What about this Darijo? Who does he know?"

His words flew out of his mouth. "Leave him alone. He's not a friend."

My eyes drifted to the shrine high on the kitchen wall. A gold-plated plaster Buddha surrounded by joss sticks in a ginger jar. A thin straw basket. A bowl of water. I pointed. "Dustin, why is there a McDonald's Whopper on that shrine?"

Puzzled, he raised his head. He grinned. "You gotta have food for the ancestors or something like that. I think that's why. For the long journey. That's what my mother says. It's—bullshit. I don't pay attention." He squinted. "A cheeseburger?"

"My question exactly."

He started to laugh. "I guess Mom was out of those blood-red oranges." He stood up and peered at the cardboard container. "My Mom's fuckin' nuts."

He caught my eye, and for a brief moment we laughed. A wonderful moment. I'd never seen Dustin laugh before. "Quarter Pounder with Cheese."

"Anyway, Dustin, back to…"

I stopped. The front door opened, and his mother walked in, one arm holding a paper bag. Her cane clacked on the floor. She deposited the bag on a table, took off her coat, let out a weary sigh, and seemed ready to head toward a bedroom when she noticed Dustin and me in the kitchen, both of us watching her.

"Anh Ky," she began. "Mr. Lam."

Her face closed up as she raised a fist in the air. "You can't come here like this. Wrong, wrong, wrong. You have to leave now." She stood in the doorway and yelled in Vietnamese. "*De cho toi yen.*" She sputtered in almost incoherent English, "Leave me alone. You. Go."

"Let me…"

"Never come back."

I hesitated, glancing at Dustin who had dipped his head down into his lap. I stood up. She waited in the doorway, her fists still clenched. As I walked by her, I noticed she was trembling, her eyes closed.

Chapter Nineteen

Hank stretched out on my sofa, his feet up on my old coffee table, his hands behind his head.

"You really should have more food in this apartment, Rick. How do you expect to entice guests into these rooms? On your personality alone? C'mon. This bagel is a year old." He pointed to the bagel he'd taken from my counter.

"Yet my plan is not working. You're here."

"I'm family."

"True. Family usually comes calling with—bagels. This hour of the morning."

"I already ate breakfast."

"And yet here you are."

He swallowed the last of the stale bagel, wiped crumbs off his chest onto my floor. "You're not the only form of life that occupies these rooms." He squinted as though he'd spotted a colony of ants nearby. "I'm feeling charitable."

"Hank, I've been thinking." I reached for my coffee. "Maybe Dustin *is* involved—but unawares. Something he said—something said to him—some association at school that precipitated a murder he had nothing to do with."

"Yeah, he'd like to hear himself described as such."

"You know, six degrees of separation."

"In this case, maybe one degree. That's all it took."

"But who is that person?" I wondered, tapping my fingers on the table nervously. "Dustin and one other person who…"

Hank broke in. "Yeah, someone using Dustin? Maybe. Someone, that one person, who knows the whole story of Dustin's battles with Winslow and decides it's the perfect plot for his own revenge. Someone who might trigger him as a scapegoat?"

"True. Maybe someone Dustin confided in."

Hank sat up. "There's Professor Laramie."

"He seemed to enjoy the fight."

"But could he fire two shots into Ben?"

"Unlikely. But who knows? Not a nice man, but a God-fearing born-again."

"Yeah," Hank sneered, "none of them ever take pot shots at their enemies."

"You know what I mean. He's seems—wimpy."

"Once again, none of them…"

I held up my hand. "I get your point. Murderers come in all shapes and sizes and states of moral cowardice."

Hank grinned. "Yeah, I remember hearing a prof of mine in Criminology saying those very words."

I shook my head. "So where does this leave us?"

He sat up, bunched his arms around his knees. "Let's make the assumption that Dustin is the innocent bystander here, but somehow integral to the murder."

"Let's talk to his almost-friend, the non-friend. Darijo Delic. Maybe he can give us a clue."

Hank stretched out his arms, yawned noisily. "Where do we find him?"

"Finals are done. Most likely Darijo Delic is home or at his father's restaurant in Hartford."

Hank rubbed his stomach. "I've never eaten Bosnian food."

"We're not going there to eat."

"If I'm weak, I can't ask intelligent questions."

Late morning, a bustling avenue in the South End of Hartford, cars double-parked and the *boom boom boom* thump of rap music from a low-slung passing car. Old Barry Square, now called Little Bosnia by locals after the migration following the bloodshed of the Balkan wars of the nineties. Vestiges of the old neighborhood dotted the street: mom-and-pop Italian bakeries and pizza shops, a few stolid three-decker homes with green asphalt siding and peeling front porches. A speckling of Spanish bodegas and groceries and nightclubs lined the avenue. Two teenaged boys running between cars hurled curses in sputtered street Spanish at drivers who refused to slow for them. But in the teeming mix was a Balkan market on one corner, a glittery nightclub called Ziveli! in the middle of the square. Cruising through the side streets, sizing up the neighborhood, I spotted a real estate company: Herkovac Sales. An insurance broker named Mastovac and Sons. *Bosnian Spoken Here.*

"There," I pointed. Hank craned his neck. "Sarajevo Café."

A small eatery in the middle of the rundown block, an elevated brick front terrace surrounded by black wrought-iron railings. Summer patio tables covered with blue plastic tarps and coated with a thin film of ice. At the back of the terrace wide wooden doors, one bearing a small sign that announced: CLOSED.

As we walked in, we collided with a young woman in the process of leaning past us to flip over the sign. "I guess you ignored it anyway." She grinned at us. Then she added, "We're almost open for lunch."

A small dining room with institutional lunch tables and helter-skelter chairs, nothing matching but somehow working—home-cooked meals from a family kitchen. Against one wall a coffee bar with an ornate Ottoman Empire urn. Dimly-lit wall sconces gave the room a shadowy feel, but someone snapped on overhead lights as we stood in the doorway, the room jumping to life. An amateurish wall mural depicted what I assumed was a scene from bustling Sarajevo: yellow-stone buildings with red-tiled roofs, a prominent minaret reaching into a blue sky.

Darijo Delic was standing by one the tables, his arms holding bunches of silverware as he watched us approach. His face was set in a grim line. "*Dobar da*n." A greeting. Good day.

"Darijo," I began, "a few words with you?"

He said nothing, simply stared, but then, as though obeying a shouted command, dropped the silverware on the table and turned quickly toward the voice behind him. "Father." Words addressed to someone still in the kitchen but immediately at his side.

Father and son stood shoulder to shoulder, both faces stoic, though Darijo at one point cast a sidelong glance at his father.

Darijo resembled his father, both medium height, the father stockier than the slender Darijo, but both with long, almost stark faces, huge deep-set black eyes, chiseled chins under flat cheekbones. Dark, olive complexion, both with pitch-black hair, wavy and swept back from their foreheads. The father, probably late forties or early fifties, had a weather-beaten face, a lined forehead, but his son had the creamy complexion of a pampered child.

"What's this about?" the father finally said, staring into my face. He spoke with a thick accent, barely intelligible.

Darijo nodded at us. "From school. The murder." Then Darijo's face relaxed. "My father Ahmed."

"I'm Rick Van Lam and this is Hank Nguyen."

"I know who you both are." Darijo's voice was slow and measured. "But I don't understand."

"You were—are a friend of Dustin Trang." I watched his father's face get cloudy. "We're trying to clear his name, Darijo. We thought—a talk with people who know him."

Ahmed interrupted, "He no part of murder." He protectively placed his hand on his son's shoulder.

"I know that," I said hurriedly. "But they spent time together. Friends."

"Not friends." Darijo said.

"Not friends." An echo from his father.

"But you've spent some time together. The College Union. In class."

Darijo glanced at his father again. "I already talked to the cops." But he lifted his chin. "A nice boy. To me. We are lost there…" He waved his hand helplessly in the air.

His father relented. "Then you talk." He pointed to a clock on the wall. "But quick please, yes? The lunch people. In minutes."

Darijo was dressed in black slacks, black tie shoes, and a crispy white dress shirt, open at the neck. "My sister and I," he told us. "The only ones waiting tables today."

Ahmed beamed. "Darijo has a scholarship. All A's Bulkeley High School." He nodded to a table in back. His laugh was boisterous, full-throated. "I time you like a factory clock." But still wariness in his tone, his eyes dark with worry.

Sitting down, Darijo leaned in. "My father doesn't like authorities. You know…cops. People who flash papers at him." He flicked his head toward the kitchen. "A hellish life in Bosnia. The death camps. Cousins buried alive. Old women raped. At night, sitting here with his buddies, they drink *slivovitz* and weep. Everything is memory here."

"You were born in America," I said.

"Yes. A good thing. A bad thing."

"Why?" From Hank.

"A good thing because it's America and I can wake up without bombs blasting in my ears and people offer me money to go to college and have a good life."

"And the bad?"

"Because I watch my father cry as nightmares wake him at night."

Ahmed carried a tray from the kitchen and placed it on the table. "*Turska kava,*" he said. Turkish coffee. Small enamel cups inserted in filigreed silver holders. A burnished silver pitcher with a crescent star on top. He poured us coffee.

"This will put hair on your chest," Darijo's father told Hank.

Hank chuckled. "Ah, puberty arrives in a Bosnian café."

Ahmed narrowed his eyes, confused, but his son said something in Bosnian. Ahmed stared, his brow furrowed, then laughed loudly, holding his sides and pointing at Hank.

Darijo shared a smile with his father. "He says you're a comedian."

Left alone, we sipped the potent brew, winced from its shot to the system. "Like Italian espresso on steroids," Hank said.

Darijo watched us both. "My father demands you stay for lunch."

"I was planning on it," Hank told him.

Darijo nodded. He downed the last of his coffee, wiped his lips with the back of his palm, and said quietly, his eyes suddenly sad, "I don't know anything."

"Tell me how you know Dustin."

He sat back, reflected. "We sort of fell in together, you know. I mean, we're both in Professor Laramie's class, and he was in the Union gazing out the window. I sat down with him, which made him unhappy." His eyes twinkled. "I don't think he wants friends."

"Interesting. Do you like him?"

"Yeah, I guess so. He's a smart guy. Can be funny, even."

"Funny?"

"He used to make fun of Laramie."

"How?" I glanced at Hank. "Dustin?"

Darijo chuckled. "Yeah. Professor Laramie sort of ends each sentence with a barely-suppressed sound—like *ehh*. Sort of. A nervous tick maybe. Dustin would read his notes from class out loud and end with...*ehh*."

"Do you like Professor Laramie?" I asked.

He deliberated his answer. Then he said bluntly. "No. He's... like patronizing. These off-hand remarks about America going down the toilet. And he'd look at the foreign students. Like me—like Dustin. He doesn't like Muslims. Bosniaks."

"He said that?" Hank's face tightened.

"You don't have to put it into words, you know."

"I'm sorry about that," I said.

A slapdash grin, delightful. "You didn't say it."

"Did Dustin talk about his home life?" Hank asked.

"Not much." He ran his fingertip across the rim of his coffee cup. "I mean, I asked him once."

"What did he say?"

"He said he had no home life."

That startled me. "Kind of extreme, no?"

His eyes flickered. "He said he was born in the middle of a highway." An unfunny laugh. "And then he added that all his life people have been driving over him."

Hank shivered. "Good Christ."

"What did you say to that?"

"Nothing. No chance to. He said that, shrugged, and walked away. It sort of told me to keep my mouth shut."

"Tell me something, Darijo." I glanced at the clock and the shadow of his father in the kitchen doorway. "Did he talk about Professor Winslow's murder?"

"No, we didn't talk after that."

"Did he ever mention problems with Winslow?"

"Oh yeah. I mean, it just exploded. Everything is okay, then—bam. Yelling at each other. Then—Winslow is dead. He did say he asked Winslow for a favor, expecting him to agree, but Winslow flipped out. He said Winslow wasn't a kind man." Darijo paused, rephrased his words. "No, I'm wrong. He said he was a kind man who didn't understand how bad things were for him. For Dustin."

"What did he mean?"

"Dunno. Then he stopped talking about it. He said it would blow over if Winslow would just get off his back."

Hank and I exchanged looks. "But Ben wouldn't let it drop."

Darijo was eager to say something. "Can you really believe Dustin would shoot someone twice?"

"No." I repeated myself. "No."

Suddenly Ahmed and the young girl—"This is Almira, my daughter, a beauty, no? And a freshman at St. Joseph's University, full scholarship"—covered our table with food, which Darijo began identifying. *Cevapi,* grilled bits of meat served with raw onion and slabs of pita bread. Some sort of Bosnian stew that smelled of exotic Arabian spices, heady, thick. *Burek,* a flaky pastry packed with meat. Platters of cold meats. Bottles of *rakija*—"brandy, homemade, not on the menu because we cannot serve because of the American laws."

Darijo grinned. "You will need to sleep on the cots in back for the afternoon after this feast." He pointed back to the kitchen. "I often do. My father does not believe in a salad with little bits of chicken sprinkled on top for lunch."

Ahmed leaned in. "We are religious, if you need to know that. No pork."

Darijo whispered, "We are Muslims who drink. We choose our laws carefully." He smiled at us.

We dug in, Hank delirious with pleasure, Ahmed standing by the kitchen, arms folded as he watched us eat. A few customers straggled in, were seated away from us, and Almira scurried about.

"I gotta get to work," Darijo said. He started to stand, nodding at us, glancing at his father. "I got to…"

"Darijo," I said quickly, "one last question. Those audiotapes released to the public. Did you hear them?"

An unhappy face. "Like everybody I know is flooding Instagram with stuff, real crazy. Someone even put a music track behind those phone conversations. *Star Wars.*"

"But I wondered what you thought of that line Winslow said to Dustin. 'You know where the body is.' What did you think?"

"Yeah, everybody's yapping about that."

"It didn't bother you?"

He bit his lip. "A little but, you know…" He looked off across the restaurant, nodded to a customer walking in. "Did you ever hear Winslow in class? I had his Social Problems. Did you ever hear that dumb expression—'Where the bodies are buried.' Like—secrets, hidden information. Winslow liked to use that phrase, you know. Talking about the hidden stories of American life, scandals, religious nuts and their…you know infidelities and transgressions. He always laughed and said—'Hey, where the bodies are buried.' It made us laugh. So, no, it didn't bother me. Said differently, true, but I could sort of hear Winslow saying it. No *real* body, sirs. I don't think he meant Dustin was hiding a body in the cellar or something."

Politely, Darijo shook our hands, bowed, and backed off. His father walked us out the door, thanking us, inviting us back.

Outside, I started the car, turned on the heater. Light sleet had fallen, a thin coat of ice covering the windshield. While I scraped the front window, Hank worked the rear window, the two of us quiet.

Finally, waving his scraper in the air, Hank said, "This is a new wrinkle, right?"

"I have no idea what it all means."

"That's not the answer I want to hear from you."

I chuckled. "I was assuming there was a real body."

"Everybody was." He shivered. "There could *still* be a body."

"Hank, I…" I stopped, alarmed.

"What?"

"Quiet."

There it was.

Ka-clunk ka-clunk. Faint yet undeniable, though fading away now.

"That sound."

I stared up the avenue and Hank followed my gaze.

"Look."

Turning a corner a few blocks away was a car with a white-primer side panel.

The noise disappeared, lost among the horn blowing, revved engines, screeching tires, and laughter from strollers on the sidewalk.

"Shotgun," Hank yelled, hopping into the passenger seat.

I sailed across a lane of traffic, sped around a double-parked car, and turned down Capon Street. A few cars crept along, but not the one I wanted. I skirted past them. At the next corner I idled, searched left and right. Nothing. Another street. Nothing. I turned back toward the avenue and out of the corner of my eye I spotted a car pulling into a driveway.

"There," Hank yelled, "that piece-of-shit car. I think…"

We pulled alongside the curb just as a young Spanish guy was opening the driver's side. He spotted us staring and frowned.

"Not the car," I said to Hank.

Yes, a heap of a car, with a makeshift front fender painted primer white. A dented back bumper. A Take No Prisoners sticker on the back window.

The young man ambled toward us. "Help you?"

Hank rolled down the window. "No," he said politely.

"I didn't think so." He turned away.

I pulled back out into traffic.

"I swear it was the same car. Did you hear the...?"

"No," Hank broke in. "But I saw the flash of a car."

"What does this mean?" I wondered out loud.

Hank settled back, still craning his head left and right, watching the street, the experienced cop surveying the landscape. "What it means is that someone doesn't want you snooping around. Someone is afraid you're gonna find something out."

"That's just what I plan on doing."

Hank pulled in his cheeks. "Even if it kills you."

Chapter Twenty

Hank texted me during his late afternoon shift. I'd been stretched out on my sofa, my laptop balanced on my lap, as I jotted in notes about Dustin Trang. His text startled me, making me sit up so quickly that the laptop slid to the floor.

> Working now. Dustin texted. Frantic. Letter suspended him from classes. Panic. Check out.

I texted back:

> Suspended? What mean panic? Frantic?

His quick response:

> I read between lines.

I typed back:

> What do you want?

His answer:

> Unlike him. He said sick of it all. Worried.

So was I. I dialed Dustin's number, but the message said Out of Service.

I texted Hank:

> Headed to Bristol now.

I dressed quickly, tried his cellphone one more time, then drove to Dustin's home and pulled into the dark parking lot. No lights on in his home, though the apartment next door blazed with light. A group of men huddled by the front doorway, coatless, cigarettes bobbing in their mouths, a run of overlapping Spanish that ended when I approached the doorway. Suspicious, they eyed me, waiting. I nodded a hello, was ignored, and knocked discreetly on Dustin's door. No answer, as I expected.

No one had washed off the graffiti—"KILLER" had dried to a dull dirty finish.

I knocked louder. Then I pounded. I leaned toward the barred window and yelled, "Dustin, open up. I know you're home."

"No, he ain't," one of the men said.

"You saw him leave?"

He didn't answer.

"Nobody's home. Go away." Another man laughed as he said the words.

"I know he's home." I rapped my knuckles on the door.

Suddenly the door opened and Dustin stood in front of me. He peeked out, his hand gripping the door.

"Let me in." I moved forward, forcing him to back up. He stepped aside and I walked past him into the dark room. "Could we have a little light, Dustin? I'm always fumbling in the dark when I visit you."

"I like it that way."

"What? Me fumbling in the dark?"

He didn't answer but I found the light switch.

At that moment I saw his face. "Christ, Dustin, what happened?"

Nervous, he backed up, but his hand flew to his cheek, then covered his left eye. I grasped his shoulder and maneuvered him under the garish overhead light. An ugly black eye. A half-closed eye socket. His left cheek sported a silver-dollar-sized welt, bright crimson and raw. A speck of dried blood. His hair was standing on end, the coarse spiky stands electrified. No eyeglasses, which surprised me.

"Dustin, talk to me."

He started coughing, bent over, and held his sides.

"I'm taking you to the hospital."

"No, I'm all right." He tried to back away. "Go away."

"You're not okay, dammit."

His back to me. "It's a couple bruises, that's all."

"Dustin…"

"No. Fuckin' leave me alone."

"Sit down," I told him.

Strangely, he listened, sitting on the sofa, his hands folded in his lap, his head turned away from me. In the bathroom I found a face cloth, soaked it in hot water, wrung it out, and told Dustin to rest his head back. Quietly he obeyed, and I dabbed at the wounds. He winced, squirmed, but finally sat still. "Quite the shiner, Dustin. Tell me."

"Nothing to tell."

I stared into his small face. "Oh good, Dustin. One more story you won't tell me. Everything is a goddamn secret with you."

"Nobody's business."

I gripped his shoulder and he jerked back. "You're wrong about that. It's my business now."

"What do you want?"

"You texted Hank. He was worried. I was worried. I *am* worried."

He rubbed his eye with a finger. "Hank called you?"

"Yeah."

That news seemed to please him because I saw the corners of his lips turn up slightly, a hint of a smile. "Nothing—shit. I got this letter from the college. They won't let me back on campus next semester until the…you know, the matter is resolved."

I dabbed at his cheek though he pushed my hand away. "Then you have to resolve the matter. To prove it—but you have to *talk* to me."

"I don't want to be suspended," he said loudly. "I got nowhere to go anymore." Panic. Frantic. I wondered how Hank, that state cop *wunderkind*, could detect such extreme reaction from an impersonal text on his cellphone. Maybe, I thought, it was generational. Hank was right—he *could* read between the lines.

"Okay, Dustin, I'll work on that for you."

"You will?" His eyes got wide.

"Now," I said, breathing in, "you tell me what happened." I dabbed at the welt on his cheek that seemed to be turning a deeper shade of scarlet.

My phone beeped. A text from Hank:

> If I got to use all 140 characters I will: talk to me.

I responded:

> I'm here. Calm down.

"Hank?" Dustin said.

"He's worried." I waited a second. "Tell me."

"Nothing to tell."

"You're bullshitting me, Dustin. I don't like that." I looked around. "Where's your mother?"

He panicked, restless in the seat. "You can't stay. Mom said you can't come here anymore. She told you…" His words ran on, sputtered.

"I know what she told me. Tell me." I waited a second. "Where is she?"

Nervously, he watched the front door. "She went to the Indian casino at Foxwoods. With Aunt Suong and Rosie. You know, Timmy's wife. They go by bus from the center…They're gonna be…Mom might come back any minute." He pointed at the clock. "At suppertime. You gotta go."

"I don't care. I'm not leaving until you talk to me about what happened to your face. Who beat you up?"

"I wasn't beat up." He fumbled on a table for his eyeglasses, putting them on, and they rested crookedly on the bridge of his nose. The black eye now seemed more ominous.

"Tell me." I grasped his shoulder and he froze. "Somebody from the neighborhood?" I waited. "Your brothers?" His body tightened.

"Timmy?"

"Shit no. That fat slob can't get off the couch."

I clicked my tongue. "Hollis."

He didn't answer but I knew. "Not here, right? He can't come here. Where were you?" Silence. He couldn't look me in the eye. "Uncle Binh's?"

"Yeah, I…"

"But Hollis doesn't talk to you. Ever."

A phony laugh that went on too long. "He didn't have to say anything, right?" His eyes kept going to the front door. "You gotta go. I don't want trouble."

"All right. I'll leave." I glanced toward the door. "You okay?"

He rushed to the front door and opened it. As I walked by him, I touched his shoulder, forcing him to stop moving. I leaned in, smelled his hot breath. "Dustin." He shook off my hand, but as he closed the door behind me I heard a faraway mumble. "Thanks."

One of the men lingering outside the other apartment took a drag on his cigarette and yelled to me. "I told you no one ain't home."

• ● **●** ● •

Standing outside Uncle Binh's apartment door, the overhead lamp switched off, I grasped the knocker, but a screw came loose, the brass knocker slipping. Suddenly the door swung open, and I faced a surprised Timmy Trang. He switched on the outside light, and squinted. He was in the middle of a sentence. "Why the hell you don't use your goddamn key…we expected you…" He stopped, a bewildered look on his face. "Shit, I thought you was my wife."

"Can I come in?"

"Yeah, sure." He made a face. "Like a party here tonight."

That made little sense because the only other occupant of the room was Uncle Binh in his wheelchair in front of a large-screen TV that was playing a Vietnamese tape. A song-and-dance routine, slender Vietnamese beauties pirouetting across a stage in front of a large South Vietnamese flag. Timmy saw me looking. "Tet festival in San Diego." He flicked his head to the side. "Pure crap, so far as I'm concerned."

He grabbed the remote from the table and switched it off. The screen went black as Uncle Binh cursed him. "*Lo dit.*" Asshole.

Uncle Binh's hands idly sifted through a stack of letters on an end table, a nervous gesture that caused the letters to flutter to the floor. Postmarks from Vietnam, I noticed. Scribbled addresses. Uncle Binh leaned over and reached for the letters. He scowled at Timmy. "Help me."

Timmy ignored him, rolling his eyes. "Crap news from the homeland. "*Khong gi ma am y.*" Big deal.

An overheated room. Radiators popping on. Yet one of the windows was cracked open, a breeze drifting across my feet. The coffee table was filled with white cartons from a Chinese restaurant, paper plates with plastic forks and cheap chopsticks still in the red paper casing. I saw pork fried rice piled on one dish within reach of Uncle Binh. Lo mein spilled out of a white carton, tipped on its side. A splash of soy sauce drizzled on a napkin. A dish of General Tso's chicken, florets of broccoli dotting the glossy meat.

"I'm interrupting dinner?" I said to Timmy.

"We're done."

He shuffled to the sofa, plopped down. Dressed in a denim shirt pulled out of his trousers, washed a few too many times because the country-western design was faded, it was also tight on his fat belly. A button undone so that worm-white flesh peeped through. His hand found the spot and scratched it.

"What?" he said, watching me. At that moment his phone rang—a loud ringtone that played the theme from *The Godfather*—and he mumbled an answer, then said to Uncle Binh, "The bus is downtown. Rosie lost fifty fucking bucks." He frowned. "That's old news." To me he said, "They'll be here in a few minutes."

"I want to know what happened to Dustin. Why was he beat up?"

Timmy acted surprised by that news, turning to Uncle Binh with a confused look, adding, "What the fuck's he talking about?"

"I just came from his apartment. He's been roughed up."

Uncle Binh was twitching in his seat. A gurgling sound escaped his throat. "Earlier..." he began.

"What the hell?" From Timmy. A bead of perspiration on his brow. "Man, I don't know..."

I heard banging from the back of the apartment, the sound of a toilet flushing, then the kitchen light snapped on. Hollis walked into the room.

"Well, well, well. The cops are in town."

"I'm not a cop."

"You look like one."

"Thanks."

"You gotta gun on you?" His eyes looked me up and down.

"Yeah, and it's registered. How about yours?"

"I can't carry no gun. As you well know. I ain't gonna go back to jail."

"Doesn't mean you don't have one."

A smirk as he walked into the room and sat in a chair. "I'm law-abiding."

He was a sharp contrast to his round brother—woefully skinny, shorter, wiry, stringy muscular arms. A white T-shirt that revealed a bony chest. A shaved head that revealed a phrenologist's orgiastic dreamscape: bumps and moon ridges and scar tissue. Green and red tattoos across his neck. The hollow gaunt face of a druggie—those wide vacant eyes. He sat with his right arm cradling his left and rocked back and forth. All of a sudden a smile on his face—whatever he'd done in that bathroom kicking in, softening the edges of his crankiness.

"Why'd you hit your brother?"

He made a jack o' lantern face, mocking. "He's a little prissy college fag."

"You beat him up. Why?"

"If you gotta know, he walks in here and sees me and freaks out and Uncle Binh tells him to leave and I say 'Get the fuck out' and he says 'Fuck you' to me."

"So you hit him?"

"Wouldn't anybody? He's a little shit who disses the world and then acts like a pussy."

"Leave him alone."

He mimicked me in a high falsetto voice. "'Leave him alone.' Yeah, sure. He's your little fuck buddy, right?"

"Jesus Christ." From Timmy, looking toward the front door.

Uncle Binh broke in, his voice quivering. "Hiep, no. Stop this." In Vietnamese: "*Lam on.*" Please.

Hollis shot at him, "You're the one talking about how he disgraced the fuckin' family. Even your beloved minister, that fat fuck Simms, shocked you at the service, and you couldn't shut up about those insults."

Binh dropped his eyes. "Our family pride."

"Hah!" Hollis bellowed. "Family pride. Do you look around your world, old man? Yeah, he's bringing fame to this family. The TV is fuckin' filled with his dumb-ass face."

Timmy cleared his throat but said nothing.

Hollis pointed a finger at me. "That boy is a waste of space on this earth, always has been, fucked up the family the day he was born, and everybody in the goddamn family knows it." A deadly grin. "And I'm called the bad boy of the family 'cause I do a little time for making a living. He walks in here and is all up-in-my-face. He's lucky he got off with a few black-and-blue marks. When they haul his ass to prison, he's gonna know what a beating is really like."

"You touch Dustin again and I'll haul your ass to jail. Hear me?" I said.

"Scared of you, asshole."

"You're on record, hear me? Trust me. The cops are on my side. I got all the odds. You'll be watching your own ass in jail."

He stood up and gave me the finger. "They teach you sign language in cop school."

"Among other things."

"What does that mean?"

"It means I can spot a coward at ten paces."

He rallied. "I'm outta here. My girlfriend's waiting for her bucket of bolts she calls a car." He grabbed a coat off a rack by the door, shot a look back at me, and left, slamming the door.

I stepped to the window and watched his back as he bustled down the sidewalk, slipping on a patch of ice. Through the shut window I could hear his "Fuck, fuck" as he kicked the ice. At the curb he tumbled into a car, a decades-old Cadillac with plastic covering a back window that had been knocked out. The car slid from the curb, bounced off a snow bank, and disappeared.

Quiet in the room.

"Nice guy," I said.

Uncle Binh was shaking his head. "Nothing is ever good anymore."

His face flushed, Timmy stood up and peered out the window. Another button had come undone on his shirt as he scratched his belly.

He was shaking his head. "You know, I ain't got much in my life, but it's a whole crap load better than that loser."

"He's your brother."

"I don't care, man. Yeah, he's my brother, but that dude scares the shit outta me."

Chapter Twenty-one

Liz phoned from Sophia Grecko's apartment, and for a second what I heard was the sound of a *beep beep beep*, a truck backing up, followed by muffled yelled voices. Then Sophia's dark laughter covered Liz's soft words.

"Come over. Now. Sophia's. You free?" A whisper. "You better be."

"What's up?" I swallowed the last bite of a tuna-on-toast sandwich I'd made, my eyes scanning my laptop screen where an itemized bill to HR at Aetna was aching for my SEND touch, and squinted at the icy rain slamming my old windows. A day to stay indoors, though Liz's call suggested differently.

"The Martin and Melody Show, act two."

"What are you talking about?"

"Martin is moving Ben's stuff out of the apartment. His friend just backed a U-Haul onto the lawn and smashed into the frozen shrubbery. The whole house shook. He's been running around like a deranged nut."

I found myself grinning. "And I should be there for what reason?"

A door slammed shut. Liz raised her voice. "I met Melody in the hallway as I came in. She's getting sentimental and talkative. She mumbled something about dreams of her father." What sounded like glass breaking. "And one of their conversations."

"So? Important?"

"You're the detective, Mr. Lam. When people are waxing sentimental about their murdered father, perhaps you might want to eavesdrop on such chatter. Useless but…" She trailed off with a slight laugh. "Sophia also made a huge pot of soul-searing chili."

"I'm on my way."

The door to Ben's apartment was blocked open with a stack of books, and as I walked past, headed to the stairway leading to the second floor, I peered in. A madhouse. A young man I didn't recognize was pushing cardboard boxes across the floor while Martin circled him. Red-faced, sputtering, he was complaining that something would break. "What are you? An asshole? Well, you must be. I wouldn't put it past God when he…" On and on, delirious, irate, while the friend—I'm assuming soon-to-be-former-friend because that's what happens when you ask a friend to help you move—narrowed his eyes and said nothing.

Sitting primly on a wing chair facing the doorway, her hands clasped in her lap, Melody watched the circus.

"Something has happened." Liz's first words to me as I walked into Sophia's apartment. "All was calm and all was bright when they started emptying Ben's apartment. But then, like bombs exploding, we heard Martin yelling at the top of his voice, cursing, foot stomping, something glass smashed against a wall. Very Joan Crawford when she became box-office poison."

Sophia added, "We heard Melody pleading, 'Think of Dad, think of Dad.'"

"The friend is doing all the work," I commented.

"Why are you surprised?" From Liz, motioning me to a table where a pot of hot coffee rested. "Have some coffee, and then you can make a class field trip into darkest subterranea."

Not talking, we sat at the table, our silence punctuated by sudden outbursts from below. What sounded like a table dragged across a hardwood floor. The rumble of a dolly as someone ran it up the corrugated incline of the U-Haul. But Martin's fury was unrelenting. Indeed, growing—at one point, he must have been standing on a stepladder, his head inches from the floor of Sophia's apartment. We heard his raspy breathing. A heating vent magnified the noises. Sophia spooned out bowls of chili as we tore off chunks of fresh-made Italian bread, warm and crusty and moist, popping them into the chili. "Dinner theater," she commented wryly.

"How long have they been here?" I asked, sitting back.

"A couple hours," Liz said.

"I've been waiting for Martin to come. Ever since I gave him the key. I'm surprised he waited."

Idly, I compared Sophia's apartment to the one below—two lovers living in such close proximity. Whereas Ben's old apartment had a ramshackle feel to it with his thrift-store couches and church-bazaar tchotchkes, with the frayed scatter rugs and piles of books and magazines in sloppy piles on the floor, Sophia's place was its opposite. A sleek, art-deco arrangement of sharp-lined furniture, black enamel finish, bronze fixtures, Frankart lamps of sleek slender women striking poses with green-and-black fans. Chase chrome-plated floor ashtrays that no one would dare to use for a cigarette. A polished, machine-age apartment. I remembered Ben joking that when he went up to Sophia's apartment he felt he was toppling into a movie set for a *Gatsby* remake.

And Sophia happily answered him. "And your apartment is the back room of a hoedown rummage sale."

Now Ben's apartment was disappearing into a U-Haul truck.

Standing at the window, I watched the friend rolling up boxes into the truck. Icy rain pelted his bare head. He stopped, rested the dolly on the side, and lit a cigarette. Coatless, he wiped his brow with the back of his hand as smoke covered his face. Then he shivered from the cold, dropped the cigarette, but still didn't move. From the apartment Martin's voice sailed out the open door. "I'm paying you to stand around?"

"I knew there had to be a reason," Sophia said over my shoulder. "Hired help. I didn't think he had any friends left. They all stayed with his beleaguered ex-wife."

"Wish me luck," I said with a smile. "I'm going down into the mosh pit."

Liz's eyes twinkled. "If you don't return, could I have that lovely Le Po watercolor you have over your desk? I've already identified it on the back with a label-maker when you weren't paying attention."

I did a half-bow.

Downstairs the apartment was quiet, Melody still sitting in that wing chair facing the open doorway. I greeted her, but a voice shocked me from behind.

"What are you doing here?"

Martin's face was flushed, his chin quivering

"I was upstairs visiting and…"

His face a mixture of dislike and wonder. "I'm moving."

"You found an apartment, Martin?"

"In Wethersfield. Near the old center. In a house. This"—he indicated the contents of his father's rooms—"is what I got to live on."

"Your divorce is final?"

"You ask a lot of questions." He turned away.

The hired help walked in, wiping his wet face with a handkerchief. Maybe one of his students in need of spare change. The boy spotted the scowl on Martin's face, grabbed a box, rolled his eyes, and disappeared. Martin's eyes followed him, and he walked out after him, grumbling, "Let's see how that minimum-wage serf destroys another box of glassware."

"I don't know why I came." Melody was not speaking to me but to a wall. "The rain is so cold."

"Melody," I began, "why *are* you here?"

"He asked me to help. He never asked me for help before."

"So you came?"

"My mother insisted. I wanted to make her happy."

I counted a moment. "Is it working?"

She eyed me closely. "Nothing makes my mother happy. You know that." Then, gazing toward a desk, the papers rifled and scattered. "Martin found the letters."

"What?"

"The cause of his…hysteria. Rage. Insanity."

"What letters?"

She pointed. A bunch of letters dumped into a wastepaper basket alongside Ben's old country-store desk. Stamped envelopes and creamy stationery, but now torn into pieces. "There."

"Incendiary?" I asked.

She smiled impishly. "You could say that. Dad kept the letters from that…that UConn intern who dragged him into bed that semester and guaranteed the end of our home life."

"Your father kept them?"

A bit of pique in her tone. "I just told you, no? There they are. And Martin read them."

I was tempted to retrieve them, patch them together. But I said, "What's in them?"

She blew out her cheeks, a weary look on her face. "That dumb affair lasted only a month or so. Dad came to his senses, and walked away. Unfortunately he confessed all to Mom. A mistake." A pause as she swallowed. "Dad loved Mom."

"She wouldn't forgive him." A flat-out statement that made her start.

A sad smile. "You've met my mother, Mr. Lam. She…she hasn't forgiven a fourth-grade teacher for calling her…a sneak. I've heard about *that* too many times." She sighed. "Anyway, Martin found the letters. I don't know why Dad kept them. They were written after they parted company. Pleading letters, begging. I love you, love you. If you don't love me, then drop dead. Over the top. References to lovemaking that was glorious, inspired, earth shattering, epic. You get the picture. Martin almost had a cow." She laughed out loud. "It was almost worth the price of admission to this show."

"So he tore them up?"

"Ritualistically, dramatically. I'm surprised there wasn't some ancient runic incantation to exorcise the spirit that flew out of those letters."

I checked to see where Martin was—outside, giving the boy the finger. Rain splashed on his head. "That's why he's in a rage?"

"You bet." She shifted her position in the wing chair. "I was afraid to move. That mover was—in fact, is—ready to run for the hills."

"Why doesn't he?"

She sighed. "He needs the twenty bucks my brother promised hm. And he knows how to drive a U-Haul."

"Martin's taking everything?"

"I came because I thought there might be something I'd want."

She indicated an accordion folder bulging with sheets of paper. A sheaf of printouts rested on top, bound with elastics. A few scattered photos. "I'm gonna keep his notes for his new book. Over there."

I walked to the table and picked up the photos. "A new attack on evangelical religion?"

"My father only sang one note, Mr. Lam."

"But he was good at it."

A melancholy shrug. "If you say so."

Among the eight-by-ten glossies were three photos taken from the Gospel of Wealth Ministry. The Reverend Simms preaching in his flowing robes, a miter clutched in his right hand. Another of the vast hall packed with worshippers. But the third surprised me—a close-up shot of one wing of the auditorium—the section where the contingent of Asian—mainly Vietnamese—sat, all with rapt, upturned faces. All holding their dollar bills up in the air. I spotted Uncle Binh and Aunt Suong, but not Dustin's mother.

"Who took these pictures?" I asked Melody.

She shrugged. "How would I know? A spy? Dad couldn't go to that carnival show and come out alive."

A spy? I peered into the photo. Dustin the spy? His story to me—the Professor wanted me to be a spy. I was a spy. Was it possible? But I couldn't imagine Dustin merrily snapping away with his iPhone. Or could I? How did I know? Maybe he was caught, and accused. Maybe that explained the Reverend Simms' public naming of Dustin as Ben's possible killer. The servant of a sadistic but righteous God.

"If you stare at the photo any longer, it's gonna burst into flames." Martin tapped me on the shoulder. "You can leave now."

"Leave him alone," Melody said in my defense, which surprised me.

Martin stepped into the kitchen and returned with a glass vase. He held it up to the light.

Melody watched him. "I've been dreaming of Dad." Her voice was so soft I could barely hear her.

"What? Not that again." Martin frowned. "I don't wanna hear it. All morning you can't shut up about it."

Melody sounded wistful, ready to sob. "I've been dreaming about the happy days."

"Shut the hell up, Melody." He shot a look at me.

A bit of fire in her voice. "I went to see him, Martin. You didn't. I snuck out of the house, away from Mom's wrath—I came here. You didn't."

"Yes, I did." A biting tone.

"Not till recently. Only because you wanted something. He told me. You asked for money."

Martin checked me out again. "He was my father."

"And you're thirty years old."

Sarcastically, "I know how old I am. Two years older than an old maid we all know."

She caught her breath. "I came here. Not you. We talked. You never talked to him."

"Maybe because he always found fault with me."

She rushed her words. "No. That's not true. He always forgave your lapses. Your wandering. Your…dumb marriages you toppled into because you…"

"Because what?" he yelled at her.

"Because you need someone to blame for your failure."

A dark laugh. "God, you got everything wrong, Melody."

She swung her head back and forth. "You think so? I'm sitting here watching you pilfer his life, a life you ran away from.

You're gonna sit on his sofa, eat out of his dishes, sleep in his bed. God, how can you live with yourself?"

The young mover walked into the room, listened for a moment, then turned on his heels. He looked back over his shoulder for a second and caught my eye. Though skittish, he was having the time of his life.

Martin snarled, "I have a life."

"You live a lie." She made a dismissive wave of her hand.

"I'm outta here." He raised the glass vase over his head and hurled it against a wall. It shattered, shards covering a counter, slipping to the floor. "Fuck you."

He left the apartment, slamming the door behind him.

Melody didn't move.

"You all right?" I asked. "How you getting home?"

"I drove my own car, Mr. Lam. I sort of knew how this afternoon was going to end."

I walked away, but she mumbled, "I have been dreaming about Dad, you know."

"Good. You have to remember your father."

She spoke over my words. "I've been trying to memorize his voice so I'll never forget it. Things he said to me." A wistful smile. "All our conversations. He talked to me, you know."

"What did he tell you?"

"He told me how much he loved me."

"That was good, no?"

"I needed to hear it, Mr. Lam." Her lips quivered.

"Did he ever talk about his students?"

"Of course. All the time. That was the problem. He lived for his students. He said things that made me want to take notes. Isn't that weird? My own father."

"A smart man."

Suddenly she studied my face. "I was here a day before he died. He said the strangest thing." A faraway look in her eyes as she remembered. "He said, 'Sometimes history falls like a ton of bricks on the innocent.' When I asked him what he meant, he said sometimes life just gets too heavy to carry on your shoulders."

"What was that all about?"

"He never told me."

"Melody, you should go home now."

She shook her head. "If you don't mind, I'd like to sit here for a while. By myself. It will be the last time."

Chapter Twenty-two

Hank's grandmother asked him to invite Dustin for supper, a request that prompted a call to me. "Have you been talking to her?"

"Hank, *you're* the gossip," I told him, laughing. "The family town crier. Okay, we had that talk in Grandma's kitchen when we talked about the Trang family debacle…"

"Yeah, I remember. But still and all."

"Still and all, Grandma is a curious woman."

"But Dustin?"

"I want to be there."

"That's why I'm calling. Grandma will go all Buddha dog day afternoon on him, and you are the only annoying Buddha pest that follows her conversation."

"Wisdom, Hank."

Dustin resisted the invitation, Hank let me know. He sputtered and hung up and Hank had to call back. Dustin claimed his license was expired and he was afraid of being pulled over—until Hank, breaking in, told him to be at his parents' house at six. "I used my state cop voice."

Not surprisingly, Dustin was late, but then we heard Dustin's rattletrap Toyota choking to a stop in the driveway. We waited. He sat in his car for a few minutes, unmoving, the interior dark, until an impatient Hank, peering out the window, flicked the outside light on and off. Dustin got out of his car and scurried up the walk.

Nervous as hell, he froze in the doorway, then stumbled in, bending to take off his spotless blue-and-gold sneakers and carefully putting them aside. An elaborate ritual, untying each lace, folding the laces in, lining the shoes up as if in a store display window. So stylized a procedure that we stopped, enthralled, watching. Worried, he picked up the shoes, held them up in front of his chest, and then, spotting a pile of shoes on a mat nearby, positioned them there—neatly, next to each other, at the edge of the mat. He smiled at me.

Hank led him into the kitchen where he blinked rapidly as he looked from one person to the next. His goggle eyeglasses kept slipping down his nose. Under the overhead light, the bruises on his cheek and his purplish black eye were fresh, scary, made dramatic by the eyeglasses.

Leaving the counter where she'd been chopping ginger into miniscule flecks, Grandma approached him, smiling, for a brief second touching his bruised cheek lovingly. *"Xin chao."* Welcome. In English: "I wanted to meet you. The boy I see all over TV."

Said, the words startled Hank, who flushed, stammered. His mother, her back to the counter as she spooned oil into a wok, started to speak but changed her mind. Yet Dustin wasn't bothered. He nodded back at Grandma. A tiny woman with a head of ivory white curls under a lace bonnet, she stood eye-to-eye with the short boy, and he stared back at her, muttering a hesitant thanks. *Cam on.* A half-bow, awkward. But Grandma suddenly grasped his elbow, tugged at him, and with an infectious laugh led him to a chair. "Sit, sit. We are all family here."

Dustin's expression suggested he didn't believe a word of that, but he welcomed the chance to sit down, spine erect, hands folded in his lap.

Hank made the introductions, ending with, "And of course you know Rick, I think. He was not invited but the aroma of homemade cooking always draws him from the street."

"Shush," his mother said as she gently rapped him on the shoulder. "A comedian—he should be on TV." She stopped, alarmed by her own words. A nervous glance at Dustin. "I mean...I mean on TV..."

Hank saved her. "Mom, it's all right." He reached out and touched her wrist.

Hank's father walked in, followed by Grandpa, who seemed unhappy there were strangers in the house. Dutifully, Dustin sprang to his feet, half-bowed, and shook their hands. Strangely, he introduced himself as Anh Ky and not Dustin. The Old Country, I thought, respect for elders. Surprisingly, Hank's father gripped Dustin's forearm and thanked him for coming. I caught Hank's eye—this was an unexpected wrinkle. But Grandpa, who barely tolerated me as the impure mongrel feasting on his bounty, simply grunted and sat down, grasping some chopsticks between his fingers.

Hank caught my eye again and mouthed: That went well. I told you so.

I ignored him.

I sat back, breathed in the smells of the Nguyen kitchen. Today the pungent scent of chopped ginger covered the room. At the counter Grandma whacked the brown tubers until glistening bits and pieces of dull gold speckled her cutting board.

I followed Dustin's eyes as he surveyed the room—the walls covered with calendars from Asian marketplaces, a redundancy that bothered no one at all. Above the knotty-pine cabinets was a carved wood clock in the shape of Vietnam, always offering the wrong time, which also bothered no one, a clock covered with gaudy stencils of peasants in conical hats carrying water buckets on their shoulders. A water buffalo. A South Vietnamese flag. A smiling cartoon-faced girl staring, for some reason, at the numeral three.

Grandma turned from the counter, her cleaver in hand. "You like ginger chicken with broccoli?"

Dustin nodded.

"Everybody likes that," Hank volunteered.

"A guest must be pleased," Grandma told her grandson, who beamed back at her.

Hank leaned into Dustin. "You hear that, Dustin? You're the official guest."

Dustin stared as he chewed his lower lip.

"Anh Ky," Hank's mother said to him, "you must tell us a little about your life."

Grandma was still waving that cleaver. "Anh Ky, we know of your problems. That foolishness. Tell us about your real life."

"My real life?" he echoed, confused.

"You're at Farmington College," she said. "A scholarship, yes?"

"I *was* at the college," he mumbled back.

Hank cleared his throat. "Grandma, this sounds like an interrogation."

She chuckled. "It is called conversation." She went on, "I met your mother, you know."

Dustin was surprised. "Where?"

"Maybe a Tet festival. The marketplace. And your Uncle Binh and Aunt Suong. There are not many young people in your family." She stopped to look into his face.

"Me." Dustin smiled back.

"A majority of one." Grandma walked over and handed him a piece of ginger. "Eat this. Taste the sharpness. They say that ginger will help you see in the dark."

He squinted at her, taking the morsel from her fingertips, putting it between his teeth, and biting.

Hank's mother was watching Grandma closely, shaking her head. "Such questions." And then, of course, asked her own. "Anh Ky, do you wish a family of your own?"

Hank swallowed a laugh as he caught my eye. Dustin waited a bit, then said clearly, "I want five children."

Grandma stood behind him, leaning in, hugging his neck. "Oh my. Five. Why?"

He angled his neck and stared into her face. "So everybody will always have somebody to talk to."

Said, the line hung in the air, naked.

Grandma flicked a finger at him. "*Cang dong cang vui.*" The more, the merrier. "Many will give you pleasure."

For the first time Hank's father said something. He'd gone to the refrigerator for a Budweiser, popped the tab, and finished most of it before turning to Dustin. "Someday you will visit your family village, no? Saigon, yes, your uncle, a man known by reputation as a hero for the South Vietnamese, but the family comes from a village."

"I don't know."

Grandpa, who looked as though he'd not been paying any attention, suddenly sat up. "Ton Dang. Outside Vung Tau."

"You know that?" From Dustin, startled.

"Folks talk. A place of fierce fighting. The Cong so cruel. The bodies piled up. Americans. Our people." He closed his eyes and interlocked his fingers.

"No one talks of it." Dustin's voice was small, hollow.

"Dead. Everyone," Grandpa murmured.

"We got cousins there," Dustin said slowly. "I mean, I think we do. Uncle Binh gets letters, writes back. We send medicine."

The most words he'd spoken. His glance swept from Grandpa to Grandma, then took in the rest of us. "Mom and Uncle Binh whispering about the hardships. Then. Now."

"Everyone carries Vietnam with them," Grandma said. "The war cut our lives in half. Before and after."

"They don't like to talk about the war. It's—like taboo. The wonderful days, yes. But not the war."

"Everyone should talk about that war," Grandpa went on, his voiced heated. "It ended a lot of our worlds."

Dustin wet his lips. "It's a forbidden topic, I think. I mean, the fighting. Leaving." He swallowed. "Like I said—taboo."

Grandpa thundered, "It should be the only topic. What now? Exile? Communists crushing lives?"

"The Commies," Dustin said quietly. "The Commies are in the way."

"In the way?" I asked.

Dustin ignored me. "People used to bow to Uncle Binh. Here. In America."

"All the answers to our lives in America can be found back in that war, Anh Ky."

"What?"

Grandpa shook a hand in his face. "Do you hear me? Why you are *here*. You. Tan"—he referred to Hank's Vietnamese name—"here. Your footprint is back in the village."

Dustin suddenly turned pale, as though he'd violated something he didn't understand. "In school..."

Grandpa shouted in English. "In school they teach you shit about the war."

"Your mother and father," Hank's mother began, frowning at Grandpa and softening her tone. "They came here for you."

Dustin straightened in his chair. "No. Not for me. Their lives ended when they got on that helicopter." The shyness had disappeared, his voice firm, clear. "Mom sits and waits. I sit and wait—she tells me to be quiet in a house where no one talks. Me—her. Like...a time capsule, you know. Like someone stopped running the camera, froze the frame, you know, like a movie, and they're waiting for someone to unfreeze them. It's a little scary because their lives are in black and white and the world is in color and..." He stopped, suddenly embarrassed, looking down into his lap.

Silence in the hot room.

Quietly, Grandma and Hank's mother served platters of food. We dug into the glistening chicken. Chopsticks sailed across the table, clicking, tapping. Cups of tea. More Budweiser for the men. Grandma with her coconut flavored water. A feast, and we were absorbed now, savoring it. Grandma sat back, her old fingers fiddling with chopsticks, on her face a mysterious smile.

Dustin relished the meal, and I wondered about his daily diet. That pasty bowl of rice on his kitchen table, barely touched. The shriveled chunks of meat. Probably Italian subs from the grinder shop on the corner. Burger King. Wendy's. A life of fast food paid for by the part-time job at the diner.

He never looked up, devouring the ginger chicken, not surprised when Hank's mother without speaking used the blunt end of her chopsticks to fill his bowl with more chicken and broccoli. He nodded at her, a hint of a smile.

Grandma finally spoke. "It is our lot to suffer." She pointed to the statue of Buddha. "War makes evil."

I added, "*Ac gia ac bao.*"

Grandma smiled. "Buddha's wisdom. Yes, evil will bring more evil in the world."

Dustin narrowed his eyes at me. "You—like follow Buddhism?"

"When I was a small boy, I was left in an orphanage by my mother, who gave me a small book called *Sayings of Buddha.* Tattered, falling apart. I carried it with me to America."

"It's golden," Grandma said, nodding at me.

Hank pointed at me. "Grandma and Rick are the resident Buddhists. They will paste aphorisms on your soul."

"They are already there, my boy." Grandma tapped her heart. "Buddha is always in your heart and tells you to do good deeds. In that village of yours, little Anh Ky, the souls of the ancestors wait. That is why your mother and uncle look back there…the rituals of the dead."

Hank interrupted. "People shouldn't suffer."

Grandma's voice had a gentle edge. "They have no choice. It is what you *do* with the suffering that matters."

"What about greedy people?" Dustin asked out of the blue.

"What?" From me.

"If Buddha is in the heart, why are people, you know, violent, mean, rotten, robbing people…you know?"

"They don't listen to their hearts," Grandma answered. "So we need to suffer." Grandma smiled at Dustin. "Remember that. But you are *not* your suffering. You hear me? You look to the sky above, where Buddha watches." She smiled. "You are a blessed boy."

That seemed to embarrass Dustin, who dipped his head into his lap.

I spoke in English, "'Life is full of misery, loneliness, and suffering—and it's all over much too soon.'"

"Buddha?" Hank eyes got wide, a smart-aleck grin on his face.

"Woody Allen."

No one laughed except Hank. But Dustin smiled. "I heard of him."

"A wise man," Grandma commented, understanding the English.

Hank pointed to the elaborate shrine up on the wall in the corner: a plaster Buddha, gold-plated, chubby and grand, surrounded by joss sticks and artificial flowers, but sharing the space with the Virgin Mary, regal in blue and white, a beatific smile, Sunday palms and a votive candle at her feet. In front a stack of blood red oranges. "Dustin, we are Catholic and Buddhist here. Peaceful coexistence. Sort of. The women Buddhists. The men Catholic. The favorite son"—he bowed—"neither."

"A heathen," his mother said, though she grinned at him. "We wait for the day of his enlightenment."

Dustin concentrated on the shrine. "Both? Wild."

I smiled. "Yeah, wild. Only in America."

"We got a shrine like that but I don't pay attention. My mother and Uncle Binh take care of it." He grinned. "No Virgin Mary, however."

"You are Buddhists." From Grandma. "The ancestors journey to America with them."

Dustin laughed. "They come for the cheeseburgers."

Grandma paused as she held chopsticks in the air. "What?"

Now Dustin was embarrassed. "I mean, when Rick was at my house, we looked up, and…I guess Mom ran out of oranges, so she had a McDonald's cheeseburger in a box and…" He waved his hands in the air, a helpless gesture. "Nothing. Nonsense."

Though everyone smiled at the image, Grandma did not, her face tense, and the chopsticks, suspended in the air, moved up and down like dreadful punctuation. She never took her eyes from Dustin's, and I glanced at Hank, worry on his face. Grandma's face looked shattered.

Hank mumbled, "Maybe a sacrilege. I don't know. Grandma takes this stuff…"

His mother leaned in. "It ain't stuff." In English.

Grandma wasn't happy. She nodded at the shrine, bowed, but then placed her chopsticks across the top of her bowl. Her meal was over. The shadow of that plaster-of-Paris Buddha cast a pall on the warm room.

Bothered, looking at his Grandma and then at his scowling mother, Hank shifted the conversation, addressing his father. "You're spending a lot of time in Little Saigon, Dad. Rumor has it."

His father, sitting back and watching the women of the family becoming somber and distant, mumbled, "I'm retired now. What do you want me to do? Stay in this house all day?"

Hank's mother bit her lip. "When he is home, he is like dust. Everywhere you look. Underfoot."

Her husband found the remark delightful. "She sends me to the market and I come back with mangoes instead of jackfruit."

"The wrong rice. The wrong brand of soymilk. He buys the kind that tastes like aluminum foil."

"Mom," Hank said, "how does aluminum foil taste?"

She grinned at him. "Like the soymilk your father brings home."

Hank faced his father. "Mom says you spend a lot of time at Minh Le's Bar and Pool Hall on Park. With your buddies. Loc and Joe. The guys from your foundry?"

His father nodded. "We have discovered we are"—he switched to English—"the hustlers."

Hank guffawed. "Good God. I'm gonna have to arrest you."

"Loc and Joe are fatter than you."

Hank made believe he was shocked. "I'm not fat. This is muscle."

"Here we go again." His mother rolled her eyes.

A voice broke into the humor. "Pool?"

"Yes, Anh Ky. Pool." His father mimicked the motion of a cue stick striking a ball.

"Dustin plays pool. I've seen him at the college." I watched Dustin's face.

Hank asked him, "Where did you learn to play pool?"

Dustin answered but he was watching Hank's father. "At the Bristol Boys Club. After school. It was there or the library."

"You good?" From Hank's father.

And then, strangely, Dustin turned his chair so that he faced Hank's father, who also shifted his position. The two of them began a spirited conversation in Vietnamese, with flakes of colloquial English drifting in, that centered on pool and billiards techniques and trick shots and banking and spotting...the way you break...the shots off the rails...the merits of eight ball over nine...the rules that are violated...this player, that...ESPN... the current Filipino champion touring Connecticut...the legend of someone called Kid Delicious—

"Kid Delicious?" From Hank.

He was ignored.

Thrilling, really, mesmerizing, the most animated I'd ever seen Hank's father—and certainly Dustin. They talked over each other. The two men, one a crotchety sixty-something and the squirrely, skinny eighteen-year-old boy demonstrated impossible shots they claimed they'd executed.

The rest of us watched. Grandma wore a satisfied smile on her face. She mumbled to me, "*Toi khong hieu.*" I don't understand this. But she looked happy.

Seizing the opportunity, Hank mentioned a pool hall on Main Street, blocks away. Classic Billiards, a local East Hartford hangout next to Hooters. He suggested we men hit balls for an hour or so, but his father balked. "I've gone by there. Only white men play there."

"Not anymore," Hank insisted.

Hank's mother welcomed the move, shooing us out the door. "Not too late. Dustin has to drive home."

"I have to drive home, too, Mom," Hank said. "Aren't you worried about me?"

She touched his cheek. "I worry about the people you will drive off the road."

As we stood, thanked the women, bowed to Grandpa who grumbled and said he was going to bed, Grandma stopped me as I began putting on my shoes. "Stay."

"Grandma," Hank laughed. "Rick has to be with us. He's such a bad player. Who else can we make fun of?"

She ignored him, though she waved him off. "Stay." To me, tucking her hand under my elbow. "Sit."

Everyone left, and I watched the two women clear the dishes, load the dishwasher, both refusing my help, though I offered. Not the job of the guest—and a man at that. Woman's work. I thought of Dustin, fiercely Old Country in his definition of marriage. *I will tell her what to eat. I will order my wife's food.*

I grinned to myself: Five children who obeyed like robots.

I sipped tea while the women talked of the wilted bok choy they'd purchased at A Dong last week.

I waited.

A half hour later Grandma and I sat by ourselves in the little-used living room on a plastic-covered sofa. Framed family photos hung on the wall: Hank and his siblings in various celebratory moments of school history—grade school awards, high school medals, college. One of Hank on the day he was sworn in as a Connecticut State Trooper, his face glowing. Next to him, Grandma clutched his arm affectionately, looking up into his face.

For a moment Grandma watched my face.

"That boy is not a murderer."

"I know."

Her voice a whisper. "I know that you know. But I watched him all night, I listened to him. He could never kill a living thing. Not a bird or anything that lives."

"I know."

"You must help him."

"I'm trying to."

"But he will not help you."

"Grandma, that's what is driving me nuts. He won't talk of his trouble with the professor. He has tons of secrets. He says he had nothing to do with the murder, and I believe him, but then he stops—like I should accept that. That the world should accept that."

"Because he is telling you the truth. Why should he explain?"

I smiled. "For one, the police have a different slant on things."
She waved her hand, dismissing the idea. "Foolish, they are."
"They have to find the murderer."
Her voice rose. "Then they are walking the wrong path."
She waited a second and then said slowly, "He wants to tell you something."

That startled me. "How do you know that?"

"The fact that he sat at supper with us. That he likes you. Likes Hank."

"Everybody likes Hank."

"A murderer would not be chatting on the phone with a state cop. Night after night."

I agreed. "That is a little strange." But I added, "Unless he's a sociopath—gets his kicks…"

She stopped me. "Nonsense. Not that boy."

"I know."

She waved a cautious finger in the air. "He's not ready yet because he doesn't know he needs to. I know why. Look at his—courtly manners. The bowing. The respect. Such an Old-Country boy who doesn't understand that Vietnam holds him to the ground, doesn't let him breathe. He's a prisoner of the past. He's a prisoner in that house that does not understand the living Buddha. He lives with his mother in a cell. It is because of *her* that he is quiet."

I sat up. "You could tell all that from dinner talk?"

"Of course. Obvious. A boy locked into his family's past. His mother has given him nothing but shame and guilt and—and now obedience. No one else. Not his brothers who ignore him. No, his mother."

"What are you saying?"

"He hates his life, but he will do anything to make his mother love him."

"It's not working."

"What else does he have? Living in a house that doesn't talk. He's alone." An unfunny smile. "Until he has the five children who will be Americans and not listen to him."

"And an obedient Old Country wife."

She swung her head back and forth and grinned. "She will bean his head with a wok."

I laughed. "So where does this leave me?"

But Grandma was distracted, her face scrunched up. "I worry because there is no Buddha in that house. That awful story of the McDonald's"—she pronounced the English word as "Madonell"—"cheeseburger at the foot of Buddha."

"I'm sorry. Offensive, I know."

"I am not offended by it."

"Then what? Dustin found it funny."

"It isn't funny. That boy lives in the shadow of a Buddha that has closed his eyes."

"Anyway, Grandma, It was just…"

She held up her hand. "This is about a cheeseburger, but it is not about a cheeseburger." To my puzzled expression she said, "I will not sleep tonight."

Chapter Twenty-three

Darijo Delic was shot the next afternoon.

I'd left my apartment, headed into Hartford, stopping at my office to say hello to Jimmy, but then spent three or four hours lost in the musty cubicles at the Connecticut State Library on Capital. Absorbing research that tickled the antiquarian in me, I supposed, as I delved into family bloodlines that collided and turned and led to contemporary swindle among the less loyal and more greedy millennials who traced their lineage back to Thomas Hooker. Fascinating, the avarice of those who were already comfortably rich. My iPhone was switched off, of course, wi-fi also silenced in the quiet rooms. Shelter from the social media frenzy surrounding us, but welcome respite—a peaceable kingdom where no one could get at me. Although my fingers twitched for at least one tweet or email blast.

My wish granted—outside, walking into wispy snow and heavy twilight, my phone pinged, the Facebook alert on my laptop sang a song, and I knew I'd reentered the world. Hank tweeted and texted and left voice messages. Liz did the same. Even Jimmy, Luddite extraordinaire, left a halting voice mail. But they all alerted me to the same nightmare:

Darijo, shot.

Darijo Delic had been shot as he stood on the terrace of his family restaurant in Little Bosnia, the hapless young man sneaking a cigarette. A passing car hesitated, a window flew open, two shots rang out. One struck the poor boy.

"He's all right," Hank told me when I reached him as he came off duty. "Winged in the left shoulder. A bullet lodged in his flesh."

"In the hospital?"

"Home now. Cops all over the place. State cops, too. The whole nine yards. Finishing up now."

"Jesus Christ," I said into the phone.

"My sentiment exactly."

"Do you think...?" I began.

"What do you think? Okay, I got the go-ahead to head there from my supervisor, especially since I've already talked to the kid. The family is terrified. So...you and me."

"When?"

"Now. Head there now."

• • ● • •

A state police cruiser was parked in front of Sarajevo Café, Hank in uniform sitting behind the wheel. He stepped out as I pulled behind him.

Yellow police tape circled the front of the restaurant, the front terrace pitch-black. A lone Hartford cop car sat nearby, the officer behind the wheel nodding at Hank and pointing to the second floor of the brick building. Although the restaurant was closed—the CLOSED sign I'd seen earlier—and another sign taped to a window—ZATVOREN. I assumed it said the same thing in Bosnian. But the second floor, the family residence, was ablaze with light, the shades pulled up so that blocks of brilliant yellow dotted the upper story. Snowflakes drifted across the windows.

The cop rolled down his window. A young Hispanic officer, nametag LOPEZ, with a crooked smile and a hint of a moustache over his upper lip. "Good luck, man. They're not happy."

"No reason to be," I told him.

"Detectives just left. They weren't happy either."

"Don't blame them," Hank said.

"I'm not happy," he said, smiling.

"You're in a warm car," Hank said.

"Then I guess I should be happy." He waved us off.

I pressed the doorbell at the side of the building. No answer. Again. Finally someone peeked out of the upstairs window, a young girl who spotted Hank when he stepped back. A buzzer clicked.

A light switched on suddenly at the top of a dark, narrow staircase, and I was surprised to see Darijo standing there, his shadowy body silhouetted against the brightness. Hank bounded ahead, though I stepped carefully, holding onto a wobbly rail that seemed ready to give.

Darijo was smiling. "I'm all right, gang." He backed up. "Come in. The cops said you'd be coming."

His left arm was in a sling, his shoulder bandaged. When he moved away, he winced, though he tried to smile. He motioned us to a sofa as he eased himself carefully into a recliner.

His mother and father sat in straight-backed chairs next to each other, facing us, in a solemn formation, their set faces reminded me perversely of Grant Wood's classic *American Gothic*. Balkan Gothic, with shrouded dark eyes, fearful.

"My parents don't want you here," Darijo said, smiling and glancing at them. "They think you brought on this…this shooting."

That surprised me. "How?"

Another quick glance their way as his father sighed. "You bring the talk of death with you. I mean, talking of Professor Winslow. Of Dustin Trang. I told them it's all nonsense but… you know." He shrugged.

"I do know," I agreed. "And I understand." I turned to his parents who'd not taken their eyes off Hank and me. "My apologies for the intrusion but it's important."

His father held up his hand and said something to his son in Bosnian. The boy nodded, then shook his head with a wistful smile. "He offers his hospitality to you. Some tea perhaps." Then he grinned. "Even though he told me your presence scares him."

"We won't take long," Hank said.

"Authorities," Darijo said. "Cops." He pointed to Hank's uniform. "Echoes of disaster in the homeland."

"I understand," I repeated. "But there's a chance this could relate to Dustin."

Darijo spoke quickly. "No, it doesn't." He drew in his breath. "I think you're wrong."

We paused as his sister scurried in from the kitchen, balancing a tray. Small teacups with crescents. A tiny urn. Slices of poppy-seed and walnut rolls. Darijo's mother nodded to us, and in a high-pitched, nervous voice said something in Bosnian.

"Eat," Darijo said to us. "Drink." Then he lowered his voice, confidential. "You have to. It's being polite."

We did, though Hank seemed to enjoy the sweet rolls more than he should, stuffing one after the other into his mouth. I read his lips as he faced me: Damn good stuff. Put some in your pocket for later.

I ignored him. "Why do you say it doesn't relate to Dustin?"

His father grunted, so I waited. The old man muttered something and pointed at Hank, who was unfortunately stuffing his mouth with another roll.

"My father says good men love good food."

Hank managed to blurt out thanks, poppy seeds collecting at the corner of his lips.

"The cops think it was a random shot," Darijo went on. "In this neighborhood there's a lot of shooting. Wild West in Hartford. Guns go off all the time. Drug battles, turf wars down at the corner. Los Solidos gang against the Soul Brothers. You learn to live with it."

"But you were shot." I pointed to his bandaged shoulder.

"I know, I know." He paused, glanced at his mother and father whose faces had taken on another level of panic. "But the first shot went wild. I heard it."

"Two shots?" From Hank, swallowing.

"Tell us what happened," I prompted.

He sat back, wincing as he shifted in the seat. "The dinner crowd was gone, I go out for a cigarette like I always do. I like to stand on the terrace over the street, watching the cars whiz by, the folks going by. Christmas—folks a little drunk. Freezing, but after my shift in the hot restaurant…it's invigorating. Anyway, I'm standing there and I see a car hesitating, an old crate, a backfire I think, but the sign on the building next door goes ping. I realize it's a shot. Nervous, I back up and at that moment I hear another shot and I jerk back, my shoulder stinging, blood on my palm. I toppled onto the terrace."

"Then?"

"I dunno. I blanked out." A sheepish grin. "Next thing I know I'm in an ambulance on the way to Hartford Hospital. And here I am. Alive."

"Thank God," I said.

"So I think it was an accident."

Hank didn't buy it, his tongue in his cheek. He said to Darijo, "That's what the cops told you?"

"Their guess. The detective said I was—unlucky. A city with lots of shooting, killings every night, they said I was lucky to be alive. Innocent bystanders get whacked all the time. Standing on the sidewalk—shot dead. Caught between rival gangs. Last week an old lady taking in her mail. A few blocks from here."

His father was grumbling. In halting English he said to me, "The gunfire. Here. America." He stood up, his hands fluttering as his head swiveled back and forth, a panicked look in his eyes. "My son."

Darijo said something in Bosnian, reassuring from his tone, but his father wasn't happy—he rocked back and forth. Darijo's mother stood and placed her hand on her husband's forearm, and he bent his head down. She whispered something, and he offered her a thin smile. When she smiled at me, I realized Darijo had her eyes: large, deep-set, coal-black.

Darijo watched his parents. "I don't want my parents to worry," he whispered, faking a smile. "I want them safe."

"So do I," I said, "but that safety involves you, Darijo."

He shrugged off my remarks. "I'm okay. I told you. A chance shooting. Random. I…"

"I don't care," Hank interjected.

Darijo's father's voice carried a trace of anger as he said something I couldn't grasp, a mixture of English and Bosnian.

"What?" I asked Darijo.

Awful sadness in his voice. "He says they came for peace. To America. In his nightmares he hears gunfire. His old village. Now—here—an American movie. Bang bang."

I didn't know what to say.

"Time to go," Hank whispered.

"I'm sorry," I said.

Darijo shrugged that off. "You gotta do your job." Then, following us to the door, he said, "Tell Dustin I said hello. Life has got real painful for him, right?"

I nodded. "He's in a lot of trouble."

"He didn't do that."

"So he says. Over and over." Frustration in my voice.

"Maybe you're not asking him the right way."

"What does that mean?" Hank asked.

"I don't know what it means, but I always felt that Dustin was desperate to talk. But something was holding him back. He was afraid of—I don't know—betraying somebody?"

"A secret?"

"But what?" From Hank, hurriedly.

Darijo smiled. "He always pulled back at the last moment. It was hard to be with Dustin, you know. He's like a…wound coil. Sometimes that scared me."

His father said something to him, a flash of anger, and Darijo nodded. A gentle voice as he said something back. Then to us, "Goodnight."

"You know, Dustin can use a friend, Darijo."

"Yeah, that's true. But somebody's got to convince him of that."

"Why?"

"I don't think he trusts that people will like him."

"Do you?"

He ran his hand through his hair and scratched an ear. He made a hurtful sound as his bandaged shoulder twitched. "I don't know. To be honest, I just don't know."

• • ● • •

At midnight my phone rang. Hank's voice sounded faraway. A rush of sounds behind him: raised voices, phones ringing, even high-pitched laughter, the clack of computer keys, someone complaining about a snow squall on I-84.

"You working?"

"I'm at Troop H barracks. Stopped in." He drew in his breath. "Listen, Rick. Forensics just spotlighted the bullet taken from Darijo's shoulder."

"That's fast."

"Hey, modern science." Another deep intake of breath. "Listen. It's from the same gun that killed Ben Winslow."

My heart raced. "I had a gut feeling."

His mouth was close to the phone. "The same goddamn gun, Rick. You know what this means?"

"Yeah, Hank. Ben's murder is somehow connected with Dustin Trang."

"Bingo."

Chapter Twenty-four

Liz took a sip from the glass of pinot grigio. "It's a simple question. Maybe a comment. You and Hank concluded that the shooting of Ben and that Bosnian boy means Dustin is involved. I don't follow that logic."

We were sitting at Zeke's. The war room, Hank termed it. Yesterday's shooting of Darijo had jump-started a chain reaction of e-mails, tweets, Instagram, Facebook alerts, Hank on Snapchat with other cops, and an old-fashioned telephone call from Jimmy suggesting an early dinner at Zeke's. "Somebody gotta talk some sense about this madness."

Leaving my apartment, I'd bumped into Gracie sweeping snow off the front steps, and I invited her. "Jimmy's idea," I'd said, and her harrumph suggested the old man couldn't possibly have an original idea—but who knew? Stranger things had happened. "You haven't see him in—what?—a day?" I'd added, stoking the fires of their unacknowledged flirtation with each other.

We'd joined Liz and Hank, already seated at a back table, Liz sipping her favorite white wine while Hank, in civilian clothes, toyed with the wet label on his bottle of Sam Adams. Liz repeated her doubt about Dustin's involvement simply because Darijo had been wounded by the same gun that killed Ben. "I was just telling Hank what I thought," she told me, "and I was amazed that his stoic expression suggested he doubted my words."

Hank groaned. "Help me, Rick."

Again she took a small sip of wine. "The dangers of your two-man tag-team testateronic play."

"How you talk!" Jimmy mumbled, coming up to the table and pulling out a chair. He struggled out of his lumberjack winter coat and dropped his gloves into his lap.

"All I'm saying…" Liz protested.

"Liz," I said. "Think about it. Darijo's connection with Ben is tenuous. One class. Nothing in particular."

"And," Hank added, "it was Dustin who had the row with Ben."

She protested. "Who knows what other stories were taking place in Ben's world? Darijo may have had more of a connection with him. Did you ever think that Dustin is—incidental? Maybe Darijo was friends with someone *else* on campus—someone who needed to kill Ben."

Hank was frustrated. "Wouldn't there have been hints— rumors? Especially *after* the killing. Somebody would talk, no? I mean, the cops investigated every story, interviewed everyone. Not a word. It's—Dustin for them. Sadly. And now this attempt on Darijo's life. What? A revenge killing?" He slapped the table with his hand.

Liz smiled at him. "Calm down, Hank. I'm only suggesting a scenario. A killer no one thought of. In the shadows. I don't want you two boys to go riding off into the Wild West with guns a-blazing, only to discover tumbleweeds blowing in your path."

"That makes no sense," Jimmy said to her. He signaled to the barmaid and ordered a beer—"Budweiser in the bottle"—while Gracie said "Ditto" and I went for a glass of pinot.

We ordered Zeke's notoriously greasy hamburgers and salty fries and heart-attack onion rings and a Caesar salad with chicken—for Liz, the naysayer in the group—and settled back, watching one another, enjoying the fact that all of us were together.

Gracie raised her glass. "A merry Christmas to us all."

Three days before Christmas, and Zeke's had dragged out last year's decorations. White lights blinked erratically over the entrance. A plastic Santa Claus had a chip of plastic missing from high on his left thigh, which made the illuminated Santa vaguely risqué—in a certain light. A fake green garland with red bulbs hung over the mirrored bar, a decoration the manager sometimes forgot to take down until someone reminded him that it was Easter.

Jimmy sat back, eyeing us all and tapping the pack of Marlboros in his breast pocket, a sign that he was ready to speak. He cleared his throat. "I called this meeting because I gotta listen to everybody asking my advice over the phone. Rick calls and doesn't let me get a word in edgewise. Hank calls and asks me what Rick has said about him. Liz and I talk all the time, which is a pleasure, even though we're talking about Rick." He started hacking, his thick cigarette cough, while we waited. Again his fingers tapped the forbidden cigarettes. "This kid Dustin is like a sun and you're all, you know, revolving…"

"Nobody talks to me about it." From Gracie, her lips set in a grim expression as she watched Jimmy. Her eyes also took in Liz, a look that suggested her alarm that Jimmy and Liz had bedtime phone chats.

Liz spoke up. "Gracie, all our conversations end up talking about you."

"Nice try, Liz." But Gracie was delighted with the comment.

Impatient, Jimmy went on. "This Dustin has become Rick's obsession. However"—he held up his hand when I went to protest—"however, I understand how he gets a little nuts with this Vietnamese stuff." He stopped. "Anyway, here's what I gotta say—nothing gets to that kid. Right? Nothing seems to scare him. I mean, the police haul him in. He keeps quiet. He's the subject of TV and social media crap. He keeps quiet. This crackpot preacher over in Bristol talks about him. He keeps quiet. Hank tries to charm him—he shuts up."

"What are you saying, Jimmy?" From Hank.

"I'm saying he is acting like someone in a war. Like in Vietnam you couldn't let anything touch you. Think like a soldier. He's like—name, rank, serial number. That kind of attitude."

"So?" Again from Hank.

Jimmy sat back, folded his arms across his chest. "So the question is—why? It would be easer for him to talk, no? There gotta be something so powerful making him hold that secret—if he got a secret, which everyone thinks he has—close to his chest. What?" Jimmy raised his voice. "Life and death. Powerful. You find that out, Rick, and you got yourself a solution to this story."

Suddenly Gracie spoke. "He's protecting someone."

"What?" From Jimmy, startled.

"His silence. He doesn't have to be quiet. A secret. If you got a secret, you are helping someone. Protecting someone. Keeping someone from being hurt."

"Or," I said, "keeping someone away from you. Or keeping someone happy."

"Who?" From Hank. "I mean, he keeps saying it has nothing to do with the murder so why does everyone want to know his business?"

"Maybe he has a point." Jimmy was nodding furiously. "Maybe it doesn't have to do with the murder."

"Or," I said, "maybe it does but he doesn't know it does. He lives such an isolated life maybe he can't put together the pieces of the jigsaw puzzle that he's in the middle of."

Liz was thinking of something. "The boundaries of that jigsaw puzzle center on the house he lives in."

"Why do you say that?" I asked.

She took a sip of wine. "Think of it. That's the world he knows. He doesn't really connect to the outside world. Alone in the library. Alone at the College Union. An occasional talk with this Darijo. He's a prisoner in that apartment."

"It's funny you mention that," I began. "Grandma used the same word. Prison. But of the past. His family's past in Vietnam. The way his family stopped living when they got to America."

"When they stopped living, they froze him with them."

"But they don't want him in the picture at all," Hank said.

"Unless he serves some purpose," I said.

"The hold of his family? Maybe? The power of his Uncle Binh?"

"I don't know." From Jimmy, shaking his head.

"They crippled the boy." Gracie watched my face. "Crippled," she repeated, furious.

"This loneliness," Liz began, "has to do with his family. Alone in that house with a mother who seems indifferent—maybe even hostile—to him. An unwanted child. A boy who finds his own way—to the library, to good grades, to college. All on his own."

"Well, he's bright," I said.

"And he knows how to survive." From Hank.

"Not only that," I went on, "but he's found a way to particularize his life. Everything orderly, precise. Even his future—the number of children he wants. Christ, you should see how he unties and ties his shoes. A ritual. Everything exact."

"Someone who is afraid of loosing control," Liz said.

"Because he has anger problems," I added.

"Well, of course he does. He's ready to explode."

"But maybe murder?" Gracie wondered.

"No," I insisted.

"I agree," Hank emphasized. "Murder is too—messy for him."

Jimmy fumed. "What the hell does that mean? Messy?"

"He likes a well-ordered universe."

Jimmy smirked. "Hey, if your world is out of whack because somebody is on your case, shoot him. Then you got the world you want. Orderly." He took a swig of beer. "Anybody here listening to me?"

"It doesn't work that way," I said.

But Liz was anxious to say something. "Wait. If he's a prisoner in that apartment, he has a keeper."

"His mother," I concluded.

She was nodding. "Who doesn't love him—or want him there."

"But he stays."

"Because he can't go anywhere else," Gracie said.

"So," Liz summed up, "maybe he is trying to curry his mother's favor. To get her to love him. To have her say he's important."

"That'll never happen," Hank said.

"It doesn't matter," Liz insisted. "Dustin probably can't believe his own mother would *not* love him. That's horrible for a child."

"So what does he do?" I asked her.

Hank answered. "He protects her."

"Or her secret." From Jimmy.

"So the secret that he confided to Ben has to do with protecting his mother?" I asked. "Seems improbable. What could be so horrible in her life—to make Ben so angry?"

Jimmy held up his beer bottle and saluted me. "Maybe you should run with that idea for a while."

"He's got brothers," Hank said.

"But," I noted, "they don't talk to him. One can't come into the apartment per his mother's orders. I met him—scary as hell. The other's a nebbish on the sofa."

"Okay, leave them out of the equation," Liz said. "View this just as a drama between an uncaring, distant mother and a hungry, lonely boy—two occupants of that cage. No one else matters. A mother who looks back to a life in Vietnam when she was happy. A war that took away the future she dreamed of. When she *had* a future."

I nodded. "Back to a time when there was no sprawling brat named Dustin who appeared one day during a highway crash that took her husband and left her with two worthless boys and a baby that got in the way."

"No wonder she runs to that godless church," Gracie commented. "False promises. False prophets. Family-sized hope and salvation. Gold as—release from pain."

"Imagine the guilt she's bred into that boy." Liz shuddered.

"And the guilt he's owned," I said to her. "An unreal obligation to her." I smiled at Liz. "An obligation to protect her secret—even to the point of fighting with Ben."

"But not kill Ben," Hank added.

Jimmy was fussing. "I've made my point already, folks—go in that direction, Rick." He signaled to the barmaid. "Do you see us sitting here waiting for the goddamn dessert menu?"

"I'm gonna have to talk to Dustin," I said emphatically. "Finally. *The* talk."

Gracie was waiting to speak. "A suggestion, Rick. Why don't you invite him to your place? Your apartment. Not the prison of his home. Not the library where he hides out. The school. But a different world from what he knows."

Hank protested. "But, Gracie, he's been to my parents' home."

Smiling at him, a little patronizing, Gracie shook her head. "He knows that world, Hank. Vietnamese. Wonderful, yes, but he needs a jolt into a calm, serene world."

Hank grumbled. "Yeah, that's Rick's apartment. Somber as a tomb. So quiet that even the mice in the walls hush each other up."

Gracie frowned at him. "We do not have rodents in my building, young man." She winked at me. "You know what I mean, Rick? A place where he can feel—warm."

"I don't know, Gracie."

My phone beeped, and Jimmy winced. "You know how I feel about phones when we're eating."

I glanced down. "It's Marcie."

"I don't care if it's the pope. We're eating."

Hank waved a hand at him. "Actually we're done eating."

"I haven't had dessert." Jimmy reached for my phone. "Rude manners, Rick."

"Ordinarily I'd agree with you, Jimmy. But Marcy sent a text." I held up the phone. Marcie's message:

Dustin sighting. Interesting. Where R U?

Jimmy smirked. "Tell her we're sitting with folks that still know how to spell."

I texted back:

Zeke's. All of us.

Ten minutes away. Wait.

Hank pulled out his phone and tapped something onto the screen. He handed it to Jimmy, who grumbled, "What the hell?"

Hank was laughing. "An emoticon for Jimmy. A good title for an after-school HBO movie." He held up the screen. A simple :) followed by a happy face: ☺

"Goddamn hieroglyphics. No wonder the Egyptians all died out."

"You're thinking of the Aztecs." Hank arched back his head.

"Symbols, signs, gobbledygook. That's how we talk to each other. Guess what country is next to disappear? Thank God I won't be around to see it."

"Always the optimist." From Gracie, leaning over to pat his forearm.

Within minutes, Marcie and Vinnie walked in. "You all look so grim," Marcie said.

"Jimmy has predicted the end of American civilization." Hank reached over and lightly punched Jimmy on the shoulder.

Vinnie saluted Jimmy. "No one told me it had arrived."

Marcie added, "It too late for civilization."

Marcie slid into a chair and Vinnie pulled up a chair from another table. "We caught an early movie, the two of us, and we stopped at the college library on the way home. I wanted to pick up an interlibrary book that came in. Deserted, as you can imagine. A few stragglers in the library, but the librarian whispered nervously that Dustin was back in one of the carrels."

Vinnie added, "That annoyed me, frankly. Like she was afraid she was going to be ax-murdered by that boy."

"Anyway," Marcie went on, "I strolled back there out of curiosity."

"Nosiness." From Vinnie, leaning his head onto her shoulder.

"Civic duty." She brushed his head away. "There he was, drowsy, it seemed, head bent into some tome. The desk was filled with volumes, stacked around him like a fortress. He started when I approached and sat up, but turned his face away."

"Did you say anything?"

She shook her head. "No, I was sorry I went back there. He struck me as so—intense."

"Intense?" Hank echoed. "What does that mean?"

Marcie's eyes got cloudy. "As I walked by, I saw that all the books—at least the ones I could see—were on the Vietnam War."

"The war?"

She nodded. "Histories of the war. Robert McNamara's book on top. Military campaigns. Like he was searching for answers. It was a little—unnerving."

"And you didn't say anything?"

Again she shook her head. "I couldn't. Really. His head jerked up and I lost my breath."

"Good God. Why?" From Gracie.

"He looked like someone who'd just seen a ghost."

Chapter Twenty-five

Sometimes history falls like a ton of bricks on the innocent.

That cryptic line from Melody Winslow came to me as I tossed in bed the following morning. I tried to get it right. The exact words: Yes, that line. A line her father told her after getting off the phone. An unsettling conversation. But was it Dustin? No matter because the line resonated, disturbed.

I sat up in bed.

The past—and probably not even Dustin's own immediate past, his deadened eighteen years. The War. The Vietnam War. Marcie and Vinnie talking about Dustin squirreled away in the college library, the young man suddenly discovering the brutal war that shifted so many lives, including those of his parents. Uncle Binh, Aunt Suong. Even, I supposed, the two little boys dragged behind them. Timmy and Hollis. Thang and Hiep. A war kept from Dustin, little spoken of, but now a war that loomed large and fierce in his consciousness. What suddenly exploded inside him to propel him to that library?

I texted Hank who texted back that he'd phone on his break. "What's your thinking about this?" His first words to me.

I emphasized Melody's recollected line, my belief that Dustin's secret was somehow connected to his mother and, more importantly, to a war he knew so little about.

"Yeah," Hank agreed. "That talk at Zeke's sort of made me sit up."

"What does it all mean?"

Hank's voice got louder. "Whatever it was, it was possibly illegal."

"Because Ben was talking about the FBI?"

"Exactly."

"I'm convinced this has to do with the war."

Hank's voice dropped off as he spoke to someone in the room. "Sorry. The citizens of Connecticut expect me to be working." A deep breath as he went on. "Maybe the flight to America? Grandma said he was a prisoner of the past."

"Something happened those last days in Saigon. April 1975. The Trang family given special treatment. Flown out in a military helicopter headed to Guam."

Hank mumbled, his voice low. "Yeah, Uncle Binh. What could be so dangerous all these years later?" Again he pulled the phone away from his mouth. "Give me a second, sir."

I spoke quickly. "That's what makes no sense. And why would Dustin turn to Ben Winslow?"

"For help. Legal advice. Maybe immigration authorities were on their case. ICE."

"No, Hank. All these years later? Uncle Binh was a South Vietnamese military honcho. A hero to so many."

"But maybe he did something that violated some U.S policy."

Pacing the floor of my apartment, I shifted through the facts as I knew them. "Still, again, Hank—more than four decades later? Old people now. Sick. A man in a wheelchair."

Hank scoffed. "Men in wheelchairs can coordinate crimes, Rick." A long pause. "Or want to cover up an old crime."

I thought about it. "David Laramie said Dustin told him that Ben failed"—I banged my forehead—"'us.' He said—us. Who was the 'us'?"

"On the audiotape Dustin says 'I gave my word.' To who?"

"But once Ben was murdered, why wouldn't Dustin simply tell us the story? The game is over."

"Because the problem hasn't gone away. His family's problem. Possibly it has nothing to do with Ben's murder—Dustin's bad timing—but the family is thinking trouble. Illegal something or other. Turning to Ben. Turning to an American professor who was sympathetic to his students."

"But Ben balked—didn't want to get involved with the Trang dilemma."

"Or, more likely, he demanded Dustin call the authorities himself—take responsibility."

I sat down, stretched out my legs, and groaned. "Yeah, a lesson in proper protocol. Ben demanded Dustin turn in his own family. His mother? That old woman?"

"A woman who fed him guilt and shame—and now demands obedience."

"Something else, Hank. Grandma's talk about the Trangs looking back to idyllic days in Vietnam, hoping to regain that paradise."

"Grandma suggested that was one of the reasons they kept Dustin out of their world. He didn't fit into the puzzle."

"A distorted puzzle at that. Grandma wasn't happy with their…I don't know, their perversion of Buddhism."

Hank chuckled. "The cheeseburger for the journey into eternity."

I laughed with him. "'This is not about a cheeseburger but it is all about a cheeseburger.'"

"Grandma's Buddhist voodoo."

"She's telling us something."

"To you maybe, the other Buddhist who spouts aphorisms from your book. Jesus Christ, Rick."

"Maybe you should listen to us, Hank."

He pulled back. "Sorry, but I always need an interpreter when the two of you wax…"

"Confucian?"

Another half-hearted laugh. "Exactly." Mumbling, his mouth close to the receiver. "People are looking at me. I gotta cut this short."

I ignored that, my mind racing. "When we first visited his home and met his mother, she said something strange." I tried to reconstruct her words. "Something about Dustin not doing something. Yes. 'I ask him one time.' He didn't do something for her. Another thought. Didn't Darijo talk of some sort of betrayal hinted at by Dustin? His mother?"

"Okay, she exacted a promise. And compound that with his mother as warden and we have a little Dustin who shuts his mouth even if the cops and the whole world believe he shot Ben Winslow twice in the head."

"Incredible." I sighed. "Goddamn incredible. The weight of that family gets heavier and heavier."

Hank summed up. "So Dustin sits in the library and reads about a war he knows nothing about, but now understands the *why* of his mother's demands."

"Hank, step back a moment," I cautioned. "We're assuming all this is true—that he's shielding his family from something that happened those awful April days in Saigon. You know, that time I overheard Ben arguing with Dustin, I talked to Ben immediately afterwards—the first thing he asked was about me being Vietnamese. He said he'd never understood what that war was about. He'd never brought that up with me before. It was the squabble with Dustin. The war, Hank."

"I believe it." Flat out, emphatic. "I gotta go, Rick."

Talking to myself, "It's time we hammered Dustin to the wall."

Hank laughed. "I have a feeling he's ready. The image of that boy surrounded by all those books on the Vietnam War. That's like—like a moment of crystallization."

"Epiphany time in the library stacks."

"But does any of this relate to Ben's murder?" I could hear hesitation in his voice. "That's what seems so far-fetched."

"Maybe not," I said. "But if we can clear up this story with Dustin and his family, the cops can stop focusing on Dustin. If we take that away, maybe they—even you and me—can see the real murderer standing in front of us."

"Waiting to be nabbed." Hank added. "Someone we've talked to." He spoke to someone near him. "All right. One minute."

"Possibly."

"So what's next, Sherlock?" Hank asked. "I have people pointing at me, and not happily."

"An invitation to my apartment. I'll call him. Tonight. Chinese takeout."

"Seven o'clock. After my shift ends. I'll pick up the food. You get him there."

"It's time the boy comes clean."

• ● ● ● •

Dustin picked up on the second ring. "What?"

I waited a moment, then said, "Dustin, that's not how you answer a phone."

An edge to his voice. "You still teaching me manners?"

"Yes."

I detected an uptick in his voice. "Everybody wants to change the world."

"Why not?"

An unfunny laugh. "Yeah, why not. It's all fucked up, right?"

"Dustin, you know why I'm calling you."

That stopped him. "What do you want?"

"Again, Dustin, your tone."

A moment of silence. "What?"

I sighed. "You need to come to my apartment tonight. Hank'll be there. Dinner. Chinese take-out."

A long pause. "Why?"

"We're gonna talk."

He didn't speak for a long time, but finally, with a deep sigh, he said, "Yeah, I know." More silence on the line. When he spoke again, his voice shook. "I know. I've been doing some thinking… reading and stuff. Now I understand something."

I waited a heartbeat. "What do you understand?"

His voice a whisper. "I understand that I gotta talk to you about something."

"Good. I'll see you…"

The line went dead. So much for manners. My Sunday school primer. I shook my head. Rich Van Lam's master class.

• • ● • •

Dustin tapped quietly on my door, waited, then immediately tapped louder. He didn't look happy when I greeted him, and he peered behind him into the hallway, down the stairs, as if he'd been followed. He walked by me, his book bag over his shoulder, which surprised me. He dropped it by the front door. He caught me looking at it. "I carry stuff." Then he removed his shoes.

Inside, he took off his winter coat, an outlandish knit cap best saved for Alpine skiing adventures, and tucked mittens with too many worn holes into the pockets of his coat. Carefully he hung his coat on a rack by the door, and then watched me. "What now?"

"Relax, Dustin," I assured him. "Hank's on his way with the food."

He'd dressed in Sunday best attire. Creased trousers a little too big and shiny in the knee, a faded white dress shirt, open at the collar but buttoned at his wrists. He'd worn old-fashioned penny loafers. I'd never seen him in any other shoes than his pristine sneakers and some muddy-brown Walmart work boots.

"You live in a strange house." He gestured toward the front window. "It's so—yellow."

Gracie's wonderful painted lady, a Victorian three-family with gingerbread cornices and octagonal windows and shutters with elaborate carvings. Every spring Gracie painted the outside a brilliant daffodil yellow. "The cheap blonde on the corner" was the neighborhood's charming appellation for the stunning house, a stone's throw from Miss Porter's elite girls' school and the town green ringed with staid Colonial white-clapboard houses. A string of Victorian upstarts around the corner from Main Street, stolid and grand. Gracie's was the only maverick in the crowd.

"I love it."

"It's like living in a dollhouse."

I pointed to the sofa. "Make yourself at home."

He didn't sit down. Instead, he walked around my living room, staring out the front window into the street below. "I like this place." He faced me. "Yeah, I do. All the books."

He stood in front of my floor-to-ceiling bookshelves. One of his hands reached out and he ran his fingers across the bindings. I have rows of nineteenth-century volumes, leather-bound, dark and faded, echoes of ancient libraries. My life collecting books at church bazaars and flea markets up and down the East Coast.

He stood in front of a watercolor. "Le Pho," I told him.

"Expensive?"

"A little."

"Vietnamese?"

"Vietnamese French."

"The French fucked us up, you know."

I didn't say anything.

"I like this one." He moved to the other side of the room and put his face close to a color lithograph of Anna Christie done by Robert De Niro, Sr. "Cool."

"A play by Eugene O'Neill."

"Whatever."

"The artist is Robert De Niro's father. You know Robert De Niro?"

"Yeah, *Analyze This*. Late night TV."

His body loosening, he strolled around, touching an oriental vase on a coffee table, picking up a figurine and squinting at the bottom as if he were an appraiser on *Antiques Roadshow*, surveying the roll-top country-store desk in the corner, wandering into the kitchen and examining the old copper-plated ceiling. "Cool."

He stared into the framed poster of a Joan Miro painting that I had hung over a cabinet. He ran his fingers down the glass, put his face close to it. His eyeglasses shifted.

He could have been a cat burglar sizing up his quarry.

Or, I smiled to myself, someone who had fallen into a warm bath.

"This place doesn't look like you," he said finally.

"What should it look like?"

He shrugged. "Dunno. Police scanners, maybe. A wall of computer stuff. Black-and-white pictures of gangland killings. St. Valentine's Day massacre. Machine-gun photos. You know, that stuff."

"This is where I relax."

A thin smile. "You did a good job of fooling me."

A knock on the door.

"Food's here."

But it was Gracie who'd spotted the boy walking up the stairs and was anxious to meet him. After all, she'd had a ton of things to say about him at Zeke's.

She carried a German Bundt cake on a platter, the icy frosting dripping onto the plate. She held it out. "A special treat." She turned to Dustin. "And this is Dustin."

He acted surprised that she knew his name. She smiled at that. I made the introductions. "This is Gracie, who owns the house and is a good friend of mine. She lets me live here."

"Your hair is the same color as the house."

She laughed. "Yes, I'm making a statement."

"What's that?"

She swirled around. Gracie was dressed in a flowing caftan decorated with outrageous purple hibiscus blooms. Around her neck huge turquoise chukka beads she claimed were given to her when she toured an Arizona reservation years back. Very little make-up, as always, but the illusion that she was ready for a stage walk-on was always there. That dramatic face, an old woman's still captivating charm.

"I was a Rockette," she told him. "I toured with Bob Hope during the Korean War."

Dustin stared at her.

"You ever hear of the Rockettes, Dustin?"

He shook his head. "No."

Gracie had a conspiratorial look in her eyes as she flicked her head around. "I stopped in to say hello."

Again, the half-bow from Dustin.

"Such a handsome young man, Rick. Quite—striking."

That news rattled Dustin, who took a step backward and almost toppled onto the sofa.

Probably no one had ever told Dustin he was good-looking. He shifted from one foot to the other, a little embarrassed but pleased. Color rose in his cheeks, and his eyes flickered. Handsome? The word made him happy. I looked at the young man—skinny as a reed but with brittle, spiked hair he obviously clipped himself with dull scissors. One side was longer than the other, and the back was a field of chopped weeds. Those oversized black-frame goggle glasses that kept slipping down his nose. A bit of tape on the corner of the frame suggested he'd snapped them. The long bony dark face. The fading black-and-blue bruises and that pale shiner. Handsome? I realized there was a good-looking boy under that mishmash of haircut and eyeglasses and bruises. Someday a woman would find him appealing.

Probably the same woman who would rebel against his dictatorial mandates and culinary fiats—and wield a wok. To use Grandma's prophetic statement...

Hank bounded into the apartment, his arms filled with bags of food. "Dinner," he announced, "is served." He kissed Gracie on the cheek as she waved goodbye, and he said to Dustin, by way of greeting, "You better like Chinese food, kid."

Dustin nodded. "Yeah."

Dustin immediately began to nibble at the corner of his thumb. His eyes drifted over Hank's shoulder as he breathed in. They rested on the book bag by the door.

Hank noticed the boy's discomfort. Putting down the bags on the kitchen table, he approached Dustin, resting a reassuring hand on his shoulder. "It's all right, you know."

Dustin squirmed. "No, it isn't."

"What's the matter?" I asked quietly.

"I caused a lot of trouble. I didn't mean to."

His eyes drifted to the kitchen, and Hank motioned us to the table. Quietly, Hank unpacked cartons of food. Too many, of course, enough to feed—in the words of my adopted mother back in New Jersey when I first arrived in America—the Russian army.

As we dug into *moo sho pork* and chicken with snow peas and beef fried rice and pan-fried dumplings, I watched Dustin's face. He grew distracted.

Finally, Dustin, dreamy-eyed, overfed, sat in the living room. Hank and I faced him, and I said, "Dustin, you know why you're here."

"I gotta tell you the story."

"About time." From Hank.

Dustin gave him a sharp look. "I didn't know the story—I mean, all of it—until last night. I mean, today. Like early morning. I wasn't supposed to *look*…" His words trailed off.

"Dustin, just tell us."

"I'm gonna get in trouble."

"We'll handle that," I assured him.

He swung his head back and forth. "I really fucked up."

I caught Hank's eye.

"Tell us." My voice sharper.

"I mean, the talk about the war in your kitchen"—he looked at Hank—"like I never thought about it—the soldiers dying and the people…" A helpless shrug.

"Dustin, what are you telling us?" I asked.

He got up and picked up his book bag. While Hank and I watched, Dustin removed a tiny box, fumbling with it, letting it slip out of his fingers. Those small fingers, the fingernails bitten to the quick, that line of dried blood.

He placed the box on the coffee table. A small cloth-covered box, the blue and gold fabric dotted with stitched white flowers, the kind of box that opened to find jingling stress balls, a popular tourist gift in Chinatown. Now, his hands shaking, Dustin clutched a piece of white napkin, and spread it open.

He sat back, his eyes closed.

Hank reached over and picked up the inch-long cylinder. Pale white, bleached almost, grayish, splintered at both ends, jagged.

His eyes got wide. He held it out to me.

"A bone," he whispered.

I took it from him, rolled the fragile piece between my fingertips. "Part of a finger."

Dustin's eyes got moist. He looked away.

"Jesus Christ," Hank said, his voice hollow. "A fucking bone."

"I'm sorry." Dustin wiped away tears with the back of his hand. "I'm sorry. Sorry."

Chapter Twenty-six

"The Commies."

Dustin's next words as we stared at him.

"Dustin, what the hell?" Nervous, I placed the bone fragment onto the table as we stared at it. "What in God's name? A bone? Christ, a body part."

His voice trembled. "I found it this morning."

"Dustin, what the hell is going on?"

Hank snapped, "Dustin, are you fuckin' crazy?"

Dustin shut his eyes. When he opened them, I saw fear. Maybe even terror. He blinked away tears. Silent, his hand scratching his neck, he blew out his lips. He began, "I got confused. I still don't know…what the hell…"

I broke in sharply. "You know enough, Dustin. And you've known enough for some time. What the hell do you think you're doing here?"

Hank softened his voice. "C'mon, Dustin, the story."

The boy breathed out again. "All right. You know, like I said, at your mom's house"—he glanced at Hank—"they were talking…asking me about the war, my family, what I knew. I knew *nothing*. Really. But I got to thinking. It was…like not real to me. All of it." His lips quivered. "Just about a month ago I learned about the body. They found the body."

"What body?" From Hank.

Dustin rushed his words. "I'm trying to tell you."

I shot a look at Hank: Slow down. Easy.

"Go on," I told him quietly.

He said something, a jumble of words, stopped, then took a deep breath. "You know how we were laughing about that cheeseburger on the shrine?" His eyes blinked rapidly. "Well, I never looked at the shrine. Why would I? Religion is—shit to me. But this morning, looking up, I realized there was a different McDonald's burger there. That stunned me. Why? So Uncle Binh and Aunt Suong were at the house having coffee and I asked them—Isn't that a new cheeseburger? Like—I thought—like a joke question. Everybody got hot under the collar, real crazy, and Uncle Binh told me to mind my own business. Mom was steamed. I hid in my room. When they all left, I snuck out to look. I stood on a chair, and I found this box." He pointed to the box on the coffee table. "I took it down and found…the bone."

"You didn't know it was there?" I asked.

A hot flash of anger. "How would I? I'm not religious—not that it's like, you know, a religious thing." Again he pointed to the bone fragment. "But suddenly I realized what was going on."

"What *is* going on, Dustin?" I asked, impatient.

"The reason for the cheeseburger."

I quoted Grandma's awful line: "This is not about a cheeseburger but it is all about a cheeseburger.'"

Dustin squinted at me. Hank was eager to say something.

"Yes," Dustin said simply. "The soldier."

"Tell us."

"Just about a month ago Uncle Binh and Mom sat down with me and told me that we had to get the reward for the body."

"Back up," I said. "The body?"

Dustin, wide-eyed. "Okay. Yeah. We got some cousins or somebody in the village over there. Loc Dang, outside Vung Tau, I guess. Farmers, poor as shit. They dug up the remains of an American soldier in the field. Decayed, mostly. Covered with stones. But some bone fragments, some clothes, a dog tag even."

"My God, Dustin."

"I know, I know. So they knew it for a while. Letters back and forth, hints in letters, I guess."

"Why didn't they call the authorities?" Hank asked, anger lacing his words.

Dustin spat out, "The Commies."

"I don't follow," I said.

He fiddled with his eyeglasses. "You know, everybody talks of finding missing soldiers. The American government is…like crazy for remains. MIAs, you know. Years after the war, you know. Organizations promise huge money. Rewards. People in the villages talk of it—whisper about it. A path of gold, they say."

Hank sneered, "Jesus Christ."

Dustin's words were clipped. "Why shouldn't *my* family have the money? They found the body, hid it away in a box, didn't tell anyone."

"Dustin, do you hear how crazy this sounds?" I said.

"I guess so. But a month ago Uncle Binh told me they didn't know how to get the reward."

Hank was confused. "What reward?"

"Promises of big money for remains," I told him. "For the return of solders held prisoners. Common enough during the war."

"And afterwards," Dustin added. "The problem is the Commies. You can't let them know."

"Of course they have to know," I said. "They run the country."

He was shaking his head vigorously, but stopped. "Could I have a glass of water, please?"

"Dustin, finish this story."

"I'm thirsty."

I got up and poured him a glass of water. He drank it down in huge gulps, slopping some of it onto his shirt, then held out the glass. "Another." I poured him another, which he sipped slowly. His hands trembled as he raised the glass to his lips.

"Okay, Dustin. Go on."

He stood up, surprising us, and I thought he was going to run out of the apartment. Instead, he walked to the front window and stared down into the dark street. "It's so quiet here," he said. "In the projects there's noise all the time. Gunfire. People shoot into the sky. Did you know that?"

"Yes," I said. "Dustin."

He walked back toward us but paused by my bookcases. Suddenly he took a leather-bound volume from a shelf, held it in the palm of his hand as if weighing it, then rubbed his fingers along the spine. "Soft," he said. "Why don't they make books like this anymore?"

"Dustin, sit down."

"Someday I will have a bookcase filled with books like these. Soft. They look like they could crumble if you open them."

I smiled. "Some of them will, Dustin."

His spun around, his face contorted. "What am I gonna do?" His face stark, pale. "What am I gonna do?"

"Tell us."

"The Commies."

I pointed to the sofa. He sat down, took another sip of the water, and then, startling me, reached over and broke off a chunk of Gracie's Bundt cake. His fingers simply snapped a piece off, and he stuffed the cake into his mouth. Crumbs dropped to the floor, rested in the corner of his lips.

"For Christ's sake," Hank stammered. "What's going on?"

"The Commies." A sliver of a smile. "In the village they whisper about people in other villages who found body remains. American soldiers. Rumors of rewards. The money promised. But everyone talks of how you gotta tell the local Commie authorities, and suddenly they are the ones with the cars, the villas on the South China Sea, the trips…you know…the guy who found the body gets squat. You can't open your mouth. The Commies call the Americans who have a committee or something to deal with this—they are hungry to get bodies back, even now, years later—and the money—millions and millions of dollars—goes to the Commies. Nothing you can do about it."

"So your family…"

"Didn't know what to do," he finished for me. "How to contact the people offering the reward and skip by the Commies until they had to know—after the fact."

"Dustin, there's lots of fakery. People show up with pig or cow bones, with phony dog tags and bits of clothing, and demand money. Not uncommon. Most turn out to be scams. Dustin, let me tell you something—the American government does *not* pay a reward for remains."

"They don't?" Wide-eyed, mouth open.

"No," I said firmly. "That's a myth. Everybody wants American money. Dishonest folks traffic supposedly real bones to innocent folks who think they'll become rich—get a visa to America. Piles of hidden gold handed over. The Vietnamese Office for Seeking Missing Persons fields hundreds of such fake remains. Manufactured dog tags. Evil bone dealers dig up Vietnamese graves—hand over the bones of old women."

Hank was watching Dustin's face. "Reward?"

I answered. "Stories of rewards up to a million or more. From private sources. Like the POW Publicity Fund. Black market dealings. Word-of-mouth promises of money."

Dustin protested, his voice strident. "But this was real. That's why they sent a piece of bone to America. For the shrine. Proof. The American—part of him—back home. In a shrine. Worship. The long journey home."

Hank grumbled, "The cheeseburger."

Dustin gave a phony laugh. "American food for the American journey. Keep the G.I. happy as can be."

"And you didn't know this?" I asked.

"I thought it was, you know, because they didn't have oranges or something. When I found it today, it creeped me out. That's why I'm *telling* you."

Suddenly Dustin shot up, pulling open his book bag. "I just remembered." He extracted a crumpled sheet and handed it to me. A yellowed, torn sheet of fragile paper. I smoothed it out.

"This was in the shrine."

A reward leaflet, typical of millions dropped by planes over Vietnam, during and after the war. A line drawing of a stereotypical Vietnamese man shaking hands with an American soldier. Much of the cheap ink had faded but what little I could discern talked of a two-million-dollar reward for the return of an MIA prisoner, proven, documented. Or proof of death. The process for contacting a committee called America Homeward. In big letters: "2,000,000 dollars. U.S. Dollar." Some of the language I couldn't understand, and I handed it to Hank.

"This is from during the war," he said. "Also rewards for information about the Viet Cong strongholds, rewards for firearms turned in, for secrets, a whole laundry list of reimbursement."

I was shaking my head. "Whole mythologies have sprung up about MIAs. Fake reports, fake leaflets, fake sightings, eating into the hopes of those back home who miss their loved ones. Foolishness. Greed."

Dustin had been following the conversation, his head going back and forth. His eyes traveled to the cake and he started to reach for a piece. I held out my hand, grasped his forearm.

"Dustin, what is your role in all this?"

He swallowed. "None—I mean—a little. They knew about this for some time, I guess. The relatives in Nam counted on them. There are lots of black market groups who work under the radar, cut around Commie crap, U.S. government crap even, to bring home soldiers. Pay out money. Private donors. But they were afraid to tell anyone."

"So they told you?" I said.

He nodded. "Last resort, I guess." He waved a hand in the air. "They couldn't *trust* anyone. Uncle Binh no longer has, you know, contacts. They…"

"Who else knows?" Hank interrupted.

"No one. Uncle Binh, Aunt Suong, and my mother." Another phony laugh. "And they probably didn't wanna tell me."

"Your brothers?"

He rolled his eyes. "Christ, no. Mom told me that Uncle Binh said they were loose cannons. Talkers, greedy. It would be all over the neighborhood." A sweet smile. "She said they could take care of themselves when the three of them returned to Nam." A pause. "In style."

"So that was their goal?"

He made a sarcastic face. "Yeah, of course. The land of soymilk and honey. My loser brothers would be in the way."

"What about you?" Hank asked.

Dustin started, then jerked his head back. "They could care a fuck about me. I'd be left behind, too." A harsh laugh. "I'm just the travel agent."

"What were you to do?"

"Use the Internet—they called it the machine in my room—to locate people to contact. Nobody in the Vietnamese community could know. Only me—I *promised* them. So they had to trust me."

"But you couldn't find an answer?"

He made a fist and slammed it into his palm. "How the hell was I to know? There's so much crap online. I didn't know where to start. Shit, a body hidden in a shed?"

Hank stood up and paced the room. When he faced Dustin, his voice was filled with anger. "Do you know what you did?"

"I didn't do…"

Hank's hand flew up, traffic-cop style. "Stop. Don't bullshit me. You're a part of this craziness, Dustin. Don't bullshit me."

Dustin whimpered, "Hank, I mean…I mean…"

Calmly, I leaned into him. "So you turned to Ben Winslow?"

Dustin gnawed at the corner of his thumb as he gazed toward the front window. Small pellets of sleet suddenly pinged the window, a *rat-a-tat-tat* that reminded me of firecrackers exploding in Chinatown. Dustin kept blinking his eyes at the windows, adjusting his eyeglasses.

Calmly, he answered me now. "I trusted Professor Winslow. I mean, he was friendly and funny and—and he liked me. He praised my paper. He told me—come see me if you got a problem. So I did. I felt good. I trusted him."

"But why ask him for help?"

"Because he was…like sympathetic. In class I knew he was anti-war, you know. He talked of protesting American imperialism, as he called it. Iraq, Afghanistan, hot spots all over the world. Fighting, fighting. He was a pacifist, he said."

"And that led you to trust him?" Hank sounded bewildered.

"That, and the fact that he talked about protesting the Vietnam War way back when. Like when he was a teenager, I guess. He protested in the streets. Carrying signs and stuff. He even got this picture on his office wall—did you ever see it?—of himself as a teenager carrying a sign somewhere. 'Hell No We Won't Go.' A riot. He looked so—young. Like one of us. I didn't really understand the war until I read about it the other day. I knew he didn't like what happened in Nam. I thought—he'd help us."

"But he didn't." My voice dropped.

He scrunched up his face. "He got real mad. Furious. I mean, he scared me. 'This isn't right,' he kept yelling. 'A family gotta have their son back home. Wrong, wrong, wrong.'"

Hank fumed. "It is wrong, Dustin. You know that."

Weakly, sighing, "I guess so. Yes. I know. But he said I had to call the authorities right away, give them the information. I said the Commies would take the money. He said, 'Who the fuck cares? Do the right thing.' But I thought of my mother and what she wanted and…"

"And you didn't want to disappoint her." From Hank.

"I wanted the whole thing to go away. He said he wanted *me* to do it, but if I didn't he would call someone. I begged him not to. I lied—told him to give me time. He said—he'd give me two days. Period. He *promised* me he'd keep quiet."

"What?" I asked.

"Because when I first went to his office, I said—'If I tell you something, will you promise not to tell anyone?' He said yes. So he was gonna break his promise."

"He couldn't keep that ridiculous promise. Dammit, Dustin," Hank swore.

Wonder in his eyes. "Why not? A promise is a promise. I trusted him."

"You were foolish."

He wrapped his arms around his chest. "I was an asshole."

"True," I said. "There is that."

He watched me closely. "I didn't know what to do. I told him—okay. I'll take care of it. But I didn't, and he kept after me. For two or three days we kept—arguing. I had to keep him quiet. He gave me a deadline. If I missed it, he was going to call the FBI. That scared the shit out of me. I was afraid my mother, the others, would get in trouble. Relatives back in Nam would get punished, tortured maybe."

"Then you'd be in trouble."

Helpless, an exhausted look on his face. "I couldn't sleep those nights. I went to his place. I fought him. Like—screaming at him. I was running off in every direction."

"You could have made a phone call."

He screamed out at me, "It's easy for you to say. You don't have a whole fucking world in Vietnam waiting for you to do something." His voice broke. "A family that asked me to do something."

"Something wrong," Hank shot out.

"Yeah, I know that now. But the last time I saw Professor Winslow I told him he was right. I said, 'The day after I finish finals, okay? I promise.' He was relieved and said he'd help me through it all. A nice guy. 'It's better if you do it. You, Dustin. I'll be there with you. We'll call together.' Dustin's eyes got moist as he dipped his head into his chest. "He wasn't mad at me any more. Like we were yelling at each other and then he smiled at me. 'Merry Christmas,' he said. 'I'm a Buddhist,' I told him. 'Sort of.' You know what he said? 'We're all Buddhists at heart.' I liked that." He breathed in. "I liked him."

"But then he was murdered."

"That's what I'm telling you. This got nothing to do with *that*. The police gotta look somewhere else. He had enemies, you know."

"Everybody has enemies," I told him. "But they don't shoot you to death."

He shivered. "Some do. Obviously."

"True."

"The funny thing is that Professor Laramie warned me to stay away from Winslow. When he saw me getting chummy with him, he talked to me. 'Don't trust him. He's an atheist.' Imagine saying that. 'He'll betray you. If you're godless, you care only about yourself.' Laramie is this born-again Christian."

I turned to Hank. "Laramie hated Ben because Ben fought against him getting tenure."

"No, not true."

"Then what?"

"He hated Winslow because he was anti-war and stuff. Especially because he opposed the Vietnam War."

"Years ago?" I questioned. "So what?"

"Because Professor Laramie told me that his father was a soldier who died in Vietnam."

I started. "What? He told you that?"

Hank yelled out. "Holy shit."

Dustin sat up straight. "Yeah, more than once. In fact, he talked about that dumb photo Winslow had in his office. How it bothered him. He asked me if I was Vietnamese. I said yes. And he told me about his dad. He was a little baby then, I guess. His dad was killed parachuting into Da Nang."

I caught Hank's eye. "A new wrinkle in that bitter man's portfolio."

Dustin went on. "You know what he said to me. He said, 'You're here in America because my father died in Vietnam. Don't you find that ironic?' I mean, that sort of made me dislike him. Like he wanted me to feel guilty for something I had nothing to do with."

"Christ, Dustin." Hank was frowning.

"But every time I saw Laramie, he gave me a look that said— you killed my father."

"Did your mother and Uncle Binh know you talked to Ben?" I asked.

"Yeah, but they weren't happy about it. I told them he could be trusted. We *needed* his help. He was on our side."

"But he wasn't," Hank threw out.

Dustin's voice dropped. "When I told my mother he wouldn't help, that he was talking FBI, they got crazy. Uncle Binh said he was probably a Communist. But I told them I'd handle it. I lied and said Winslow said it was up to me—that I told Winslow it was a story I made up. Like for English. A stupid story. I told them the matter was dead. They relaxed. I even found some dumb address on the Internet and said I was contacting the people. Me, taking care of it." He waited a moment. "So they were okay. I was taking care of things. My mother said God was answering her prayers. The key."

"The key?" From Hank.

"Yeah, the Gospel of Wealth Ministry, you know. My mother told me that the first letter from Vietnam arrived about the time they were going to hear Reverend Simms. When he talked of God hiding the key to vast wealth and waiting for you to discover it, she thought the letter was a sign from God." Dustin smiled. "I guess Buddha could only take you so far. Jesus has to pick you up for the rest of the journey."

Hank smirked, "A cheeseburger is a cheeseburger is a cheeseburger."

"A shrine to greed and evil. McDonald's."

"Mom thought she was doing the right thing."

"Yeah," Hank was sarcastic, "a human bone resting in the belly of Buddha. Talk about your indigestion."

A gust of wind blew a spray of ice pellets against the window. Dustin jumped, nervous.

"Dustin," I was ready to end this talk, "you did a wrong thing. Not only this plot with your relatives but keeping your mouth shut. By holding back on this story you messed up the police investigation into Ben's death. Everyone assumed you were involved because…"

He broke in. "That's why I'm telling you. Something *else* is going on *there*."

"But your stubbornness clouded the investigation."

"I couldn't betray—my promise." He closed his eyes for a second. "Okay, tell them. The cops."

"Oh, I plan to." I added, "Here's what's going to happen. Tomorrow I'm making a few phone calls. It's Christmas Eve and then Christmas—there may be a day or so delay here. But I'm going to get the ball rolling. FBI. Whoever. You're going to have to talk to people. You're going to have your mother, maybe Uncle Binh, tell what they know."

He was antsy. "What about the money?"

"Fuck the money," Hank shouted. "There is no money. There shouldn't be any money. This is a man's life, Dustin."

"I know, I know. But the money."

"Stop it," I yelled at him. "This is over now. Your family has to reveal the remains to the authorities. Get that body back home. Assuming it's a real story and not a fake story. A real MIA."

"It's real, but my mother…"

"Wrong," I said forcefully. "Everything is wrong about this."

Dustin, scratching his cheek, shaken. "I don't know what to do."

"I do." I stood up. "I'll also tell the Farmington cops. Hank'll take care of the state cops." He nodded at me. "They can refocus their investigation. If need be. The detectives will follow up on this."

Dustin jumped up, then reached down and gulped down the rest of the water in the glass. He spun around, a dervish, looking at the front window where the sleet pinged and rattled the panes, then at his book bag on the floor. He grabbed his coat and pulled on his knit cap.

"Can we wait a bit?"

"No."

"The money is a…my mother…"

"No."

Suddenly he lurked toward the coffee table, grabbed the bone fragment and began wrapping it in the tissue. I grabbed his hand and unfolded his tight fingers. "No."

"I gotta put it back."

"No, you don't."

"You can't have it."

I held his shoulder. "You're not taking it out of here. This is evidence of something. A body most likely. Maybe. It stays here." I gripped the bone fragment in my palm. "Sort of degraded, maybe not viable DNA but…maybe mitochondrial DNA. It stays with me."

"You can't steal it."

I didn't answer.

"Goodnight, Dustin." From Hank. "We'll talk to you tomorrow. Okay?" He tried to soften his voice. "It's gonna be all right. This is gonna come to an end."

"But I can't go home like this."

"Yes, you can."

"I'm gonna be in trouble with Mom. She's gonna notice it's gone."

"You're a big boy," I said. "Deal with it. Tell her what we talked about."

An arch laugh. "You think she's gonna believe me?" Fire in his eyes. "I can't mention I came here."

"No, Dustin."

Suddenly he pumped his fist in the air and scrunched up his face. "I thought you two were my friends." His voice broke at the end.

I reached out to touch his arm but he backed off, pulled away.

"We are, Dustin. We are your friends."

"You're…you're fucking losers like everybody I ever met in my life."

His eyes teared up as he stumbled to the door, fought with the knob, and then rushed out of the apartment, leaving the door open. I could hear his furious steps flying down the staircase. The front door slammed with a thud.

Chapter Twenty-seven

At first I had no idea who was on the line. Indistinct words. Finally a high-pitched "Rick." More silence. The sound of banging in the background, a door slammed, then a run of rapid-pace Vietnamese, furious, shrill, rising and falling.

"Rick, it's me." Swallowed words, a mouth close to the receiver.

"Dustin, what's going on? Who's screaming?"

Silence.

Then a loud whisper. "Mom is losing her fucking mind."

I glanced at the clock on my computer screen. Five o'clock. Christmas Eve. Darkness had fallen, snow had begun to fall, and I was idly playing solitaire on my laptop. From the apartment above me wafted the choral sounds of "O Little Town of Bethlehem." The other tenant in the building was a taciturn retired librarian who'd been playing Christmas carols too loudly since—I'm exaggerating only a little—early October. I'd planned on a light supper because I'd promised Gracie I'd go with her to Midnight Mass at St. Timothy's down the street. She liked to hear Christmas carols. When I told her all she had to do was sit in my apartment, she told me I would burn in hell. In her gritty falsetto: "On the first day of Christmas, Rick was sent to hell…"

"Dustin, what?" Silence, more screaming. "Dustin, are you okay?"

He breathed into the phone. "She's flipping out, man."

"What happened?"

An edge to his voice. "What do you think happened? She goes to do something with that damn shrine and she finds the box missing. Freak out. She comes pounding on my door. She's—like hysterical for hours now."

"She knows you took it?"

"Who else? The ghost of Christmas past?"

"All right. Calm down. Tell me about it."

He yelled into the phone, his voice cracking. "You know, it's been a shitty day. I shouldn't have gone to your place with—you know—it. A goddamn mistake."

"Dustin, what do you want me to do?"

Silence, more screaming in the background, his mother pounding on his door. He yelled something at her, sort of like *couldyoustopthisnow*—one long word, said so fast it was nearly incomprehensible. Silence again. Then, "This is all your fault."

"Dustin…"

A long sigh. "Nothing is good around here."

"Did you tell her that I have it?" Silence. "Dustin?"

He hissed into the phone. "God, no. You think I'm nuts."

"What did you tell her?"

A raspy laugh. "I told her I hid it in my locker at the college."

"You don't have a locker at the college."

"Really, Sherlock? She doesn't know that. I didn't mention you or Hank. That would have sent her off into outer space. Nobody can know about the two of you."

"So what did she say?"

"I gotta bring it back. Taking it was a curse, a crime. Stealing. I took the key that God gave her. The fucking key. Gospel of wealth crap. Christ, I knew something was wrong when I came out of my room. She's like—evil eyeing me, miserable, moody, but she didn't say anything. Timmy and Rosie and one of my cousins had stopped in, yammering about Christmas shit. So Mom couldn't say anything."

"She wouldn't let on?"

"You crazy? When I walked in, she throws me a real mean look. I knew something was up. I mean, she practically threw them out, and then the screaming started."

"Dustin, again—what do you want me to do?"

"Give it back."

"Impossible."

A long silence, silence in the background. "She called Uncle Binh. I heard her. They're on the way here." A sardonic laugh. "He's gonna run me over with his chair."

"What are you gonna tell them?"

"I don't have a fucking clue, man."

"You said it was a bad day, Dustin. What do you mean?"

I could hear him breath in. "I was at the college library real early this morning. I had to return some books. Otherwise they won't release my lousy grades, you know. When I was leaving, there was…like I felt someone was tailing me all the way home."

"How do you know that?" I caught my breath.

"Like in the rearview mirror this car was always there. I mean, always two cars back or so. I first saw it in the school parking lot, didn't pay any attention. But then one street, then another, another, all the way home. I stopped for coffee and I swear it was behind some parked cars. Then I pulled over at Walmart to buy Mom a Christmas something-or-other, and I swear I saw a flash of that car turn in behind me, four or five car lengths away. I'm not imagining it, Rick."

"Coincidence?"

"Yeah, sure."

"What did it look like?"

"Dunno. Cars are cars to me. But it had this white door. A black car with one white door. Dark windows. So tinted so you can't see the fucker."

"Did you hear any noise? Like a…*ka-clunk* sound."

"That makes no sense." He paused. More pounding on his door. "I came home and hid in my room—made believe I wasn't here."

"Dustin, I want you to meet me somewhere right now."

"Yeah, what? Knock over my mother to get out. I can't climb outta the window. The projects got bars on all the first-floor windows. It's a prison, you know."

I counted a heartbeat. "Get out somehow. Meet me at the Burger King down on Route 6, the one near your house. Wait there. I'll see your car, then I'll follow you out of there, see if that car is following you."

"You're scaring the shit outta me."

"Good, Dustin. You've been scaring the shit out of everybody else."

He broke in, angry. "I'm gonna go now." His lips close to the phone. "This is all your fault."

The line went dead. I dialed Hank, filling him in. "Where are you?"

"Finishing a shift. Southington. I'll head over. Meet you there. I'm in my cruiser."

"No sirens?"

"Not unless my public demands it."

"I don't like the idea of that phantom car following him, Hank."

"Maybe this afternoon we can find the creep. If he's trailing Dustin, we can do our own little dance up that avenue. The Grinch who got caught on Christmas."

It took me twenty minutes to get to the Burger King parking lot. Snow had begun falling, so folks slowed down. Parked near the entrance, I waited. No Dustin. I'd checked inside when I first arrived, moved through bunches of shoving teenagers in a holiday mood, but no Dustin. So I waited. Cars streamed through the drive-thru, idled in the lot. A popular teenage hangout, souped-up Toyotas and Hondas and loud-muffler cars with tinted windows. Booming rap music, an incessant bass line punctuating the lazy afternoon.

The snow fell harder now. The blizzard they'd predicted. A Christmas Eve postcard from New England, but a bad night for driving. Cars skidding off the road. Drunken revelers filled with road rage. All is calm. All is bright. Hank texted me and I replied:

> maybe still in his room

A horn blared. Another beat-up Toyota that reminded me of Dustin's bucket of bolts. But not Dustin. His phone went to message over and over. Two boys threw snowballs at each other, while a third kept yelling in a singsong voice, "Strike one, strike two, strike three."

Strike three: time for me to leave.

Hank's return text:

> head to his house. I'm almost near BK. Home of the whopper

A traffic jam on Route 6, the falling snow hampering movement. I inched along, but finally turned off toward the projects.

A car zipped by on the narrow road, swept past me, headed in the opposite direction. Dustin's rinky-dink Toyota.

Through the blur of falling snow and the shadowy light from a streetlight, I spotted his face, his body hunched over the steering wheel. A gust of wind hurled a wall of thick snow against my own windshield, and I braked. I glanced up in time to spot another car speed by. The black car with the white-primer door. Dark tinted windows.

Ka-clunk ka-clunk ka-clunk.

Loud, then fading away.

A car behind me, a few in front, all creeping slowly. Desperate, I pulled to the right onto the shoulder, and the car behind me swerved, braked, and slid on the slippery pavement, the driver raising a fist at me, cursing, but pulling away. I waited to make a U-turn.

I called Hank, switching on speakerphone. "Dustin's headed toward Route 6."

I could hear Hank's radio beeping. "I'm turning off the avenue now."

"He's being followed."

"Christ."

I maneuvered my car into the passing lane in order to get by a slow-moving car, nearly sideswiped an oil delivery truck whose driver gave me the finger. At the end of the street, up ahead a hundred yards, a suddenly loud bang. The whiny scrape of metal against metal. A fender bender. The cars crawled to a stop. Horns blew.

Peering through the wet windshield, I spotted Dustin's car careen to the right, tires dragging on the ice-slicked curb. Bouncing off the curb, he pulled into the Gospel of Wealth Ministry parking lot. He disappeared from view.

I inched along.

Up ahead the white-primer car pulled around a stalled car, sped into the lot, and disappeared from my sight.

"The church parking lot," I told Hank.

"Christ, I'm bottlenecked. Some yahoo jumped a stop sign and hit an SUV. Nobody is happy."

"I can't see Dustin." I stretched my neck. "This isn't good."

"I'm gonna use my siren to get through the crowd. What we call a perk of the profession."

In the distance the sudden wail of his police siren, which comforted me, though it didn't seem to be getting closer. A horn blew. Another. A gust of snow blew against my windshield. Close enough now, I swerved out of the driving lane, hugged the shoulder, jerked the car across some frozen lawn, and sped into the parking lot.

The wide doors of the church were open, crowds streaming out. The end of an early Christmas Eve service. Clusters of excited folks worked their way through the lanes, dusting off cars, starting motors. I cruised around the front, weaving through people who'd stopped to chat, but no Dustin. He'd vanished in the vast parking lot. Frantic, I rolled my window down, stretching my neck out, my eyes flicking away the snowflakes. A trio of old women interlocked arms and walked across the slippery pavement. The women were laughing, looking up at the snow. They stepped in front of me, moving slowly, and I waited, my heart racing, my palms wet.

Suddenly Dustin's car appeared at the far end of the lane, hesitated, started to turn left, then switched to the right, indecisive. Too far from me to see his face. He paused as a group of parishioners shuffled in front of him. A few hundred yards away from me now, he backed up, then lurched forward as he tried to squeeze between two parked cars. For a moment his car disappeared, but then popped into view. His car jerked forward, stalled, sputtered, inched along.

Snow clouded my windshield.

A motor revved. Dustin's car jerked to a stop.

A loud burst of gunfire. *Pop pop*.

His front windshield blew apart. His car careened to the right, smashed into a parked car.

"Hank, shots fired."

"I'm in the lot."

I stopped my car and jumped out, ran.

Another shot. *Pop*.

Sudden panic. Madness. The easy-going holiday crowd began running, screaming, ducking behind cars, pushing their way back into the church. Folks hurried by me, horror on their faces. An old woman fell, rolled on the ground. I heard her weeping. Too many people, chaos, and Dustin's car up against a car, steam coming out of the radiator.

The wail of Hank's siren as he maneuvered the cruiser up another lane, headed around the back.

I ran toward Dustin's car, my gun drawn, but a man pushing past me spotted my gun and howled, "He got him a gun." Loud, crazy, his voice sailed out over the heads of the crowd. "A gun." People hit the ground.

Yards away now, Dustin opened his door and stumbled out. For a moment he leaned against the open door, as if uncertain what to do, then he wobbled away.

"Dustin," I yelled, but I doubted whether he heard me. "Dustin."

Hank's cruiser came from behind.

Dustin staggered toward the church doors. Stunned, I realized his face was covered with blood. He was wearing a white T-shirt and baggy pants, one hand pulling up a pant leg as he ran away. No coat. He slipped, regained his balance, started to run.

"Dustin." He didn't look back.

For a second he paused, his hands fluttering in the air—but almost in slow motion, floating, a body suspended in space.

Then, deafening, another shot burst from somewhere deep among the parked cars, the shooter crouched down, out of sight. Dustin spun his body around, and I saw the front of his white T-shirt turn bright red. He doubled over, staggered, and reached for the fender of a car that had pulled up near the front entrance. Someone inside, already bent over, hiding, quickly peeked but then ducked down, out of sight.

Dustin took a step toward the church steps, feeble, halting.

Running, I slid on a patch of ice. A flash of movement, someone slinking through the parked cars. Suddenly I spotted an arm outstretched, the gun aiming at Dustin. Poised, ready, sure of itself.

A parishioner, crouched down, hidden, screamed, and the hand wavered.

Dustin started to sink to the ground.

The gun pointed.

Another shot rang out, explosive, but from a few cars away.

I watched a body stumble into view, stagger, slip to the ground. In seconds Hank appeared, his face tense, his hand gripping his gun.

I hurried near.

Hank flicked his head toward the body on the ground. "Wild Bill Hickok's got nothing on me."

The wail of an ambulance turning into the lot.

Hank nodded at me. "I called ahead." He pointed. "Dustin."

He stood over the body while I rushed to Dustin. Nosy folks, gathering, leaned in. A woman who said she was a nurse was holding Dustin's head in her lap, but she looked worried. Slowly she stoked his hair and rubbed his cheeks, rocking back and forth. A wadded handkerchief pressed against the hole in his chest. He wasn't moving. His legs stretched out, covered with a haze of falling snow. She cradled his body as she tried to breathe life into him. Frightened, holding my breath, I touched his bloodied wrist. A faint pulse, almost nonexistent. My fingers were sticky with blood. I caught the eye of the nurse. She was shaking her head.

"No," I said. "No."

EMTs pushed me and the others aside as the nurse whispered to them.

I walked over to Hank who was watching me closely.

"Tell me it's okay," he said.

I didn't answer.

"One day something has to go right for that boy, no?"

I didn't answer, afraid my voice was too foggy. I felt like crying.

Some stragglers approached us, but Hank waved them away, puffing up his state trooper chest. A wail of sirens as police cars turned into the lot. Hank nudged the body lying between two cars, the shooter's gun kicked away from his extended hand. I noticed a wedding band. A man bundled up in layers of winter clothes. A head buried under a ski cap pulled low on his forehead.

"He dead?"

Hank nodded.

"The car with the white primer door."

After Hank's shot zeroed into his chest, the shooter fell on his side, his face buried in the snow. I watched Hank slowly maneuver the body, righting the head.

"You know this loser?" he asked me.

"Yeah. Timmy Trang."

Chapter Twenty-eight

Late afternoon on Christmas day at John Dempsey Hospital. The cafeteria was mostly deserted. Liz, Hank, and I huddled by a window, staring out at the banks of snow from last night's blizzard. The state had been closed down until mid-morning, crippling Christmas services at churches and families headed out for holiday cheer—and crippling the investigation of the shooting in the Gospel of Wealth Ministry parking lot. The lone cashier said she was surprised anyone showed up. Late afternoon, the winter sky darkening and the snow turning to ice. "Just the three of you. Go figure."

Hank teased Liz because of the huge box of chocolates she'd placed on the table.

"I thought I'd die when I got that phone call," she was saying. "Imagine. The two of you racing around that parking lot like Wyatt Earp and Doc Holiday."

Hank grinned. "More like Road Runner and Scooby-Doo."

I sat back. "He made it. That's what matters."

Dustin lay in a bed upstairs, room 315, heavily bandaged and medicated—but alive. Bloodied, drifting in and out of consciousness, but alive. Superficial wounds to his face and neck, the bullets that shattered the windshield had found their mark. Another shot struck him in the chest, dangerously danced around his heart, ricocheted against his rib cage, caused internal bleeding, and effectively knocked him out. He was fading as the EMTs took over, but Dustin wasn't ready to die.

"His own brother," Liz said now.

"I would have thought the ex-con. Hollis. Hiep. But it was Timmy who overheard a conversation that Uncle Binh had with Dustin's mother—and learned about the dead soldier and the reward."

Liz stressed, "Yes, according to Uncle Binh, as relayed to me earlier by Detective Manus. He was at Binh's house until late last night."

Hank was nodding. "Yeah, that's one story the old man is telling. But the cops figure something else was going on. Uncle Binh, alarmed at the way things were working out with Dustin and Ben Winslow, might have panicked, confided in his nephew. Take care of the Winslow guy—he's trouble. There was so much money at stake."

"We'll never know," I said. "It doesn't sound like a plan Timmy could hatch on his own. I agree—Uncle Binh from that wheelchair probably felt powerless. Unable to control Dustin and Ben once things started falling apart. He'd need an ally. Someone who had no qualms about…"

"Brutal murder." From Hank.

"Even his own brother."

"Once his mother told Binh that he'd stolen the bone fragment, that set off a chain reaction. They didn't believe Dustin had told anyone"—I caught Hank's eye as he nodded—"but they couldn't take a chance. Dustin had become a wild card—he might spill the beans. Get him out of the way."

Liz shivered. "But to kill your brother."

"What brother?" I said hotly. "Timmy and Hollis didn't talk to Dustin. They disliked him."

"Cain killed Abel, Rick," Hank said. "It was on the news."

"But Dustin's mother?" Liz wondered.

"Look. Dustin was in the way since the day he was born on Route 6."

"So Hollis was the only one kept in the dark," Hank said.

I nodded. "Too dangerous. Uncle Binh had to trust Timmy, but only so far. Reluctantly, probably. Timmy is a little nuts.

When Dustin told his mother that Ben wouldn't play games with them, that Ben gave Dustin a window to comply and talked of the FBI, something had to be done. Time to let Timmy trail him, shoot him to death."

"And he shot Darijo," Liz added.

"Crazy, Timmy was running off in all directions. Suddenly he'd been told of millions of dollars available. A goldmine. The key. Probably he heard echoes of Reverend Simms' promises of paradise from his mother. From TV he learned that the cops questioned Darijo. What had Dustin told him?"

"And he was following you," Hank added.

"Yes, and our path led to Little Bosnia. *Ka-clunk ka-clunk.*"

"The car with the one white primer panel." Hank laughed out loud.

"Don't take any chances. Kill Darijo. Just in case. But Timmy was no marksman. Yes, Ben at close range. But not from a car window."

"Which," Liz went on, "was a lucky thing for Darijo. Otherwise he might be dead."

"*Ka-clunk ka-clunk.*" Hank mimicked my dreadful onomatopoeia.

"It turns out," Liz informed us, "Timmy worked part-time in a used car lot down on King Street. He borrowed that old wreck. Otherwise Dustin might have recognized Timmy's own rattletrap Honda."

"One question I have." I looked at Liz. "Dustin talked about Timmy stopping over with his wife and son—and his mother cooling her heels, waiting to explode after they left."

"Simple," Liz noted. "Uncle Binh, crafty old fool, told the cops he never told Dustin's mom that Timmy had found out about their scheme."

"So he says," Hank added.

"That could be a lie," Liz said.

I added, "Also, think of it, Timmy was with his wife and kid. Maybe that's a reason for her silence."

"The bottom line," Hank summed up, "is that Binh and Suong and Dustin's mom Mai reluctantly trusted Dustin to follow through on something. They didn't like him. They wished he weren't around. They probably wished they didn't need him. But they did—and it backfired. More guilt for Dustin—obey your mother. They felt he betrayed them by telling Ben, who turned on Dustin. Ben was a threat."

"And Dustin was a threat. A powder keg, especially after the bone fragment went missing." I shook my head back and forth. "Dustin didn't believe Ben's murder had anything to do with him—or his family. That's why he kept protesting his innocence—and his surprise that anyone would point a finger at him. Because it was only the three old folks—and him. He never considered Timmy."

"What now?" Liz had a faraway look in her eyes.

I sipped the last of my coffee. "I've put a call into the FBI. The gears are grinding. More questions for Uncle Binh about the remains in Vietnam, real or fake. There's protocol involved—complicated, I understand. No matter— there'll be a punctuation mark placed at the end of that long periodic sentence."

"Paragraph," Hank insisted. "Long paragraph."

"And Dustin?" From Liz, concern in her voice.

"God knows. Home to that toxic environment. Hated before. Hated even more now. Can you put hatred on a graduated scale? Whatever it is, he's a boy without a country. He took away the golden egg."

"The golden key," Hank stressed. "Blessed are the sleek…"

"Let's go," Liz stood up, tucked the box of chocolate to her chest.

My fingers touched the red ribbon on the box. "Did I ever tell you about my first taste of chocolate?"

Both Liz and Hank glanced at each other. "Every Easter when you bite into the chocolate bunny we give you." Liz gave me a peck on the cheek.

Hank punched me in the shoulder as he walked by. "Happy Easter, Buddha."

Upstairs Dustin watched us through groggy, half-closed eyes. So tiny, this dark skinny boy lost in clouds of white. A white bandage on his neck and jaw. Bandages across his chest.

"You." One word that took all of us in.

Liz leaned in and gave him a kiss, though he winced. The bruises he'd gotten earlier from Hollis were fading now. No eyeglasses, I realized, probably lost during his manic flight across that parking lot.

"I hope you like chocolate," Liz told him. She dropped her voice to a whisper. "You'll have to keep them hidden from Rick."

Dustin squeaked out two words. "Hey, Liz." A sloppy grin.

"Rick and Hank are here, too."

Dustin was smiling. "Hey, Liz."

I grinned at Hank. "I guess he's on the mend."

But Dustin was fading, his eyes closing. I squeezed his hand and whispered in his ear, "Everything is going to be all right, Dustin. We'll take care of you."

His head jerked to the side. But then a slight wheeze escaped his throat. He was sound asleep.

Hank and I pulled into the driveway of the rooming house on Federal Hill. I parked my car alongside a rotting wooden shed, the back wheel of my car sinking into a pothole. The January thaw the past few days had turned frozen ice and filthy snow into rivers of sluggish run-offs. Muddy fields, slippery sidewalks, tree boughs sagging under melting snow. I backed the car up, sloshing through a puddle that probably dropped two feet. I groaned. Bits of broken asphalt and sand sprayed up into my windshield.

"I hate this place," Hank mumbled.

We stared at the ramshackle Victorian house, sliced into smallish one-room homes for local transients. Cracked windowpanes, lopsided shutters, roof tiles slipping into the gutters, porches missing railings, a plywood sheet nailed on a door panel. The house had given up after the brutal winter.

"Let's get the hell out of here," I said.

Two weeks before, just after New Year's, Hank and I had visited Dustin in his single room on the third floor. Released from the hospital, he'd returned home to find the climate in his mother's rooms arctic. Uncle Binh had repeatedly been questioned by the Bristol cops, the state police, even the FBI stepping in after my call about the mystery hidden in that Vietnamese village—and he resented the implication that he'd orchestrated Timmy's murder plot. He protested a little too hotly, and finally he chose silence. Dustin's mother, stunned by the death of her son and refusing to believe that he had tried to kill his own brother to silence him, wailed that Dustin had single-handedly stolen their chance for happiness. The key to riches. So when Dustin was settled in his own bed at home—I had delivered him from the hospital to the projects—she hammered away at him, furious, bewildered, unforgiving.

At night she woke him by pounding on his locked bedroom door. One time, talking with him a day or so later, mid-afternoon, I heard the pounding begin. A high, piercing voice hissed through the door—"You took away our happiness."

Dustin hung up the phone. He didn't say goodbye.

A day later she told him he had to move, and the next call I received was from the grungy rooming house a half-mile away. His cellphone sputtered, staticky, lost connection, but later he called back from the street. "My new address. But I don't want you to come here."

Of course, we did, Hank and I. Dustin's Spartan room held a single bed with a lumpy, dark-stained mattress, a nightstand missing a leg, and a maple chest of drawers painted a hideous deck green. Dustin sat on the edge of his bed, still bandaged but healthier, color in his cheeks, and told us we couldn't stay. "I don't want people to see this."

Hank pointed at the pale green shag carpeting probably installed when Richard Nixon waved goodbye on the final helicopter. Forty dollars a week, no meals. The crunch of flaky cockroach bodies crunching underfoot in the carpeting.

Marijuana seeds in the crevices of the warped bed railings. Folks wandering the hallways all hours of the night, wailing, sobbing, blaming the world.

"Christ." Hank was steamed.

Two weeks later Hank and I climbed those dark rickety stairs again and knocked on Dustin's door.

"You ready?" I asked Dustin.

He nodded. He reached for his winter coat, carefully buttoned it, slipped on his knit cap, and reached for a case that held his laptop. An army canvas bag with camouflage coloring was next to him. A plastic Shop-Rite bag held some pairs of shoes. A old leather briefcase with buckles and straps—I was reminded of the old Russian émigrés I'd seen wandering Washington Heights in Manhattan a thousand years ago—held papers and books.

"That everything?"

He nodded. "Everything I want."

I caught Hank's eye. A lifetime collection of stuff that could fit into the trunk of a small car—with room to spare.

"Let's go," I said.

He hesitated, his eyes focused on Hank. "You sure?"

Hank said nothing but reached for the duffel bag, slung it over his shoulder. Finally, grinning, "You bet."

When we arrived at Hank's family's home in East Hartford a half-hour later, the front door swung open and Grandma beamed at us. Behind her, Hank's mother was trying to maneuver around Grandma, who refused to budge. As Dustin neared, Grandma reached out and touched his shoulder. "Welcome to your home."

His eyes flickering, Dustin stiffened, his head darting back to look for Hank.

Hank was grinning. "Actually *my* old room. I'd hoped it would get national landmark status, but I guess the Fates had different plans."

Grandma leaned into Dustin. "You must be hungry." She nodded at Hank's mother. "We need to feed him immediately."

The kitchen table was covered with food. Platters of fresh summer rolls, bowls of fried rice, bowls of fish sauce, a roasted chicken hacked into pieces, barbecued pork strips. Grandma pointed, "For you, Rick. A happy pancake. But save some for Dustin." And on the counter a massive sheet cake in a Costco box, brilliant red piped lettering that was supposed to say, in Vietnamese, "Welcome, Dustin." *Chao mung, Dustin.* But the unfortunate and doubtless harried bakery clerk at the store had switched a letter. What I saw was: *Chao dung.*

Of course *dung* is pronounced *yum.* As in *yummy.*

But the error ironically translated as: *Welcome brave one.*

I smiled.

In the two weeks since Hank and I visited Dustin in that Dickensian hovel, all sorts of family machinations happened. Hank's family—particular Grandma—had followed the story on TV and in the newspapers, demanding translation into Vietnamese of whole paragraphs that baffled her. And Hank's own recitation of Dustin's woes, including his exile from his own mother's home, had alarmed Grandma. For a couple days the women of the household, a solid voting bloc, had discussed Dustin's fate, only to discover that Grandpa was indifferent to their schemes—and Hank's father sat back, a Budweiser in hand, and mused that Dustin was a remarkable pool player and perhaps his presence in the house…now that Hank was gone… perhaps his buddies Joe and Loc had a few surprises waiting for them when next Hank's father cued up the balls at Minh Le's Bar and Pool Hall in Little Saigon.

Hank's old room, now Dustin's.

Grandma was gleeful. "A house must have young people in it. You know what I always say."

"Yes," Hank answered in Vietnamese, "*Cang dong cang vui.*" The more, the merrier.

Hank's mother added, "I'm assuming he'll keep it cleaner than you did. Those grimy socks hanging off the lamp."

"I needed to air them out," Hank protested.

"Yes, and the Board of Health nailing notices to our front door."

Hank, delighted, kissed his mother on the cheek.

So Dustin found a new home, though he was skittish about it. After his name was cleared, the college reinstated him, though Professor Laramie still had qualms and registered his dismay. Steadfast, Marcie and Vinnie trumpeted Dustin's return, and managed to garner him scholarships—full tuition and books. He could be a full-time student, and the work-study job that the college offered—twenty hours a week in the college library—gave him spending money, gas money, and the nominal boarding costs Hank insisted he pay at Grandma's. "He doesn't want charity. Nobody does."

During all these late-night or Sunday-dinner negotiations, Dustin moved mechanically, hesitantly, and at one point he expressed a fear that he'd fail everyone—that he'd stumble, bungle his classes, disappoint Grandma, betray Hank's confidence.

Hank shrugged that off. "It's your turn, Dustin," he told him one night as the three of us ate hamburgers at Shady Glen in Manchester. "Just remember that."

"I don't know," he said.

I answered him. "We know."

• • ● • •

On the first spring day in April we sat in Hank's parents' living room watching the TV screen. Hank diddled with his laptop, accessing a live podcast from Washington and streaming it onto the TV. We sat in a regimented line, Hank's parents on the sofa, with Grandpa dozing on the end, his head resting on the arm. Grandma sat in the wing chair, her small body lost in the oversized chair. We'd carried in chairs from the dining room, putting Dustin on her left. Hank stooped in front of the TV. We waited as he adjusted the sound, the feed. "Okay, then," he announced. "Ready set go."

We sat in reverential silence as the solemn ceremony took place at Arlington National Cemetery. The camera panned the breathtaking sweep of white marble headstones. Quietly, the announcer narrated the ceremonial internment of Private First

Class James "Jimmy" Dodson, the MIA whose remains had been located in the small hamlet a few kilometers outside of Vung Tau.

The young black enlistee from Biloxi, Mississippi, was then the young husband of the old woman dressed in black who now stood stiffly next to her son, Jimmy Junior, the toddler left behind when his father went overseas in 1968. A tall lanky man, Dodson's son, he stood with one arm around his wife, the other around his mother. He whispered something to his mother, who was sobbing. Twin girls, perhaps ten or eleven, dressed in identical pink dresses, stared at the confusing scene. At one point their grandmother bent down to embrace the girls after they started, nervous, when the gun salute began.

No one spoke in the living room. We held our breaths. I could sense Dustin's body tense up as the casket was interred. The casket that held bone fragments, but also a dog tag. I reached over and grasped his shoulder. He flinched but turned his head for a second and smiled at me.

When it was over, Grandma was the first to speak.

"I never expected to die in America."

"Grandma," Hank said nervously.

She held up her hand. "It's not a bad thing. You have to die somewhere. But we're all exiles in America. Wars are like a hard wind that blows flower petals far and wide." She sighed. "But it's the people who are blown across the earth."

Dustin's words were scratchy. "That war will never be over, will it, Grandma?"

Grandma reached over and squeezed his hand.

"Flower petals," she whispered. "Blown by the wind."

To see more Poisoned Pen Press titles:

Visit our website: poisonedpenpress.com/
Request a digital catalog: info@poisonedpenpress.com

CPSIA information can be obtained
at www.ICGtesting.com
Printed in the USA
BVOW03s1717230717

490043BV00002B/114/P